Tales of the Spinward March.

Book One: The Great Khan

By David C. Winnie

Thank you Rene
Please Enjoy!

[signature]

2017

To Mom and Dad

And to the Eleven

Forever separate. Never separated.

Acknowledgements

Thanks to the following:

Cover art: Bogdan Maksimovic

Book Cover Design: Creative Publishing Book Design

Author photograph by: John McAlpine

I would like to acknowledge and offer my heartfelt thanks to some of my inspirations:

-Isaac Asimov

-Ray Bradbury

-Arthur C. Clarke

-Frank Herbert

Thank you for opening my boy's mind to worlds, universes, peoples and cultures unfamiliar. Through you I could close my eyes and see the Mules ships race through the stars, talk to Martians, understand other realities and witness the spectacle of a messiah.

-Richard Adams

Thank you for my favorite book of all time,

-Gene Roddenberry

-J. Michael Straczynski

-Glenn A. Larsen

You brought me your visions, first to a thirteen-inch black and white TV and later to a 40Hi-Def for an hour each week. Thank you.

-Finally, a special thanks to my friend, mentor, Mom, (after my own Mom died) visionary and editor. The literary world knows her as J.R. Nakken; I am lucky enough to know her as Judith. Thank you for being strong enough to tell me the truth when the writing (and the story) was bad, and loving enough to support me through the painful years when I suffered through my writer's block. Thank you for showing me there is a right way and a wrong way. Thanks for the goosebumps, the shivers, the hair standing on end and the "NO, NO, NO, NO, you cannot do this or that!" Thanks for the chuckles I got when you chewed me out with your editing notes.

You were right. I needed you.

Then I saw the Beast and the Kings of the Earth and their Armies gather together to wage war against the Rider on the horse and his army…" Revelation 19:19

10,908,136,910 A.D.

Hard radiation wrapped the Enderii ship as it punched its way out of otherspace. It would be minutes before the radiation cleared enough for the sensors to give clear information.   Doctor Boradt's cilia flushed from red to violet and back again in excitement and anticipation.

This very well could be the system of the legend. It met the criteria. It had nearly spun its way out of the galaxy, soon to join the nimbus of debris that surrounded the Temple Galaxy, as his people called it. The brown star glowed bravely, a dying ember in a fire pit.

His trail to this star came from an obscure report he had found thirty years ago while studying ten-thousand-year-old records in the archives of Hecate University. A naval cadet scout ship had chanced upon the system, dutifully studied and cataloged it. They estimated it had once been a bit smaller than the average yellow star. Thirteen billion years ago, it had consumed the last of its hydrogen fuel and begun to consume its helium. It swelled, then collapsed on itself, now growing smaller and colder.

A ring of frozen planets spoke of an ancient civilization. Four gas giants whose accompanying moons also showed scars of former life passed. Two planets were closer still. The outer showed the same signs as the moons, but it was the inner planet that garnered Doctor Boradt's entire attention.

It was in the right orbit for life to have developed. Sensors showed it was covered with water ice, so the planet had once had oceans. Rocky mountain peaks penetrated the ice, evidence of the land masses of eons ago.

The Enderii captain cleared its throat. "Well, slug," the furry creature asked, "is this the one?"

Boradt waved his cilia in irritation. Of all the species this ship carried, the Enderii captain seemed to enjoy taunting him the most. And after he had been paid, quite well, thank you very much.

"We will know more when we move closer," Boradt said, his irritation clear. "Mister 379, please set course for the inner planet." The artificial being acknowledged and the ship entered the system.

Boradt blinked, stared, blinked again. Yes, the bridge walls were gone, replaced by walls of stone and fire. The consoles and rails melted into a pool of shimmering acid. He took a breath and gagged; the room was acrid and foul. A figure rose from the pool - Urethral, the Dark Lord of the Underworld. Urethral's skin rolled and boiled as it burned, brilliant flames replacing the Vaudoo cilia.

"Leave this place!" Urethral demanded. "It is not for the likes of you. Leave or suffer my wrath."

Boradt blinked once again. Urethral was gone. The whole of the bridge crew, save for the artificial life, wore countenances of incredulity.

"Quickly, what did you just see?" demanded Boradt.

"Graaarg, Lord of the Underworld," responded the Captain.

"No," insisted the navigator, a Sympodial. "It was Shierachan, Queen of the Damned."

"I saw Veer-ko, the Dead Lord," said the Ioman engineer.

"Curious," 379 said. "I saw nothing. Ship, do you have any record of a visitor or visitors on this vessel in the last five minutes?"

"Negative, Brother," the ship responded. "I do have queries throughout the crew. But I sensed nothing."

"A mind weapon, then," mused the Captain.

"It could be," Boradt said. "But we are dealing with legends and gods."

The captain waved his clawed paw and spat anger. "I am not interested in fairy tales and myths. I am interested in treasure and payment. Remember, slug, my crew and I are entitled to fifty per cent."

"I haven't forgotten," Boradt responded. "Mister 379, the inner world, if you please."

They scanned the worlds and moons as they passed. Foundations for buildings, road beds. But no buildings. No satellites. No vessels or hulks. Nothing outside ordinary space debris. Truly, if this was the home system of the legendary Terran Empire, where were its remains?

Boradt selected the inner world to start. The ship entered a polar orbit, angling each orbit slightly so the ships sensor array could map the petrified globe. Boradt and the students he had convinced to accompany him studied the icy world below for hours, matching what they saw with the collection of maps he had purchased or stolen. The artificial, 379, interfaced with the ship, orientating the sensor suite when the scientists asked.

For three days, the ship dissected the frozen hell below them. On the fourth morning, Boradt sent them all to bed while he stared at the piles of data they had gathered. The answer was here, he was certain. Did the data support his feeling? He couldn't be sure. He had searched for so long. This was the end of the journey. He felt it. Deep in his founal gland, he knew it.

He had found Terra. Homeworld of the Mighty Terran Empire.

"There," he finally said, pointing. "That mountain range there."

There were five in the landing party: Boradt, the Captain ("to make sure you don't try and cheat me out of my earnings") and three students of Boradt's. The ship landed crookedly on the uneven surface, rocked in the barren planet's stiff wind.

One assistant stayed behind as they exited the ship in their extravehicular activity suits. Boradt's, since he was a Vaudoo, had a small hover unit and manipulator arms attached. The rest, as bipeds, stepped on the icy surface.

"What are you doing here?"

A Biped stood there, just a few meters from the ship. Female, it appeared. Wearing a golden jacket, the skirt a rainbow of color, cream trousers and boots. On its head a fur cap. It was not affected by the bracing wind or the frozen temperature.

Or the lack of breathable atmosphere.

"I did not give you permission to land. In fact, I told you not to come at all!" Brilliant emerald eyes glared at them. "Why did you not heed my warning?"

The captain started forward, then froze. "Ah, you expected to find treasure here. Would you have stolen from me? There is a price to be paid for stealing in the Law, is there not?" Her green orbs stared at him. His suit disappeared. He had no time to scream as he froze immediately, and vanished nearly as quickly.

She shifted her gaze. "You two are standing on my world. The Founder banned aliens from my world." The two assistants and the shuttle disappeared without fanfare. Though he couldn't see the Enderii mothership, Boradt knew it was gone as well.

She turned her gaze to Boradt. He could feel her probe his mind. "You, on the other hand, are seeking the most valuable treasure of all," she admonished, "that of knowledge. Why are you seeking the Terran Empire?"

Boradt found his voice. "Because it is legend. There are signs of it throughout our galaxy and stories that tell of the great Empire which once ruled. I have followed those stories since I was a boy, believing when others mocked me. I have traveled long and far, Lord. Tell me, is this the legendary world, home of the Gods of Terra?"

"Ah! You seek redemption and validation for your life's quest! The reward you seek is academic acclaim! You want your peers to revere you for finding the home of Gods!" She roared as a

11

thunderclap, growing hundreds of feet tall, her fists shaking to the heavens. "Ego!" she raged. "Hubris! That is what my masters warned me about. The younger races might come here seeking their gods to fulfill what they thought were their dreams, when what they seek is only validation of their egos!"

She clutched him in her mighty hand, shaking him as a vicious cgormatth would shake a hapless pupa in its teeth. Her mind filled his and he wanted to scream.

"I am the Guardian, assigned by the Last, to guard the World and the Temple of Angkor Khan. Do you truly wish to see the splendors of the Terran Empire?"

"I do," Boradt croaked.

"Very well," she said. The world began to melt away. "I warn you though, legends are not always what they seem. To meet the Last, you must see the truth of the First…"

Chapter 1

They were in a great cavern, the ceiling sloped and peaked into the dark. "Behold!" cried the Guardian, "the birth of the lies!" The walls shifted and melted away...

The Third Millennium early years begat the pathway to the Terran Empire. The dust of the World Trade Center had barely settled when dozens of wars broke out across the globe. Ancient feuds based on race and religion turned into wars and unspeakable horrors upon the innocent. Refugees ignored borders as they fled the conflicts. Economies strained and collapsed supporting the war machines and trying to provide necessities for their populations. Vigilante groups, under the aegis of nationalism, performed horrendous acts of violence on the refugees.

The Americas fractured into a hundred separate states. Africa saw empires rise and fall; whole tribes were slaughtered in the name of race and gods of a dozen names. Europe collapsed.

"There was no limit to their greed..."

Russia and China engaged in a bloody war over Siberia and its immense resources. In 2119, Uighur separatists in western China obtained four thermonuclear devices. Beijing, Shanghai, Hong Kong and Canton disappeared within hours of each other. The ever-fragile world economy collapsed.

"...No limit to their lust for power..."

The winners in this new Dark Age were central and southwest Asia. Mongolia declared itself neutral during the last Sino-Russian war. After the two armies fought to collapse, they withdrew, leaving the whole of Northeast Asia and all its riches to Mongolia, along with megatons of abandoned military equipment. The Mongols put it to use swiftly, invading China in 2125, placing its boot squarely on the neck of the population.

Mongolia's smaller neighbors, Tibet, Nepal and Bhutan, allied themselves with the growing power of Ulaan Baatar. In the southeast, Viet, Khmer, Laos and the Kingdom of Thailand unified, then joined the Mongolian alliance.

"They created themselves brave words, like freedom. No matter..."

Not all of Asia could accept the New Order. The Hunan population of the former China chafed under the Mongolian law. By 2130, war erupted between the remnants of the Chin, as they renamed themselves, and their Mongolian overlords. It was a mismatch. Mongolia had modernized its Army through its alliances in North America and Imperial Japan. The war was short and decisive. The remains of the Chin found themselves a conquered people under a ruthless and brutal regime.

"There were moments sublime…"

India and Pakistan had fought ten wars since the mid-twentieth century and were preparing for another. Both the Mongolian Empire and the Sultanate of Ottoman/Persia had offered to mediate. Both combatants had their nuclear forces armed and ready to attack.

On a beautiful spring day in 2345 A.D., the Sikh Prime Minister is said to have watched the sunrise from his home in Delhi. He was certain it would be the final day of the conflict. Either Pakistan would concede or both nations would die under nuclear fire.

He sipped his tea and studied the red sunrise. In his soul, he knew he didn't want to die today, nor did he want to be responsible for the death of millions. He made his decision and picked up the phone.

"My friend, there must be another way," he told the stunned Prime Minister in Islamabad. "I offer we allow the Mongols occupy Kashmir, then meet with both the Empire and the Sultanate to finally negotiate a permanent solution."

"You would do this?" asked the amazed Paki leader. "Allow our Asian brothers to facilitate negotiations?"

"With your friends leading the talks and our mutual friends holding the territory, I pray we will find a solution."

"…Moments of hope…"

15

Thus, after three hundred twenty years of unease and war, the bulk of Asia was at peace. Imperial Japan and the Kingdom of Korea joined the talks, which quickly became negotiations for a new, vast union. The smaller nations in the southeast eagerly joined. The Philippines, the Pacific island nations and finally, Australia, joined the Pan Asian Alliance.

The new alliance brought pause to the warring planet. Europe's countries sent observers, then ambassadors. The Americas, now calling themselves by an ancient title, Occident, had formed forty nations. The largest, Cascadia, sent observers, desiring to find a way to reunify a fractured continent.

"…Moments of brilliance…"

The burgeoning alliance was abated by three significant events at the start of the twenty-third century.

First was the development of Space Fold technology. Travel through space was limited by light speed. No matter how massive the drive, no matter how clever the designs, simple physics couldn't be overcome in normal space. .99 c was the normal space speed limit.

Theoretical scientists in Bern found the solution. They proved that if *time/space* were folded, then entered, travel through the *otherspace* could reach distances in less time than travelling at light speed. The downside was the amount of energy required to fold space and make the transition. Giant vessels, known as rail fold transports for their appearance, were built. The ships were mile and a half long skeletons, with power plant and fold drive engines at one end, the command pod and sub light engines at the other. Ships would fasten to the skeleton between the pods and be carried through otherspace.

... " In their enlightenment, they discovered allies who fed their hubris... "

Secondly, scouts found Rea-galle, a trinary system of fifteen planets. Fourteen of the worlds orbited normally around one or two of the stars. But there was one world that orbited all three of the stars in an unusual and unpredictable orbit, a small, clouded world, three quarters the size of Earth.

Scouts were discharged to the odd little planet. Their instruments could detect a high level of energy but the clouds and the energy deflected their scanning beams, meaning direct observation from the planet surface would be required. The *Curiosity* landed near a large energy pattern and soon reported contact with the residents.

They called themselves the Mithranderer. Their world, Mithranderer, was a living being, conscious and self-aware. The blue skinned people lived in commune with their world. At the age of sixteen, they would adorn themselves with a stone offered by

Mithranderer and spend their lives in service to the intelligence who ruled their world.

For reasons of her own, Mithranderer had taken a liking to Earth. She dispatched representatives to study the new world and in turn, encouraged human students to study her and her people. She took a particular interest to the Mongols, viewing them as natural leaders of Earth.

She asked the Headman of the Khalkha to commune with her. Tsao Khan, son of Quziea Khan, journeyed to the misty world. There he met with Chamenade Meyer, a wise appearing blue woman with long, steel-colored haired. She wore a white robe, exposing the stone of Mithranderer on her chest.

"Mithranderer has studied your world," Chamenade told Tsao. "The past, the present. It is with great certainly she tells me your line will take your people to walk among the stars as gods. But, that is contingent on the second son of your great grandson. Should the elder survive, then you are doomed. It is that second son who is the future of your people.

Terra faces many wars, Tsao Khan, Son of Quziea Khan. You have made enemies of the others. You will do well to prepare for war."

"What others?" pressed the Headman.

"The Galactic Council is aware of you, for one,' "she responded. "Mithranderer sees great wars with them and soon. The second war I see will be the arrival of your great, great grandsons. Most assuredly, after the boy of the fountain becomes a man, I see

18

the future of the newest gods of our galaxy." Without another word, she shimmered and disappeared.

"...But in the end, they were who they were, always returning to their brutal ways..."

Terrans were never known for their subtlety, even when colonizing their own world. Alien races were encountered, ones less advanced than Terra. Negotiations were considered and attempted. The aliens proved to be less open minded and more obstinate than the Terran negotiators believed possible. Terra returned to what had worked on their own world centuries before; asking the savages to join the Union. If they refused, then they were attacked and their culture destroyed.

This drew the attention of the government of the greater Sagittarius Arm, the Galactic Council. Comprised of two hundred seventy races, the Council watched with concern the spread of the Terrans. In 2512, they authorized the Solarians, a race of a similar technology, to destroy Terra.

The war was short and vicious. Earth had been continuously at war for over eight thousand years of recorded civilization. The Solarians quickly found themselves overwhelmed. In 2516, the Earth fleet orbited the Solarian home world and bombarded the Solarians to near extinction.

Not only was Earth victorious, most of the world had unified. A central government was established in Zurich. As the millennium continued, Earth continued its expansion and Mongolia absorbed more and more power within the Terran government. In 2983, Mongolia, with the support of its old friends; Persia, India, Pakistan and the Ottomans, seized control of the Terran Council. The Leader would be the Headman of Mongolia, the Khan, an ancient God/King title from the days when the Mongolian Empire spread across Eurasia.

It was just in time. Once again, the Galactic Council decided to move against Earth.

"You have been chasing a Legend, small thing. Now see the truth of thy Legend..."

Doctor Boradt was exhausted, his cilia lying flat across his body. "No, please!" he whimpered. Then screamed as the malevolent Guardian poured the story into his head...

Chapter 2

June 3015

PITTH!"

The two small boys startled. "It's your mama," exclaimed the older boy. He looked at his muddy brother. "You're in for it now! You were supposed to stay clean to meet Father."

Today was Pitth's fifth birthday. By tradition, he would be meeting his father for the first time. Headman Tenzing of the Khalkha tribe, first of all the tribes of modern Mongolia. Pitth was excited to be finally meeting the greatest man in all of Mongolia, if not all of Pan Asia.

That he was the second son meant little to the young boy. His older brother, Sui, would one day be headman. Pitth was relieved he would not have to live up to that responsibility. He could largely become what he wanted to be, provided he lived honorably and brought great face to his family and his father.

He swirled his hands in the water, trying to clean them. Sui had suggested they go play down by the slow-moving river. There, they had found sticks and leaves they fashioned into imaginary boats, pushing them along while they scurried along the muddy bank. It was great fun until Pitth's mother called the young boy.

Sui shook his head. "You're gonna get it," he informed his younger brother. "Your mama is going to punish you for sure. And Father..." his voice trailed off.

Pitth stifled a sob as he ran back to the encampment. While his mother was second wife to the headman, she preferred to live

21

amongst the small group of the Khalkha who still roamed the steppe, driving the herds, migrating from the highlands in the summer to the winter pastures. Pitth loved the life of a nomad. He could ride a pony even as he was learning to walk. The outriders kept any predator at bay (no fools, they were armed with modern needle rifles instead of ancient bows) so Pitth could spend the day with his friends riding and practicing with their bows. In an encampment like this, there was the river with its endless games and swimming.

But now he was five and would have to start attending classes. As first son, Sui lived in the Keep and attended classes there. When he turned ten, he would be going to Ulaan Baatar, the ancient capital of Mongolia, to attend school there.

Pitth, the second son, would attend classes in the Keep until the time came for him to attend university. Pitth didn't want to move to the Keep; his heart would always on the endless steppe.

Today he would meet his father. He would ride Father's car to the Naadam Festival, the ageless jubilee dating back to the Great Khan, Genghis. In modern times, the tribes would be joined by allies from around Pan Asia and friends from around Earth. Pitth hoped aliens would be there, too.

He raced through the trail between the yurts that made up the camp. A sleek black air car was parked in front of home where he and his mother lived, with important looking men wearing shiny city clothes standing around it. The boy stopped, staring at the tall, dark suited men. His father's guards. That meant his father was here already. Sui strolled up behind him. "Oh, you're in for it now," he told Pitth. "Well, go in, you mustn't keep Father waiting."

Mother was standing by the door, angry. She spied her son and waved. "Come here, silly boy. Look at you! I tell you to stay clean. Your father is here and you are filthy." She tsk'd a few times, dragging him inside. "Tenzing! Here is your son."

Pitth was in awe. His mother had showed him images of his father and he had seen him on the vid. And now he was here. Tall, long dark hair, the drooping moustache and goatee popular across Pan Asia. He was swarthy, as were both his sons, and had large hands, which he clasped behind his back and leaned down, inspecting his youngest son.

Finally, he asked, "So, my young son, have you been out rolling in the mud with the cattle?"

"No, Father," gulped the child. "Sui and I were down at the stream, racing boats."

"Boats, eh," mussed Tenzing, "and on the Altai river. Astounding. Well, go clean up, boy. We can't have you going to the Naadam looking like a street urchin." He spun the boy about and swatted his behind, sending Pitth on his way.

His mother, Qui, gripped his arm and half pulled, half carried Pitth to the back of the yurt, where a heated pot of water sat. Pitth stripped and his mother roughly scrubbed him clean, admonishing the boy for getting so dirty and warning him to behave for his father or she would punish him severely when he got home.

23

He dressed in fresh trousers, shirt and jerkin, pulled on his boots, kissed his mother on the cheek and scurried out the door with his father. One of the men in the shiny suits held the door for the car as Pitth and his father climbed in.

The interior of the car was smooth leathers and rich woods. Pitth looked about, wide eyed at such luxury. A tall being sat opposite of Pitth and his father in the shadow of the interior.

"Pitth, this is Ryder Finn. He is my advisor and friend. Ryder, my number two son."

Ryder Finn extended a blue hand. Pitth, slack jawed, looked at the long fingers, then grasped and shook it in western fashion as he had been taught. "I am pleased to meet the son of my good friend, Tenzing," the blue man said in a low voice with a clipped accent.

"Are you an alien?" breathed Pitth. "Father, is he a real alien?"

Both men laughed. Ryder leaned to the boy and pulled back his cowl, exposing his gentle, handsome blue face and steel hair. "I am Ryder Finn of Mithranderer," he explained. "She has sent me to know your people. That your father and I have become friends is a welcome result. Meeting his son is an honor."

"Uh-huh," was all Pitth could say. The men laughed again and ignored the boy as the car sprinted across the plains. Pitth twisted and stared out the window. How fast his father's car was! The landscape was a blur as they raced toward the celebration.

Naadam Festival was said to have started in the ancient times of the Great Khan, Genghis and his son, Kublai. Three days in the summer, the tribes would gather to dance and eat, competing in horse racing, archery and wrestling. The festival had developed in the mid-twentieth century as a celebration of Mongolian independence.

Today, the festival lasted two weeks. As the largest and most prominent nation in Pan Asia, Mongolia hosted the event, of course, and invited all the nations of the world. Of late, the celestial colonies attended, along with friendly worlds in the Sagittarius Arm.

Soon, the air car slowed and entered a yurt village at the edge of the festival. A city had grown up of temporary habitations, each a representation of the state of the residents. Hence the Mongolian yurt village sat next to North American tipis, which might be beside a Persian dawah. The car parked next to an ordinary yurt and Tenzing led his son out. "I shall see you tomorrow," Tenzing told Finn. "We can discuss the African situation." The car sped off.

The smell of roasting meats made Pitth's tiny stomach growl, remembering it had been hours since he had eaten. Dutifully, he followed father into the yurt. On a table at the center of the tent sat a steaming pot of *buuz,* dumpling*s* stewed with chicken gravy. "Only one bowl, son," his father said. "We have many pleasures to indulge today! I do not want you being too stuffed to enjoy them!" Tenzing began to change into traditional garb. "It is important we honor ancestors, Pitth," he explained. "Our planet is going into the cosmos now. You are growing up in a world with one foot on Terran steppes, the other in the stars. If you lose your footing with ancestors, you will become lost. So, today, you and I will honor our ancestors on your special day."

There was a shout outside the door as Tenzing finished dressing. He pushed back the door and waved to Pitth. A group of musicians and dancers in colorful clothing cried out and began singing, patting drums, crashing cymbals, and wailing stringed instruments. The dancers kicked and twirled, kneeling and leaping. "They are dancing the Tashi Sholpa for you, son," Tenzing told the wide-eyed boy. "Our dance of good luck and fortune."

A dancer held out her hand and pulled Pitth along, showing him how to stamp his feet and spin. It was great fun!

The song ended with a clash and everyone cheered and wished Pitth a happy birthday. Tenzing smiled and surreptitiously handed the troupe their payment. He took his son's hand and they wandered into the fair.

Pitth never had a better day in his short life. His father led him through the fair, showing exotic animals not just from here on Earth, but from the planets Earth had colonized and from planets friendly to Earth. They laughed at the tiny, orange furred monkeys from Centauri, marveled at the shape shifters from Galamon 3. Pitth backed away from the pen holding a fierce meat eating cat from Vespa. It stood when it saw the small boy and crept toward the bars of its pen. The boy was mesmerized by the cat's slitted golden eyes, its blue tongue panting hungrily over a double row of yellowed teeth. Pitth slid behind the protection of Father's leg, certain Tenzing could

26

protect him from the leering creature. Tenzing chuckled, picked up the small boy and sat him on his shoulders as they moved to the next display, that of a pink tufted bird from Luftstra.

After the menagerie, they went to the games of skill. Father demonstrated his prowess with a bow to his young son and was proud when Pitth showed he could shoot a child's bow with skill. Tenzing entered Pitth in a pony race. He didn't win, but finished a respectable third among the hundred five-year old riders.

They ate a hearty beef dinner and Tenzing allowed Pitth two sweet cakes for dessert. The child grew tired. Evening fell and Tenzing awoke his sleepy son to watch the dazzling fireworks. Pitth fell back asleep as Tenzing carried him back to the air car.

The great man delivered the sleeping boy back to his mother. "Thank you, Husband," she told him. "He was so looking forward to meeting you."

"He is a fine boy," her husband answered. "He will make a fine addition to the Khalkha. You will have him ready in the morning?"

"By the sixth hour, as agreed," she replied, but pursed her lips. "I am not sure he will understand."

"He does not have to understand. He has to fulfill his duty." He took her in his arms and they kissed. "Until morning, my wife," he breathed.

"Until morning, my husband."

Pitth woke with a happy groan, to the sound of his parents' voices in the next room. He stared at the roof of the yurt, remembering the wonderful birthday he had spent with his father. At the chamber pot, he stood when he finished. The adults went silent.

His father regarded him and said, "It is time now, my son, to discuss what my plans are for your schooling. Doubtlessly, you expect to come with your brother and me back to the Keep."

"Yes father," Pitth exclaimed.

Tenzing shook his head. "No, Son, I have plans for you. You will accompany Ryder, who will take you down to Khmer, there to enter their great temple, Angkor wat."

"Father!" gasped the boy, struggling to hold back tears. "I do not wish to be a priest!"

Tenzing pounded the table with a fist. "You will go to the temple as I have ordered," he thundered. "You will go there, work hard, and study hard. You will be an example of my Khalkha tribe and you will bring honor to your people!"

Pitth lowered his head, hiding the tears in his eyes. "Yes, Father," he answered. He would not lose face by crying in front of him now.

"Your mother has gathered your things and placed them in Ryder's car. Say good bye to her and go."

Pitth hugged his mother fiercely. "I don't want to go, Mama," he wept.

She patted his back. "It is time for you to learn and grow into a man," she whispered. "Your father is showing you a great honor sending you to the Khmer. Go now, I will see you return a man."

"Yes, Mama," he replied and kissed her soft cheek.

Pitth rubbed his tears away with his sleeve. He marched across the room to the door, stopping only to glance around the room where he had spent his whole life. Mother's sleeping area where he would crawl for protection when the terrifying thunderstorms swept across the steppes. His own sleeping area, the soft furs he would nest in when it became too dark to read or too late to stare at the stars. Mother and Father sat at the table in the middle of the room watching him leave. Father gave a small, understanding nod. Pitth brightened and left his childhood home.

The village was already bustling. Goatherds snapped their switches, directing their flocks to the feeding grounds. Women and girls sat in the morning sun, their hands slapping the loaves of the day's bread. Night watchmen shuffled wearily to their homes, their needle guns over their shoulders, to eat, to sleep and ready themselves to protect the community at the next dark.

"Boy, come along." Ryder Finn was standing beside the shiny air car holding the door. Pitth set his jaw and marched to his future.

They made the long journey in silence. Pitth watched out the window as the steppes turned to mountains, then into forest. The mountains returned as they approached Khmer, poking their white tips through lush jungle.

Ryder Finn circled the vast temple complex. The center was an ancient cluster of stone buildings with domes and spires. Further out were modern building surrounding the ancient complex. All the buildings were of grey stone, brightened by colorful gardens, banners and garlands. From each spire and many poles around the place, prayer flags lazily hovered and danced with the breeze.

The air car settled on a flat grassy area. A tall, bald man wearing a bright yellow robe with a red sash bowed as Pitth approached. "Greetings, Pitth, son of our benefactor Tenzing who is a great friend of my master, Tok. I am Adept Nom Ng, and I am to be your proctor during your time here at the temple." Two bald boys appeared. Older than Sui, they wore only wrappings over their privates. Adept Ng spoke to them in a language foreign to Pitth. They took his belongings and raced away.

"Thank you for delivering my charge, Master Finn." Ng bowed deeply to the blue man.

Ryder Finn returned the bow and said, "He is a good boy. You will, of course, notify us when he is ready."

Ng nodded. Satisfied, Finn turned and re-entered his air car. It whined to power and flew away as Pitth followed Ng's path leading away from the grassy knoll. Their path twisted through the ancient stones, revealing patios and gardens. Males and females intersected their path, and not all the beings were human. A green, feathered girl (at least young Pitth *thought* it was a girl) smiled at him and bowed her head as they hurried past.

They arrived at a large garden, a fountain mounted along the wall. Another bald man, wearing the classic saffron robe but with a green sash, sat on the grass, his eyes closed.

He was old, older than even Grandmother, Pitth could see. He was shaven as any other in this place, but with heavy white eyebrows and a long, thin strand of white sprouting from his chin, reaching the middle of his stomach. "Enter, my young friend, Pitth." The ancient priest's voice was thin, but strong. "Please, sit here with me."

Pitth sat close to the priest, Ng kneeling gracefully at Pitth's side. "I am Tok, master bonze. Your father has requested that I oversee your education while you are with us. My student, Ng, will be your proctor, but I am here to show you your path and lead you to becoming a pious, modest man."

"I do not wish to become a priest!" blurted Pitth.

"I am pleased you can see that much of your path," Master Tok's answer was kind. "Though a shame. I can see you have a powerful spiritual center, even if you cannot. Pity. So, where does your path lie, young Pitth?"

Pitth stared at his fiddling fingers. No one had ever asked him that. There were many things he liked to do; ride horses, hunt, and play with his friends. His future was as clouded as the winter sky. "I don't know," was his weak response.

"Excellent!" Tok exclaimed, "It leaves us so many more venues to explore if you have no idea where you want to go. Come then, young Pitth, Ng and I will accompany you on your journey."

Chapter 3

September 3022

Pitth awakened to rain pattering on his window sill. The words of
Master Tok echoed in his mind, "The rain is just the rain. It is how
you perceive the rain that causes you discomfort." He stretched and
sighed, listening to the rhythmic hiss as the seasonal storm poured its
life-giving gift from the gods.

The familiar *pat-pat-pat* brought a satisfied smile to the
boy's face. A tiny channel lay in the stones that formed his window
sill. Every rainfall, the water would find the channel, wind its way
along the mini cataract, pool, and then drop to the lower sill with a
cadenced beat. *Pat-pat-pat.* He had studied the channel closely
during the dry days, but could never find the diminutive stream bed
unless it was raining.

It would slowly work its way down the wall, along the upper
sill, a single drop to start followed by countless others, forming a
pool at the base of his window. One such storm, he placed a tea cup
under the drip. The tone turned from *pat-pat-pat,* to a musical *plink-
plink-plink* at the same rate. The cup filled quickly, so Pitth drank
the rainwater and replaced the cup, enjoying the small song the gods
provided.

The second gong sounded. Sighing, Pitth rolled from his
warm bed, dressed and hurried to breakfast. Today was oatmeal and
fruit. Pitth missed having savory meats in the morning. Most of the
residents of Angkor wat were vegetarian. Being a student entitled
him to some privilege, but meat every day was not one of them.

Following breakfast, he was allotted an hour for meditation. Adept Ng had walked Pitth here his first day to meet Master Tok. He enjoyed the sheltered grass glade with the small tower of a fountain. He and his masters had spent many hours here meditating together. He had balked once, on a rainy day much as this one. Tok had chided him. "The rain is just the rain," he had said. Pitth had gotten soaked that day and many others, but had learned how refreshed he felt after a good rain shower.

Another boy sat on the glade this morning. Odd, he was wearing a yellow robe and saffron sash normally reserved for a Master. Pitth quietly found a spot and sat, opened his arms and began his meditations. He focused as proctor Ng had instructed him, not paying attention to the gentle rain, concentrating inward for his center.

"Can you hear it?" The other boy's question irritated Pitth. He cleared his head and started again. "Pssst, I said can you hear it?" repeated the adept.

"Be quiet," Pitth hissed. "You are disturbing my reflection."

"Yes, yes, but listen! Can you hear it?" The other boy was nothing but persistent.

"What?" asked Pitth.

"Shhh, quiet, find your center." The adept's voice was soothing and penetrating at the same time. "Now open your mind. Feel the clouds above us. Do you see the water vapor? Each drop, focus on a single drop."

Pitth was cognizant of the cloud. He found a droplet and focused on it.

"It's cooling now, drawing other droplets to it. One touches the other, breaks surface tension and they join," droned the adept.

Pitth watched as other droplets were joined to his. Each would touch, joining the two surfaces, wobbling slightly as the fluid in the tiny drops swirled together. Another drop joined and the process repeated again and again.

The adept guided Pitth's vision. "It is heavier now, too heavy to float along in the cloud." "It's falling, falling, falling. It strikes the leaf on the birch tree there. Surface tension breaks and the water inside bursts forth. The leaf vibrates from the impact. This vibrates the air around it. Do you hear it, young Pitth?"

His raindrop fell and struck the leaf. There it was! The light *tah* as the raindrop splattered across the leaf, making it vibrate, creating the barely audible *schwaaa*. It drew his breath away for a moment, then repeated the experiment, again and again. He listened to the orchestra, so different than the song from his room.

On his own, he listened to the droplets fall from the leaves and strike the grass beneath the tree. Each in turn added a softer *tah* to the symphony.

The hour was over too quickly. There was a rustle of robes and the adept patted Pitth's shoulder. "It is time to go, young Pitth," said the adept. The boy stood and regarded the other boy.

"Thank you for such an enlightening lesson, young master," Pitth bowed low to the adept. "Please, I may I have your name? I should like to meditate with you again."

"Oh, up, up, up," admonished the adept. "Look me in the eye, not at my feet. I will be pleased to meditate with you again, master Pitth. As for my name, well, I think you know who I am."

Pitth straightened and looked deep into the brown eyes. He searched the face. It was so madding familiar! His sloe eyes, the firm chin…It was his own face!

"Master?" he stammered.

"Yes, Pitth, I am who you seek," his spiritual center responded. "I am one with you now, always and forever."

Pitth kowtowed as his mother had taught him. He raised to see his center had copied the gesture. "Hurry, now," his center admonished, "we barely have time to shower and get to our first class."

Seven years before, Pitth had dreaded entering the classrooms of Angkor wat. While most of the students were human like himself, there was an upsetting number of off-worlders whose parents or governments wanted their children to better know humans.

Grrrscnk was one such being. She was Hecht, from a distant system Spinward. Her species was closely related to Terran dinosaurs, specifically predators. She was ten, two years younger than Pitth, and stood nearly as tall. Her green and blue pebbled skin was covered with fine pinfeathers. As adults, the Hecht were an explosion of color, ranging from black as a singularity to brilliant white as a nova at detonation. She walked erect on reverse knee legs like a bird and her long, three fingered hands were tipped with fierce claws. Pitth marveled at how the scythe-like weapons could be handled so delicately by the girl.

Her elongated face ended in a wide mouth rimmed with a triple row of razor sharp teeth and her snout was tipped with a heavy beak. She explained it would fall away as she entered puberty. Small, bright eyes adorned each side of her head and a crest lay flat along its top. When Grrrscnk was surprised or angry, it flared scarlet and snapped up.

Many of the other students avoided Grrrscnk. She was a meat eater; as such she didn't live or eat with the other students. As often as not she would return from her meals, carrion still hanging from her jaws, blood smeared across her snout. She was becoming aware of the effect her hygiene had on her fellow students, so recently she haphazardly cleaned herself some of the time before she returned.

Her presence caused quiet fear and paranoia amongst some of her classmates. Several times a year, students would whisper the question, *"Is she sizing me up? Am I to be her next meal?"*

She and Pitth were best friends. They would sit together in class. In between lessons, they would find a quiet place to study or discuss their lives.

Today's first period would be biology. Grrrscnk referred to the class as "learning about the galactic menu." Pitth found he loved

37

the sciences and Angkor wat was perhaps the finest school he could hope to attend. The Buddha had written that the pursuit of knowledge was a sure path to enlightenment. The priests of the wat hired or trained the finest teachers for their students. And charged a steep price for the excellence.

"How was your sleep-wakening this morning?" asked Grrrscnk. She had tried meditation once. Sitting still had proven difficult for her. Relaxing and listening to her Te was impossible. "We have those who sit quietly on Hecht," she had said. "Mother calls them supper."

Today's study was cataloging a mystery sample using an older electron microscope. Pitth took the eyepiece and manipulated the controls as Grrrscnk could barely twist her head about far enough. She recorded as he read and deciphered the strands of data. They worked quickly, the routine comfortable and *au fait.*

"She's big," commented Pitth.

"Are you sure it's a she?" questioned Grrrscnk.

"Sure. Look at the indicator here."

Grrrscnk twisted her head to the eyepiece and squinted. "I dunno," she stated, "the third tertiary looks like it could be androgynous."

They switched places again. "I think you're right," admitted Pitth. Grrrscnk snapped her jaw twice, the action that passed for a Hecht giggle.

The rest of the morning passed quickly. Pitth declined Grrrscnk's invitation to lunch. He had seen what the Hecht did to

38

her lunch. The glade was empty, so he ate his cheese and fruit under the soffit and napped.

"Pitth!" the voice was insistent. "PITTH!" His center was there in the glade. "Wake up! You'll be late for class!"

"Thank you, Master." Pitth gathered himself and ran back to his classroom. The afternoon proctor was just arriving as he slid into his seat.

The afternoon period was mathematics. The proctor insisted on a silent classroom, so Pitth pulled the lesson up on his data pad and began his work. Grrrscnk had wiped her snout, but there was a trace of red stain on her thin lips and teeth. She smacked her mouth, her black tongue probing her stained teeth and lips in the first minutes of class. An unpleasant odor emanated from it.

Pitth ignored her and focused on his work. Like the sciences, he found he had a knack for mathematics. The two disciplines worked well with each other. At twelve, Pitth was starting to ponder his future. Befriending Grrrscnk had opened his mind to worlds outside the Earth. Their mutual studies, particular classes like this morning, had him considering a future in science or medicine. Maybe both. Certainly, he would have no future following his father's lead. Tenzing was a lawyer and a politician. As eldest son, Suishin would one day be head of the Khalkha tribe.

As Khan, Tenzing was the head of the government by the Great Khural. There was talk on the news channels that he would soon lead the Earth Council. Pitth was immensely proud of his father and pleased to be his son. But it would be Suishin who would lead the Khalkha one day. So Pitth needed to study and work hard, bring honor to his family through his hard work and achievement.

The late afternoon gong rang. Pitth startled; he had been thinking of his future rather than focusing on his lessons. The class had risen, gathered their things and were leaving when Grrrscnk appeared at Pitth's desk. They left the school together, chatting. At an intersection, Grrrscnk raised her head to Pitth's. He rubbed her cheek with his, the Hecht farewell to a close friend. She made a purring noise and snapped her jaws again. "I will see you tomorrow?" the alien girl asked.

"Of course. Good hunting, friend Grrrscnk," Pitth told her.

"Good hunting to you, friend Pitth." She stalked through the portal, her head waving to and fro, stopping as a movement caught her eye. She would momentarily freeze, then continue on her path. Other students crossing her path would freeze, praying she wasn't hunting.

He dumped his things in his room and hurried back to the Glade. The meeting this morning with his center was profound; he wanted to study the effect more.

The rain had faded to a mist. Pitth was a bit disappointed to see Ng and Master Toc waiting for him. He wasn't certain his center would appear if there were other beings present. Nevertheless, he kowtowed and entered.

"Your center has revealed to you," Ng said.

Pitth nodded. "Yes Master, just this morning. And during my lunch meditation."

"Ah!" Toc said, with a happy tone. "Summon him for us, please?"

"Can I? Wondered the boy. He sat and centered himself, then opened his mind. Momentarily, he felt the presence beside him. "He is here, Master," reported Pitth.

"Yes, I can see. I greet you, young master," Toc said. "Here are the nucleus of myself and my student Ng."

Pitth opened his eyes. Two glowing figures sat next to Toc and Ng.

"These are our nuclei," explained Ng. "They are there when we need them, whether we acknowledge their presence or not. Master Toc and I will show you how to access your nucleus and make the best use of it."

"Does this mean I have to become a priest?" wondered the boy.

Both of his masters burst out in laughter. "Pitth, my boy, always with the silliest of questions!" chortled Toc. "Boy, rest assured, your path does not lead to the priesthood. Though Ng and I would not be displeased if you chose to follow us in this fashion. No, your nucleus is the personification of your inner voice, the quiet breeze in your mind that keeps you awake when you are puzzling over a problem. Tell me, did he show you the challenge of the raindrop?"

"Yes Master."

"And what did you learn?" pressed Ng.

Pitth pondered. *Listen and see* came the soft voice of his center. Again, he watched the droplets coalesce and fall, break apart on impact and the quiver of the leaf.

"Events occur because of chains of events." said Pitth. "And these events lead still to other chains and other events."

"Yes," breathed Toc, "you do see. Now, attend."

They were at the fountain's edge. "Regard the fountain," instructed Ng. "Alter the fall of a single flow, using just what you see."

Pitth chose the pour over a pair of stones that fell a foot into a pool. He focused on the spot. He could see the water, feel as it rushed over the edge and landed in the pool below. But he couldn't affect the flow. "I cannot, Master," he surrendered.

Toc bent over and picked up a stone. "Here, try this," handing it to Pitth.

The boy took the stone and placed it at the junction of two stones where the water was pouring through. Immediately, the flow split, two cascades pouring into the pool below.

"Yes better," commented Ng. "Do you hear?"

Pitth closed his eyes again. The sound was more pleasing. "Yes, Master, I hear."

"But it is still not right," noted Toc.

Pitth twisted the stone slightly to the right. He listened.

"Yes, that's it," commented Ng.

Toc's face brightened, his almond eyes widened, a beatific smile split his face. "Yes," he declared, "That's it right there. Perfect. Well done, young Pitth!"

"What did you learn, student?" pressed Ng.

His center nodded. *You understand.*

"I cannot change events," Pitth said in a cool, even voice, "but I can manipulate and control events by manipulating and changing the conditions around the events. If I listen to my center, I can even get the events to occur precisely as I want them to occur."

"Well done," Toc said, raising to his feet. "Ng, discuss with him about the alien, then leave him to his meditations. I will see you this evening at last prayers. Good night, young Pitth."

For the next hour, Ng told Pitth many things. About his friend Grrrscnk, and about the secret of the Hecht. About his father and his brother.

Proctor Ng then left Pitth to his meditation.

Chapter 4

Six years later

The incense wafted through the temple. The Buddha sat cross legged, hands in his lap, looking serene in his eternal meditation.

Pitth was seated, matching the Buddha's position. Beside him was the familiar adept, his bald head reflecting light from the hundreds of candles surrounding the two young men.

"Would you believe me if I told you part of me wishes to stay?" asked the Mongol teen.

"I would," answered the adept. "Just as you know I must insist you leave."

"Funny, a dozen years ago, I begged my father not to send me here," Pitth mused. "Now I love this place and would stay forever, even taking the vow and walking the path to priesthood."

"And after a dozen years, I believe you would," the adept replied. "But your father has summoned you; you must go. We both know you have a destiny.

"Besides," the adept grinned, "you are past time to select your name. In your culture, it's time to become a man. Finally, I will know you as something other than Pitth. Have you decided on your name?"

Pitth nodded. "I believe it is the only name I could have chosen. I will miss you."

"As will I," his center replied. "But you know where to find me, I will be where you need me the most."

The rear door of the temple slid aside; the soft sounds of slippers shuffled across the ancient stones. Pitth turned; his spirit center had faded into the ether.

"Your shuttle is here, my son," his ancient mentor announced. "Are you ready to leave?"

"I am now, Master."

The view from the rail-less balcony was every bit as spectacular as Pitth had anticipated. The major domo of his father's Keep had sent a list and diagrams of the available suites. This one sat at the highest vista, the view of the Gobi Desert unobscured. As the suite was unoccupied, he claimed the apartment and moved in.

While there were many priest wearing the same saffron robes he wore, it was unusual to see a resident of the royal chambers in Tenzing's Keep dressed so. Many sideways glances were directed at him as he made his way through the Keep. His shaggy hair marked him as the son of Tenzing; whispers followed about the robes worn by the son of the Khan. Perhaps he had become a priest while with the Khmer. But with that hair?

Still, until his father ordered otherwise, he was most comfortable in them; let the other residents of the Keep whisper. He scratched at his shaggy hair. Last year, he had started growing it back out into Mongol fashion, knowing he would be returning.

He was trying to meditate on the edge of his balcony, but there were so many distractions. The hot breeze blowing off the desert was one. The commotion throughout the Keep, another. In

45

temple, everyone tended to move in silence. Here, there seemed to be a constant buzz that permeated the very stone walls. And the smells! Pitth had missed eating meat in temple. Here in the ancient home of his fathers, his mouth watered at the smells of beef, goat and chicken floating in the air.

"So, my perfect little brother has returned home, finally." It was Sui, striding into Pitth's room unannounced.

"I am hardly perfect, Brother," answered Pitth, raising.

Sui was a large man now, thickly muscled. He wore traditional boots and breeches. Shockingly to the modest Pitth, his brother was bare-chested, opting only a traditional vest. His head was shaved, save for a long queue.

"Not what I hear," he sneered. "Little Pitth, returned to the Khalkha, looking like a priest."

"I am not a priest, Sui," Pitth responded in an even tone. "Why are you so angry? I hoped you would have been happy to welcome me home."

"I am Suishin now, Boy," his brother replied. "I am a man; you will refer to me by my man name. I am not the child you recall." His massive form towered over his slighter brother. "Your mother is expecting you to escort her to the Naadam Festival. I suggest you change into something acceptable."

Pitth stood at the edge of the vegetable garden. The Keep had many such gardens, fed from the river that flowed deep under

46

the mountain. His mother was bent, plucking weeds from the narrow rows of radishes.

She was a plain woman, of peasant stock. Pure Mongolian, Qui was a member of the Khalkha tribe who had shared her yurt and her bed one freezing night on the lowland steppe with Tenzing. He had married her as one of his minor wives until Pitth was born. He then elevated her to the position of second wife, after Suishin's mother. This changed the tiny peasant Qui little. She now lived in the palace and had servants available, but she preferred to work the garden or ride out on the vast steppe to visit friends and families in the migratory camps.

"Mother?" called Pitth.

Callused hands set her trowel down. Bright eyes glowed as her weathered face broke into a wide smile. "My son!" She cried as she opened her arms. They embraced, Qui covering his face with kisses and rubbing noses.

"Enough now," she said after several moments, "I need to finish this row. Then we can go to festival. We have much to do before your Naming Day tomorrow."

Pitth joined his mother in the muddy dirt, plucking the weeds from the soil. Father had once said how mother was a perfect Mongolian woman, shy and demure when in public, a chatterbox around friends and family. "Everyone is talking about how auspicious it is that your Naming Day is on the first day of the festival," Qui said. "Your father has invited all the headsmen of the tribes to attend and a great many of the leaders of Pan-Asia!

47

Certainly, the leader of Khmer will be there, as you have lived there for so many years. And India, Persia. All of them. We'll have to find a special robe for you, something quite magnificent for such a special day!"

"Mother, please," he replied, "don't make such a fuss. A plain robe will be just fine."

"Nonsense!" she shot back. "Everyone wants to see the son of the headman of the Khalkha named. Members of the Kurultai Council will be there. Your father is counting on you to gather much face."

She leaned over the row of green shoots to whisper. "Three years ago, that spoiled brat, Suishin, embarrassed his father and the whole tribe, showing up immodestly with his chest bare and wearing that Chin queue! It was clear he had been drinking. I have promised Tenzing you will be the very son he deserves."

The air car swept over the massive yurt city assembled on the steppe. It was as his mother had promised, thousands of the traditional homes of the nomadic Mongols from as far back as history recorded. (Although nearly all were of modern materials, sculpted and painted to resemble yurts.) They surrounded a central pavilion, avenues radiating out like the spoke of a giant wheel. To the west were more shelters of foreign design housing many of the friends and allies of the Pan Asian Confederation.

Pitth and Qui were escorted to a yurt near Tenzing's. After tomorrow, of course, he would have his own yurt, as an adult should. But tonight, as a child still, he was expected to stay with his mother.

48

The yurt was roomy, large cushions and blankets sorted about. Mindful of Pitth's modesty, his mother had ordered a screen set up in one corner. They were served a savory bowl of spicy beef strips with vegetables. He wanted to wolf down the food, so much more exciting than the plain fare he had eaten for the last dozen years in temple. A dozen years at the temple had given him restraint. Savoring the well-seasoned dish added to his enjoyment. The meal finished with a warm custard. Pitth patted his stomach and belched appreciatively. "Thank you, my son," Qui beamed at Pitth's burp. "I was afraid all those years amongst the priest would have dulled your manners. Now, no sitting about, we must go shopping for tomorrow!"

There were dozens of markets set throughout the encampment. Merchants from across Asia hawked their wares: bolts of rare cloth, squawking creatures from Earth and beyond. Jewelry sparkled in all the stalls, forged Terran gold with firestones of Mercury. Strange art from any of a dozen worlds adorned the walls of the makeshift businesses.

Pitth sniffed and savored the odors wafting through the market. It was well his mother had fed him! Any number of merchants were serving steaming meat, rice of every color, fruits and vegetables of every shape and size!

He had stopped at a bookseller, leafing through an ancient text from the Americas, when his mother called, "Pitth! Come here! I have found it, it's perfect!" He set the book down, memorizing the title, *Confessions of a Martian Schoolgirl...* " He would have to come back for it.

Qui grabbed his arm and dragged him to a clothier. "Here, look what I have found!"

It was hideous, gaudy. A stiff-looking golden brocade, high collared. It gathered at the waist, then flared out a foot of narrow, rainbow stripes. The cuffs were large and white, a dragon embroidered on one cuff, a leaping horse on the other. Cream-colored breeches and soft boots would complete the outfit.

"It's er, a bit much, don't you think, Mother?" Pitth ventured.

"Nonsense! It is perfect!" she declared. "It shows just the right amount of audacity and panache demanded from the son of the Khalkha, without being overly ostentatious or immodest."

"I designed it from images I found of the last Chin Emperor from the twentieth century," the seamstress said with pride. "It's more modern, of course and of a fashionable cut. His was called the Rainbow Robe. Wearing this modern version, you will certainly be remembered."

"Oh, yes I certainly will," mused Pitth. *"But not for the reasons you think."*

He reluctantly conceded to his mother, allowing the tailor to take his measurements with the promise the clothing would be ready by sunrise.

The ceremony was to take place outside the city, on the steppe. A dais had been raised, a hundred seats arranged. The leaders from across Pan Asia had arrived in air cars and been

50

escorted to their seats. The Mongol leaders, of course, rode in on fine steeds. Tenzing arrived, Qui riding at his side. They took their positions at the center of the dais.

There was a great shout. The crowd roared and parted as Pitth rode in on a warhorse, a shield on one arm, his bow in the other. A quiver of arrows was strapped to the saddle at his knee.

"Who is this?" shouted Tenzing. "Who disturbs this gathering of the Khalkha? What manner of intrusion is this before our brothers, the Oirats, the Durigan and the Boryats? And my friends from throughout Mongolia and all of Pan Asia?"

"I do," answered Pitth.

"And just who are you to interrupt, Boy?" thundered Tenzing. "How dare you appear here in the clothing of a man and carrying the weapons of a Mongol warrior? By what madness is this?"

"It is by no madness, Father. Today, by the laws of my people, and before the leaders of my people, I declare myself to be a man," Pitth recited from the age-old script.

"Pah!" Tenzing turned, "I see no man! I see a child wearing a man's clothing on a man's horse. Begone, child, run back to your mother."

A whisper of fletching's followed by the solid *thwock*. An arrow buried between Tenzing's feet. The crowd knew the symbology of the arrow and *HooooOOOO*-ed their appreciation of the shot.

Pitth stood tall and proud in his saddle, the next arrow nocked. Tenzing knew it was aimed at his heart.

"I claim my position as a man of the Khalkha!" stated Pitth, "You will acknowledge my place at the table of warriors!"

"A man?" asked Tenzing. "Who is this man who claims to be my son?"

He stood tall in the saddle. "I am your son and a man. My name is…Angkor."

The crowd roared.

Tenzing opened his arms and shouted. "Come to your father then, Angkor, my son." No one could hear, the cheers were deafening. Angkor leapt from his horse and strode confidently onto the dais. "A fine man you are Angkor. Tall, proud, modest. Yes, I am proud to call you my son." The two men embraced.

"Come, my friends and I have laid out a warrior's breakfast," Tenzing said. "Then you and I will go enjoy the festival."

It was a resplendent board. The tables groaned under platters of meats and fruits. Large cheeses were scattered about along with outsized loaves of bread. Servants scurried about with pitchers of tea and butter mead. Musicians played gay tunes as entertainers juggled, sang, and performed acts of bewilderment and amazement.

Tenzing dragged his awestruck son to the head table. "Friends!" he cried, "I give you a new Khalkha warrior, a man and my son." The assembly of Mongols and their allies stood and cheered, saluting Tenzing on his great fortune. Only Suishin was silent, standing near the rear of the tent. His dark eyes burned holes through Angkor as he cleaned his fingernails with a thin, tapered blade.

Chapter 5

Tenzing and Angkor strutted down the streets of the temporary city on the steppes. "Come, my son! Let's go see the games!" his father insisted.

The Naadam Festival had its roots in the ancient times when the tribes were spread across the whole of Asia. Yearly, they would gather for feasting, settlement of arguments, exchange of goods and gifts. And the Games.

The Games had started as demonstrations of warrior arts, horseback riding, archery, and wrestling. But as the centuries progressed, more games were added and contests of singing and poetry.

Now all the nations or Earth sent representatives and their games to the festival. Hellas, famous for its Olympics, sent its version of wrestling and foot races. Occident, nearly as large as Pan Asia, sent a great variety. Tall poles they threw, the lifting and throwing of heavy weights. Sliding stones across slippery sheets of ice. Each region had its favorite and drew great crowds to hoot and cheer at the skills of their neighbors.

Only the games of Earth were allowed. While many aliens attended, their games would never be permitted.

"This is who we are," declared Tenzing. "This is what it is to be human! Our songs, our games, our struggle with each other. We fight and squabble amongst ourselves, yes. But in the end, each looks to his enemy and declares 'you are my brother!'"

They joined the crowd at the children's horse race. Angkor recalled riding in the race years ago, the first time his father brought him to the festival. With a shout, the next race of five hundred leapt from the starting gate, as the tide rushes through a channel. Tiny voices screamed out dozens of tribal war cries as they broke from narrow bleachers and onto the open plain. Tenzing and Angkor jumped and cheered with the crowd as the horde raced through the course, riding miles out and back. A small girl from the Oirats tribe took the race for the five-year olds. The cry went up and the next race, for six-year olds began to form up.

Tenzing led his son away, wandering toward the archery range. He was deep in thought. "Answer me, Angkor, one question…What is the best form of government?"

"Democracy, father," Angkor replied.

"Why?"

Angkor considered for a few steps. "Because it allows participation for all of the governed," was his uncertain response.

"Does it?" Tenzing pressed. "What of the man or woman who doesn't participate? Doesn't vote? Doesn't engage in their local politics? Does democracy work for them, too?"

"They are fools if they don't participate," came Angkor's stern reply.

"Yes, fools." Tenzing walked several steps, then offered, "Yet these same fools cry out the loudest when the policy they support isn't enacted or when the politician they oppose win elective

55

office. Usually quite noisily, if my experience is to have any weight."

An announcement thundered from the fairgrounds tannoy. The men's competition in archery was about to begin. "Shall we?" Tenzing beckoned to the line of men who waited to compete. Angkor was thrilled. His father's prowess with the bow was legendary amongst the Khalkha; to be invited to shoot with his father was incredible. He would gain much face with the gesture his father was offering.

Several of the other participants recognized the headman of the Khalkha and whispered to themselves. One ran to the front of the line, excited, and whispered into an official's ear, pointing. The official scurried down the line to Tenzing and kowtowed.

"You honor us with your presence, Exalted One," he groveled. "Would you honor us with a demonstration of your skill?"

"I came here to shoot a quiver with my son," explained Tenzing, "not to show off before all our fellow Terrans."

"Please," a bystander asked, an Egyptian by appearance and dress. "I should like to tell my children how I saw the Great Tenzing shoot a bow." Other men and women around them insisted as well.

"If those in front of us do not object?" asked Tenzing. None did, of course. Indeed, most applauded as Tenzing led Angkor to the front.

They each searched though the bows available. Many varieties, from modern composite bows to ancient weapons from many cultures were neatly organized for participants to select from.

Angkor had learned on the Mongolian short bow, and selected one that felt right. When he looked to his father, they both grinned. Each had selected the weapon of their ancestors.

Angkor wanted to examine each arrow as carefully as he had the bow. However, Tenzing walked over and selected the first quiver of arrows he found, slung them over his shoulder. "A warrior knows his weapons as he knows his own arm," explained Tenzing. "Poor is the warrior who blames a warped arrow or a bent arrow head. When he draws, he knows these things and adjusts to compensate when he fires,"

A youngster led them from the tent to the target range. The path was well trod, tamped down by the feet of thousands of participants for centuries. Whispers flew up and down the line, the legendary Tenzing Khan, headman of the Khalkha and Khan of all Mongolia, would be shooting today! As the great man and his son passed, the crowd pushed forward, climbing on any object for a better view. Fathers held their sons on their shoulders.

Targets were set at ten-yard intervals, ranging out to one hundred yards. Two further targets were at one hundred twenty-five and one hundred fifty yards. "It shall be Khalkha rules," announced the official. "Odd distances out, even distances back. Scores for target and speed. Contestants ready?"

The two men, father and son, stood at the firing line. The signal was given; both loosed at the ten-yard target. Then the thirty. Again, and again. At the ninety-yard target, Tenzing asked, "So, my son, if you see a lack of participation as the single biggest issue with democracy, what would you offer as a means to replace it?" He let loose his arrow and hit the target dead center, as he had all the rest.

Angkor hesitated. He pondered the question, then focused on his target and let fly. "Mandatory participation," he said as his arrow flew down range. "Or a different form of government entirely." His arrow struck center.

"Indeed?" Tenzing's one hundred twenty-five-yard arrow flew from the bow. "What form would that be?" The missile struck center, to rousing applause from the gathered throng.

Angkor struggled to focus. Clearly his father meant to distract him with all these questions. He ignored the sound of the crowd, focusing only on his breathing, his heartbeat and the arrow. He exhaled, waited for the slight pause in his pulse and released his · arrow. "I'm not sure, Father." His arrow flew true. It hit dead center.

"Ah, then we have much to talk about." Almost too swift to see, Tenzing lofted arrow after arrow until his quiver was empty. He tossed the bow to the stunned official as the striking of the six arrows sounded of an even ripple across the six targets, each perfectly centered. "When you are finished, my son, I'll see you at the starting line for the Great Race."

The crowd parted in awe as the headman strode past.

The Great Race was the oldest of all the traditional and most grueling of all the competitions of the Naadam Festival. Riders from every corner of Terra participated, with the horses of their nations.

Tenzing stood on the starter's platform, Angkor at his side. "This is the race of champions!" declared Tenzing. "The race above all races. Only the bravest men and women, only the heartiest of beasts may participate. You shall ride across the open Gobi for seven days to the temple on the edge of Mongol lands. There, the bonzes will award you your pendant. You return here to receive acclaim and honor for completing the race! This sword," he held a gleaming silver blade, "is the prize for the victor. The first rider, with their pendant, who grabs this sword is champion! Make ready, when the sword strikes." Tenzing suddenly threw the sword down into the turf, where it buried itself several inches.

The riders raced off. Many of the elders, Tenzing included, shook their heads. "The swiftest runners the first day won't finish," an elder told Angkor. "He will whip his horse out the first day. The beast will die within the first few days. No, the winner comes from the sure and steady rider, who has thought out his race and conserves his horse at the start." He pointed to the small band that was trotting away, just barely in sight. "One of those will be the winner."

Angkor watched the group trot away. One, from Occident, wore an unusual hat, flat and brown, mangled looking.

Father and son walked the streets again, heading to Tenzing's yurt for supper. "Have you considered my question?" asked the father.

"I have, Father," replied Angkor, "but I reserve the right to study the question more."

"That would be fair," agreed Tenzing. "I myself have considered the question for more than forty years. I cannot expect you to answer in a few hours. But, please, tell me your thoughts?"

"Certainly, Father. My first impression would be a monarchy. The leader can educate the successor, preparing him to attain the throne. Continuity can be maintained with proper training and education; a Council like our own Kurultai and Great Khural can advise the leader by informing him the will of the people."

"Ah, and the weakness of your great Khan?" queried Tenzing.

"The inevitable weakening of the Imperial line. The leader would have to have multiple avenues of partners to insure the purity and vitality of the family line."

"Could this be done with a single family?" asked Tenzing. "Is there a way to manipulate the family genes to ensure this weakening doesn't occur?"

Angkor pondered. "Possibly," he said. "Genetic engineering has been going on for centuries, including our own genome. But to map and create a superior being…" his voice trailed off in thought.

"But it could be done."

"Yes, almost certainly," responded Angkor. "To be prudent, though, it would require a committee dedicated to the design of such an heir. Perhaps each generation created would have multiple candidates, each being trained to assume the rule of leader when the leader passed."

Tenzing held his arm up at the door of his yurt. "We will speak more of this later," he told Angkor, "but for now, I wish you to keep today's conversation secret. These people at supper tonight are some of my closest friends and allies, but not all would understand what I am going to achieve. Always remember, my son, if you don't want something known, don't say it."

The heady days of the festival passed to quickly for Angkor. Some days, he and his father wandered the streets and venues, admiring the goods displayed or the talents shown. Tenzing was quick witted and clever at the poetry competition.

Angkor, to everyone's delight, excelled at singing, his voice deep and rich. He had studied the customs of the Khalkha and knew most of the songs of his people. He sang the riding stories, the stories of the encampments during migration and the songs to the gods. His father was proud when Angkor won a small silver cup for his voice.

It was the day of the Warriors Ride. Each rider was given two quivers of arrows. They would ride the course as rapidly as they could, firing their arrows at the twenty-four targets scattered about. Speed was important, but accuracy was critical.

Angkor had not planned to ride. He had found a good spot to watch the race and settled in when a familiar form found him.

Suishin stood before his younger brother, thick arms crossed over his bulging chest. Although still early in the day, he had a light sheen of perspiration. His jaw moved slightly as he chewed on a string of khat.

"So, Little Brother, you have come to watch a man's game," Suishin's voice was silky, insulting. "I heard you had won an award for singing. Did you sing about doing the wash or perhaps for your monthly cycle?"

"No, I sang a better song. I sang of the great oaf who was clumsy and drunk and he soiled his pants as he crawled to the privy." Angkor smiled and tilted his head. "It reminds me of you," he needled.

"Clumsy?" roared his brother. "CLUMSY! I will show you clumsy." His great bulk weaved and bobbed. "I challenge you! Here, before these people! I challenge you to the Warriors Race! Let us see who the greater Khalkha warrior in this family is!" He swung a massive paw at his brother, stumbled and fell face first into the turf.

Angkor grabbed Suishin's topknot. He slapped his brother's face a few times, perhaps harder than he should, and stated, "You are in no condition to ride, Brother. You would only serve to embarrass yourself and our father. Nonetheless, if you wish to continue this charade, I will be too glad to best you." He released his brother, whose head bounced off the turf.

Suishin glared at his sibling as he scrambled to his feet. Together, the brothers marched down to the officials table. "The sons of Tenzing have a matter of honor they wish to dispense with,"

Angkor told the head official. "I think we should get it out of the way so the rest of the race can continue uninterrupted."

Tenzing heard the commotion and approached calmly. "Can this dispute be settled in any other way?" asked the official. "With mediation, perhaps?"

Tenzing shook his head. "No. They have made an honorable request. I know my sons. If Angkor says it is an honor request, then there is good reason for this race. Though," his voice lowered, "I would have expected better of my own sons. Let the race be done," he declared, "so we can get to the important business of the day." The crowd cheered.

Catcalls and jeers surrounded the brothers from the unruly crowd. Gamblers immediately set odds. Business was brisk with Suishin being favored by a wide margin. The commotion continued as they entered the equipment tent. Suishin selected a modern bow, all plastic and exotic materials. He thumbed the bowstring and leered at Angkor, who had selected a traditional bow.

The corral was next. Twenty fine mounts were trotted out and run through their paces while the sons of Tenzing watched. Suishin gave a shout as he chose a massive war horse from Europe. The beast was impressive, with a large chest and confident stride. Angkor selected a traditional pony. The warhorse, he knew, would be fast and provide a stable platform for firing the bow. But his pony was quick, agile. Its eyes were bright and Angkor could feel it quivering beneath him. The horse was excited to be running this race too, he knew. Perhaps its ancestors rode with the great horde in ancient times and the beast could feel it in his blood.

They trotted to the start line. "Once around the course," the starter told them. "One target per arrow. There is a penalty for a missed target. Are you ready? GO!"

The crowd roared as the sons of Tenzing tore from the line. Suishin's horse thundered to the lead, as Angkor thought it would. Confidently, his brother twisted from left to right, firing bolt after bolt into the targets as they presented themselves. Angkor matched him, arrow for arrow from just behind, watching for the opening.

A tight turn to the left and Angkor and his pony darted past. Now his brother was behind, watching as Angkor twisted with smooth grace and fired arrow after arrow into the targets as he passed. The bottom half of the course was even more convoluted. Suishin's steed was bred for charging across an open battlefield carrying a heavy knight. Angkor's pony was nimbler and quick; his lead grew at each turn.

Angkor screamed a cry of victory as he and his horse dashed to the finish. Suishin abandoned his shooting at targets and began to whip his horse, desperately trying to catch his younger brother. Angkor and his pony hunkered and sprinted the last hundred yards to the cheering crowd, crossing the line easily ahead of his brother. He stopped past the line, patting the horse appreciatively.

"The winner and point of honor for the sons of Tenzing goes to the younger, Angkor," declared the official.

"NO!" roared Suishin, "He cheated, he must have cheated!" Before anyone could respond, Suishin's last arrow was knocked and fired. The aim was true; it went through Angkor's thigh and into the heart of the pony. Angkor was able to leap clear of the dying horse, which screamed and writhed as it fell.

Tenzing appeared, knife in hand. In one motion, he cut the dying pony's throat, relieving its misery.

Now only a concerned father, he knelt and checked Angkor's wound. "Thanks to the gods it was a target arrowhead, not a flared war arrow," Tenzing breathed. The wound was clean and while bleeding messily, could be repaired by a few passes of a surgeon's stitcher.

His eyes blazing, he strode to Suishin, grabbed him and threw him from his horse. "You have dishonored me and our entire clan!" he growled. His fists rained down on his firstborn. "I cannot, and I will not have such a display of cowardice from my own family on display like this." He began to kick the cowering Suishin, who curled into a ball as Tenzing released his fury.

Finally, tiring, Tenzing stopped his assault and spat on Suishin. His attention turned to Angkor. "You have won today's point of honor, my son." Tenzing said. "And your brother will not long forget this. Come, let's get your leg fixed. Then you will leave for your university."

"But Mother, I must say good bye to my mother," Angkor protested, his voice weak from the blood loss. "And the Great Race will be over in two days. I must see the end of the Great Race."

"I will speak to your mother," Tenzing said, "and there will be other Great Races. A rider from Occident is two days ahead anyway; it is a foregone conclusion he will win." Angkor remembered the Occident rider with the unusual hat in the group that trotted away at the beginning of the race.

"As you wish, Father."

"Bring that," Tenzing ordered his guards, pointing at Suishin, as he tromped away.

It would be twenty years before Angkor witnessed another Great Race.

Chapter 6

April 3031

They were the oddest quintet crossing the market square in the old city.

Xaid Singh, a native Indian from Calcutta, led his classmates through the throng. A charismatic young man, his chubby frame could be found at the center of any social occasion. He was accompanied by close friend, Dawlish Zultan, a giant, brooding Turk from the Persian Empire. Unlike his classmates, Dawlish attended Delhi University to prepare for a military career. His uncle was the defense minister and Dawlish was expected to replace him one day.

They were joined by a new friend from Egypt, Salaam Sarkis, a nervous second year from Thebes. The diminutive Egyptian boy scuttled about, eager to please his older classmates, cowering if anyone paid direct attention to him. Angkor and Grrrscnk brought up the rear. Grrrscnk, now at full grown Hecht, seven feet tall with a four-foot tail lashing back and forth as she strode through the crowd. None but the bravest being would say anything to the toothy alien. She was only matched in height by Dawlish and her sleek feathers were a stunning white, intermixed with amber and opal stripes.

Delhi was a modern city, the jewel of Pan Asia. The largest of all the Asian metropolises to survive the wars of the Third Millennium, it boasted great skyscrapers and vast conglomerates while still maintaining its old-world charm. Air cars, private and public, raced along carefully regulated lanes in the skies, while oxen-drawn wagons and handcarts rolled through clean boulevards. Cries to prayer rang from the various temples throughout the city, alongside billboards advertising their ecclesiastical wares.

Delphi Market was the melting pot of Earth and alien culture. Pepper pot stews and curry were hawked next to *stoocha* root and *granth* steaks. Grrrscnk would grumble good naturedly (they thought :) "I cannot fathom why you monkeys insist on burning delicious meat before you eat!"

Bolts of cloth, gems and jewelry, sublime and prosaic knick-knacks and gee-haws, it was all there. Music from dozens of worlds filled the air, from graceful lilting to teeth grinding screeches and howls. Aerialists hung from ledges and lamp posts performing acts of derring-do. Street performers blew fire, juggled, sang songs and told jokes. Magicians marveled with cards and coins, scarfs changing into canes or beasts.

Pickpockets and other criminals preyed on the tight crowds. The police were ever-present, more inclined to keep order than monitor low level criminal activity. But woe to the being who was caught with its hand (or whatever appendage they had to use) in the pocket of another. Indian law frowned heavily on thieves.

That particular Saturday, they were pushing their way through the crowds, arguing as always about the latest law or news story back home, whether Ankara or Hecht. It was mostly good-natured chatter between young friends on a beautiful day.

And then Angkor saw her.

He happened to turn toward the tea seller in the sari of seafoam green, just as she also turned to face him. She was as tall as Angkor, fair skinned to his swarthy. She gasped under her breath at the sight of him, then found her voice. "Tea, sahib?"

He felt foolish, standing there staring at her. Her features were Hindi, long face tapering into a pointed chin. She had a golden halo of surprising soft, curly blonde hair. Her eyes were crystalline blue, perfect almond shaped that startled his heart. Her brow raised as she leaned nearer to him. "Tea? Sahib, would you like some tea?" she asked as speaking to a child.

"Tea? Ah, uh, yes, I would like some tea. Yes, please," Angkor fumbled. She gave him a shy smile as she pulled a paper cup from her bag. She wore a plastic jug on her back and poured the warm drink through its hose, offering lemon and sugar as she twisted to face him again. Afraid to speak, Angkor just nodded, admiring her lithe form as she prepared his drink. She handed the cup to him and held her thin, delicate, ring-less hand out.

"Three rupees, Sahib."

He handed her his credit chip, her pale hand ran it through the scanner at her belt, and she smiled again, melting Angkor's young heart. Before he could speak, she had bowed and gracefully melted back into the crowd.

"An interesting looking monkey," hissed Grrrscnk. "Is the she a friend of yours?"

"What? No, just a street vendor," Angkor answered. "Oh, my, she's beautiful, isn't she?"

"Oh, yes, delicious," grumbled Grrrscnk.

Xaid, Dawlish and Salaam appeared. "Hey, who's your friend?" asked Salaam.

"A tea girl," responded Angkor.

"What's her name?" pressed Salaam, "She's very pretty."

Confusion swept across Angkor's face. "I-I don't know," he said, "I forgot to ask."

Dawlish shook his head. "Angkor, my friend, you are going to die a virgin." He stretched his long frame above the crowd, spied the tea girl and moved to her. A few minutes later he had a steaming cup of tea, and information.

"Her name is Sophia; she is a resident of the city," he reported. "She is eighteen and hopes to get a job as a secretary or receptionist." He took a sip of tea and made a face. "A new job would be a good idea," he moaned as he spat it out. "This is horrible! Oh, and for whatever reason, she thinks Angkor is cute."

Dawlish straightened. "Clearly, if she finds a lowly Mongolian preferable to a magnificent Turk man..." his voice trailed off, a sparkle in his eye.

Angkor sipped the tea. It was terrible, too cold and too much lemon. But he imagined he could detect her aroma on the cup. Inhaling deeply, he said, "It's not so bad. Come on, we're here to shop; let's go shopping."

Try as he might, Angkor couldn't get the tea girl out of his mind. Her Hindi face with such pale skin and blond hair was so unusual. He would lie in his bed, staring at the ceiling, visualizing her lovely face and blue eyes.

He struggled in his classes all week. Normally, he could push distractions to one side while studying. Not this girl. Sophia! Such a lovely name. "English," he thought. But how would an English girl look Hindi?

The end of the week finally arrived. Without waiting for his friends, Angkor raced to the market on Saturday morning. Two hours and he was beginning to feel desperate when he felt a tug on his sleeve.

"Tea, Sahib?" She stood there, in a blue sari, her head tipped demurely, a faint smile on her face. He stood as stone again, dumbfounded and staring. She was every bit as beautiful as he remembered. "Would you like some tea?" she asked again.

"Tea, yes, I would like some tea," he stammered. Her smile got bigger and she pulled the cup from her bag, poured the tea and added lemon. She added a bit of honey and handed him the drink. The tea was worse than the week before. He grimaced.

"I am sorry, Sahib," she said, lowering her head. "My master reuses the leaves; it makes the tea weak and bitter. Please, take this poor cup for free."

"No, it is fine," he lied. He handed her his credit chip. "Please, take the money. I do not wish to cause you trouble."

She nodded and scanned his card. "Thank you, Sahib. Your kindness for this poor girl is more than generous."

Angkor struggled to find just the right words. He swallowed and stammered, "Think nothing of it."

He shifted from foot to foot, looking up and down, tasting words and then discarding them. He wanted to be glib, he wanted to appear confident. He looked into her opal eyes and felt his courage sink. "Yes?" she queried. Her mouth opened slightly, her eyes expecting.

"I, uh…um," he was frantic now, "Uhhh…"

Her face fell. "I have to go now," she said. "I must sell the rest of my tea and pay my master for the jar for today."

"Wait!" he cried. He brushed his hands on his pants, then held one out. "I am Angkor, son of Tenzing."

She took his hand. "I am pleased to meet you, Angkor, son of Tenzing," she replied. "I am Sophia Marshall. Perhaps I shall see you again here at the market another time."

She released his hand and strolled away. She looked over her shoulder and mouthed, "'bye."

Angkor watched her back until she disappeared into the crowd. "She certainly has nice hips," he decided.

"I cannot believe how stupid you monkeys are!" Grrrscnk tossed another piece of meat in her mouth and smacked her jaws as she chewed. "The Hecht way is much better."

"How is that?" argued Salaam. "How would you know? I have never seen you with a Hecht male, so just how do you know your Hecht way is better?"

Angkor's friends had found him at the market. They were eating lunch at one of the few eateries that would serve raw meat for a Hecht. (Although many patrons left when the six-foot meat eater entered.) They were discussing Angkor's failure that morning with the tea girl, Sophia.

Grrrscnk snapped her jaw in irritation. "Hecht females select their mates when they are ready to lay eggs. She selects the male and they *fffschrt*. He then builds the nest and the female lays the eggs. Both take care of the eggs until they hatch. The male hunts when the first egg starts to hatch. He must bring food, because we are born hungry."

She chomped down another piece of meat. "My father failed to have food when I escaped the shell. So, I ate my first brother as he hatched."

Her friends made faces and voiced disgust. "What did your father do when he returned?" asked Salaam.

"Mother took his kill to feed me," Grrrscnk responded. "It was clear he was inferior; therefore, his male children were inferior as well. Mother drove him away, along with his inferior sons."

"So, how is that better?" pressed Dawlish.

"Silly monkey!" Grrrscnk chuckled, "Look how selecting a mate has unsettled friend Angkor. Hecht do not get unsettled. If the male is unworthy, then he is driven off. Mother than raised me as the superior Hecht female who you see today." She ripped a mouthful of loin, and chewed noisily, her snout in the air, blood running down from the corners of her mouth.

73

"I'm not looking to mate with Sophia," Angkor protested. "I just think she's very pretty."

His friends hooted and laughed, (in Grrrscnk's case, snapped jaws.) "Angkor," chortled Xaid, "if you were any more obsessed with this girl, I'd say you were in love."

"How can that be?" answered Angkor, "I can barely speak to her."

"I repeat, friend Angkor, you're going to die a virgin," laughed Dawlish. "Listen, go find her this afternoon and walk with her. Don't think what to say, just walk with her and listen. She'll ask questions; just answer her honestly and *ah-HA!* You'll have a conversation."

"Do you really think that will work?" Angkor was anxious.

Xaid slapped him on the back of the head. "Quit thinking," he admonished. "Just go talk to her."

Grrrscnk tossed another bloody haunch into her mouth. "Take her to get something to eat," she suggested.

He found her near the restaurant. "Hello, Sophia Marshall," he said, with the slightest tremor.

"Angkor! Son of Tenzing. How wonderful to see you!" her voice was as radiant as her smile. "Would you like some tea?"

"Please, "he answered, "and, uh, may I walk with you?"

She lowered her gaze as she prepared his tea. "I would like that very much, yes."

They walked for hours. In silence at first. Then she asked him about school. He told her of University and of Angkor wat, where he had spent so many years. "How did you come to be named for the school?" she asked.

He explained the naming day ceremony and of his people, the Khalkha. He told her of growing up on the steppe and mountains in a yurt with his mother. His chest puffed as her spoke of his father, now headman of Mongolia and soon to be Chairman of the Earth Council.

"And, Sophia," he asked, "tell me how a Hindi girl came to have an English name?"

"My grandmother, Sophia, came from London," she explained. The grandmother had moved to Delhi to attend school, where she met Sophia's grandfather. Her own mother had been as dark as any Hindi, but Sophia had come out pale and blonde. Her parents and grandparents had doted on the curly haired child. Sadly, the rest of her family and neighbors did not. Classmates would pull on her locks. Small boys had held her down and poured ink in her hair.

Normally, even in modern times, a middle-class girl in Calcutta would have been betrothed by sixteen. Try as he might, Sophia's father couldn't find a suitable husband for his daughter. Eager suitors would meet the pale, blonde girl and not return. Heartbroken, she had fled to Delhi, determined to make a life for herself and perhaps one day find a good man.

Despite Delhi's modern and cosmopolitan image, there were few opportunities for a girl like Sophia to succeed. To be sure, men (and a few women) had made unsavory advances on the girl. She never wavered and resolutely applied for every honest job she could find. The tea jar she carried paid poorly and she often went to bed hungry, but it was an honest day's labor.

Before either of them noticed, evening began to fall. Sophia had to return the jar. Angkor followed her to the storefront of her employer, a dour little man with a pinched face and bandy extremities. He complained about her meager earnings for the day.

"Perhaps if you gave her better tea to sell, she would make better money for you, old man," Angkor cut in to the tea man's complaining.

"She will sell what I give her!" the tea man shouted. "If she would smile pretty and use her charms, she would sell more tea. Walking about with a barbarian such as yourself doubtlessly scared off her customers. Who are you anyway, young pup?"

"I am Angkor son of..." Angkor started in a loud voice, then quieted. "I am Angkor and Sophia is a friend of mine. You are worried about money? Here, here is the money you think I cost her for walking with her friend. Maybe now you will give her a fresh jar to sell instead of that week-old swill." He threw his credit chip at the old man.

The seedy merchant fumbled the chip, caught it and rubbed it in his fingers. He swiped it, then handed it back to Angkor. "Thank you, young man," he said, "but she will sell what I give her."

Angkor stiffened. Sophia placed her hand on his chest. "Angkor, go," she ordered. "Let me handle this. Thank you for a wonderful conversation; we'll talk later."

Outside, Angkor seethed. "If he so much as looks at you improperly," he said.

"Yes, yes, I know," she answered, "Truly, thank you for a wonderful afternoon." She kissed him on the mouth and hurried away.

Chapter 7

Years later, Angkor and Sophia would tell their friends that it must have been any one of several factors that lead to their actions that fateful week. Monsoon season was approaching, so the weather was oppressively hot. Or perhaps it was getting close to finals and Angkor wasn't thinking clearly, given the stress of the upcoming examinations.

Or it could have been as simple as the fact that the two were deeply in love.

Daily, Angkor was finishing his studies and racing to the market to find Sophia. The tea sales were good, given the heat and that the seller, perhaps unnerved by Angkor's visit, had started giving her a better quality of tea. Often, the jar was nearly empty by the time Angkor found her in the late afternoon.

They talked as old souls, discussing the events of their day, their plans and dreams. Sophia wanted little more than a steady job and nice place to live. Angkor was certain of his future; already he was applying to medical schools to earn his doctorate in genetics.

They would find a restaurant or food stall and have supper together. They had an occasional squabble. Sophia, being a proud young woman, would insist on paying her way. Angkor would take the position of a gentleman and a gentleman never allowed his partner to pay for her meal. On days, she had excellent sales, she prevailed. Most days, she would acquiesce. Partially out of practicality, but mostly because he was so gallant it was cute. She often suppressed a giggle as she argued about paying before allowing him to present his own credit chip.

The fateful day happened in late summer, weeks before the monsoon season. Angkor had spent the morning studying for his final exams with his friends. Only Grrrscnk was in a good mood; the high temperatures were more to her liking. While Dawlish, Xaid and Salaam were from torrid regions, the sweltering heat of this day was too much for them as well.

Finally, Angkor punched his pad off and declared, "Screw it. I know this stuff backwards and forwards. If I'm going to be miserable, I'd rather it was with Sophia."

They all agreed it was a good time for a break and wandered down to the market. It was bustling this early; later everyone would be seeking shelter from the blazing sun. Angkor searched in all of Sophia's usual spots, but his girlfriend was nowhere to be found.

The five had lunch at their favorite eatery (one that served the Hecht) while they commiserated with Angkor and planned the rest of their day. It was getting closer to noon; the already oppressive temperatures were moving toward unbearable. They could go to the air-conditioned library at the university and study. Or perhaps go to the cinema and enjoy a movie. Grrrscnk declared, "Monkeys are weak because they melt away in a little heat. You can go cower in an ice box if you want. Me, I'm going out for a walk and enjoying this marvelous weather."

Angkor stood. "Look, you guys do what you want. I'm going to find Sophia." He excused himself and left.

Dawlish narrowed his eyes. He had that curious feeling his uncle had told him, the feeling a warrior gets when battle was near. Without a word, he rose and followed Angkor at a discreet distance, staying just out of sight. When Angkor arrived at Sophia's apartment building, Dawlish used utmost care. There were few spots of concealment in the tenement.

Here, Angkor tapped on Sophia's door. "Who is it?" came the muffled cry.

"It's me, Angkor," he replied.

"Angkor?" He heard shuffling feet. "Go away."

He was confused. Go away? Sophia had never told him that. What had he done wrong? He knocked again. "Sophia!" he cried, "it's me. Angkor. Open the door."

"No."

He got angry. His fist pounded the rickety door. It creaked and splintered under his assault. "Sophia," he yelled, "this is silly. Open the door this instant."

He heard the lock rattle and she slowly opened the door, just a crack. "I don't want to see you today, Angkor," she sniffed, "Please go away. I will see you tomorrow, perhaps."

She started to close the door, but he blocked it with his foot. "Why won't you see me today?" he asked, exasperated with the exchange. "Is it something I said? Something I did? Something I didn't do? Please, just talk to me, Sophia!"

"Do you promise not to be mad?" her voice quivered.

"Of course. Please, just open the door for just a minute. Let's talk about whatever this is all about," he pleaded.

She relented, allowing Angkor to open the door. While she held her veil over the right side of her face, he could still see the bruising.

"What is this?" he demanded as he pulled her veil down, revealing one blackened eye and a large, swollen welt on her face.

"Angkor, please," she pleaded. 'I was clumsy; I dropped the jar and spoiled a whole day's tea. It was my fault, not his."

"He touched you?" Angkor's eyes narrowed. "He struck you? My woman, he struck my woman?" His breathing slowed, his nostrils flared and he furrowed his brow. He whirled without a word and was gone in an instant, ignoring Sophia's cries.

Dawlish observed his friend's exit, Sophia close behind. He wasn't sure what was going on, but was certain it was time to call for reinforcements. He followed Angkor and the crying Sophia while communicating with Grrrscnk, Xaid and Salaam. He was certain now where they were going.

Angkor didn't bother knocking. The door of the tea shop exploded from the force of his shoulder. The tea seller fell backwards from his stool, the terrifying visage of the enraged Mongolian stealing his breath. He scrambled back, whining and wetting himself as Angkor advanced. He was trapped at the rear wall of his tiny shop. "No," he whimpered, "Don't hurt me."

"You touched my woman," Angkor hissed. His fist pounded the seller's face. "You struck her," he said as he punched the smaller man again. "You dared raise your hand against the woman of the son of Tenzing." The fist struck again, and blood spattered on the limed wall. "You struck the woman of a Khalkha warrior." He punched again and released the blubbering, bleeding tea seller.

Red rage overcame Angkor's senses and he kicked and punched the prone form. Sophia screamed, pulled on him and begged him to stop. Dawlish and the others rushed in when they heard Sophia's screams. Dawlish wrapped powerful arms around his friend and pulled him into the street. "Hold him," he instructed Grrrscnk.

Salaam was leading the frantic and crying Sophia from the shop. Xaid knelt over the beaten shop owner. "He'll live," he reported.

"The police will doubtlessly be here soon," Dawlish announced. "Go take care of them, friend Xaid." The Singh nodded and left the room, helping Salaam lead Sophia away.

He grabbed the tea seller by the collar and sat the semiconscious man on his bed. "You are fortunate," he said, "Had she been the woman of a Turk man, your belly would be spilling your innards on the floor right now.

"The police will be here soon. You can tell them what you wish, but you will not forward any charges against my friend. Nor will you give his woman any more trouble, understand? If you see

82

her in the street, you will turn and run the other way, lest I see you and come visit you with my knife."

Dawlish extracted a handful of plastic rupee notes from his pocket and stuffed the bills in the seller's shirt pocket. "For your injuries. If it's not enough, well, that's the cost of doing business, yes?" He patted the little man's bloody cheek and smiled. The seller nodded and smiled, exposing his broken teeth.

Dawlish stood, then announced, "Oh, lest I forget, Sophia is my friend as well." He spun about, his foot catching the seller squarely in the head. Dawlish heard the crunch as the older man's skull fractured and his body toppled onto the bed.

The Turkman fished his money back out of the man's pocket. "I changed my mind," he said. "The likes of you don't deserve the mercies and generosity of a Turk man."

In the street, Xaid was handing a policeman a handful of banknotes and speaking with a lot of gestures. Grrrscnk and Salaam were leading the crying Sophia away. Angkor sat on the sidewalk, his head down. Dawlish pulled his friend to his feet and led him away.

"You know, Angkor," he told his friend, "your one quality I admire most is your restraint."

Sophia sat on her sleeping mat, crying. "What am I to do now, Angkor?" she asked, "Don't you understand how difficult it is for me? Now that you have assaulted the tea maker, I have no job.

What am I to do now for money? Where will I live? How will I eat?"

He stood there, chewing his lip. When he saw the bruising on her face, the only thing he could think of was to smash in the face of that wretched man. He was responsible for her plight. It was up to him to find the answer. He made the decision quickly. "Gather your things," he told her, "We have a train to catch."

"A train?" she puzzled. "Why are we going on a train ride?"

"I need to speak with your father about this," he explained.

"I don't want my father involved with this," she said. "I moved here so my father had no more influence on my decisions."

"Nevertheless, I must see your father," he said.

"Why?"

Angkor knelt and took her hands. "I am a Khalkha man," he said, "bound by our traditions. I must ask for your father's blessing before I marry you."

"Marry…me?" she whispered.

"Of course. I see no one else in the room," he answered.

"Are you certain?" she asked. "You don't know me that well. How do you know there aren't things about me…things you might regret?"

"In temple, I was taught we are all half people looking for our other half," he said. "Our search may be long and it may be short. I think I knew the very moment I laid my eyes on you that you were my other half." He lifted her into his arms. "Join with me," he whispered. "Let's journey together, first to Calcutta, then to our future."

The mag-lev train took only an hour. She held his hand the entire way while staring out the window. In Calcutta, the sun was low on the horizon. The walk to her home was short and anxious. An older version of Sophia, save for darker skin and hair, answered Angkor's polite knock. "Daughter!" her mother cried, hugging Sophia tightly. "What has happened to your face?"

"There was an incident in Delhi," Sophia explained. "Mother, this is Angkor. He wishes to speak to Papa."

"Did you do this?" Sophia's mother squinted her eyes and glared at the tall Mongol.

"Madam. I am Khalkha," Angkor stood at his full height. Mindful of Suishin, he continued, "We do not strike our women."

"Our women. "Sophia's mother took notice. Her face softened slightly and she escorted them to the garden, next to the small household shrine to Bhadrakali. She returned minutes later with her husband and a servant carrying a tray of refreshments.

"I am Ham, Sophia's father," he said, offering Angkor a glass of lavender juice. "My wife says you wish to speak to me."

"Yes, sir. I am Angkor, son of Tenzing. I am a student at University in Delhi, studying to be a doctor." Angkor swallowed, then went on resolutely. "I have known your daughter for some time now and have grown quite fond of her. My people's traditions demand I come to you and ask for your blessing, for I wish to marry Sophia."

Ham stared for a long moment, then shook his head. "Impossible," he told the couple, "I am afraid you have come a long way for nothing. Good day." He rose.

"May I ask why, sir?" Angkor questioned.

"I will not pay any aaunnpot your family asks." came the explanation. "You should go find yourself another."

"I am not requesting a dowry, sir, or asking your permission." Angkor stood, tall and proud. "I am only asking for your blessing."

"It is not given!" Ham thundered. "My daughter is not a suitable wife for a gentleman such as yourself. You may not marry her."

"What do you mean, not suitable?" Angkor asked.

Sophia had turned and began to weep, embraced by her mother. Ham glared at his daughter and asked, "So, you have not told him? Do you add to your shame by becoming a liar, a deceiver now, trying to entrap a husband?" He stomped to the door, calling over his shoulder. "Tell him. Warn him so he can come to his senses."

"Sophia?" asked Angkor.

She sat up, her mother holding her hands. "When I was eleven, some friends and I went to the cinema," she said, "We had such a wonderful time, but the movie ended late. The other girls left the cinema, but I wanted to stay for one more movie. When it was over, it was dark out. I would be in trouble when I got home. I

86

should have called Father, but decided to run home instead, so perhaps he might not know I was out after dark.

It is not safe for a girl on the streets after dark in this neighborhood. There were five of them, older boys I think, maybe young men." She lowered her head. "They did…things. To me."

"I was in hospital for a week and in bed at home for many more. They never caught who did this shameful thing to me. The doctors said I could have a happy, normal life, except," she looked Angkor in the eye, "I can never have children. I still ovulate, but the woman parts in me will not allow me to have children. I am sorry, Angkor. You must hate me now."

He knelt and took her hands. "This was done to you," he said, "not by you. Amongst my people, nay, our people, you would have been taken to temple and cared for. Your attackers would have been found and your family would have decided the punishment. In cases like this, the punishment is usually quite severe."

Angkor was almost through talking. Pulling Sophia to her feet, he announced, "We will find lodging in the city tonight and in the morning, we will go to city hall and perform the *Prajapatya.*"

Sophia's mother shot her daughter a glance. *A barbarian,* she thought. *How does a barbarian know of our laws?* "Ham!" she called, "The boy is still here."

"I have studied your laws," Angkor told them. "That is why I asked for your blessings rather than your permission. I wish you had given your blessing, sir and performed the *Vivaha* wedding. My wife would have appreciated and revered you forever for that. But if

87

you chose to deny Sophia your blessing, then you can go your way. We will go ours. You cannot stop us from getting a civil wedding."

Hand in hand, their future before them, they left the house.

Chapter 8

October 3043

Of all the vistas on Ganymede Station, the view from the window above Angkor's lab station was his favorite. He could straighten in his chair, tip his head up just a few inches and the magnificent maelstrom that was Jupiter was right there. The polar orbit of the station and the lack of rotation meant he would have the unobstructed view throughout his work day.

Brilliant colors, ranging from pale yellow to vibrant pinks and orange raced in never- ending swirls and rivers of gas. Unfiltered, he could see cloud formations hundreds of miles down into the gaseous giant. Lightning bolts ten thousand miles long would arc, leap and twist as the atmosphere, forever in chaos. They writhed and roared past the scientist's slacked-jawed awe.

He would admire the chaos outside his window, then focus on the organized world of cellular biology. Ganymede station was the leading research station in the Earth Union. Angkor counted himself fortunate to be working here.

A tap on his door caused Angkor to check his chrono. He beamed and called out, "Enter, my love." The greatest blessing of his life was there to have lunch with him.

Sofia floated in, bearing the tray with the containers of their lunch. She wore a jumpsuit of green, eschewing her sari (to his chagrin) because of the low gravity. They embraced and kissed as she set the tray on his work station.

She looked to the window and commented, "The god appears angry today."

"Eh?" he asked.

Sofia pointed. A sustained bolt of lightning, thirty thousand miles long, writhed as a serpent under and through the clouds. He admired the show, idly wondering if the combination of chemicals in the clouds contained any aminos, jolted into life by the epic charge, living their lives in the upper reaches of the gas giant.

It was possible. Collector drones had dropped into the upper atmosphere and returned with samples that qualified as life, albeit barely. It was clear, though, that the lightning was far too deep in the atmosphere to collect a sample.

Pity.

Having Sophia on the station was a godsend for Angkor and a delight to the scientists. She had struggled at first with the micro-gravity. But she adapted. While having no formal job on the station, she determined no job to be beneath her or too small for her attention. Her cooking skills, tempered on the streets of Delhi, turned the ordinary, plain algae foodstuffs into exotic, savory meals. Small bits of color began to appear throughout the station, whether a painted surface that suddenly appeared and was just right, to bits of art or a knick-knack in just the aesthetically perfect place.

She was never seen without her little bottle of cleaner and rag, always erasing a smudge here or a spill there (something very difficult to do in micro-gravity, but still it happened). Always with her genuine smile, twinkling blue eyes and soft voice: "I am pleased to serve, Sahib."

They had agreed early on their assignment where the floor was in Angkor's lab. She arranged the containers of their lunch (curried protein and rice, a favorite). They tapped tea filled bulbs and began to eat. Angkor looked out the window irritably as a shadow passed by the window, cutting off the glow of Jupiter for too long.

The shuttle sat right there, outside his window. "Go away," he growled at it. "I am dining with my wife." He shook a futile fist at the window.

Sophia covered her mouth with her hand and giggled. It was indicative of a trait he found most attractive about her. While she wasn't shy or withdrawn, she displayed modesty and humility. When they arrived on Ganymede, for instance, the toilets were all unisex. Sophia quietly designated individual units for all three sexes. While there was some grumbling, everyone followed the change by the quiet Hindi woman with no questions.

The shuttle moved away. Their meal was quiet. In ten years of marriage Sophia had learned that Angkor would still be thinking about work during lunch. She had little understanding of genetics or DNA, so she would sit quietly with her husband during lunch, enjoying his company and basking in his adoration.

"Attention on the station," came the call over the tannoy. "Doctor Angkor, you have a visitor in the Administration module."

Angkor shrugged at his wife's questioning look. "I shall know when I get to Administration. I'm sure it's nothing," he assured her. Earth was over two hundred million miles away.

He floated over the table and kissed Sophia while hovering above her. "You've outdone yourself again, my love," he cooed. "I will see you later in our quarters." He swam through the door as she began to clean up their meal and straighten up his lab.

Ganymede Station was nearly five square miles of modules in a variety of sizes. To the casual observer, it appeared a haphazard starburst of oblong pods, cubes, globes and pyramids. The largest cube was on the "top" of the station on a half mile rail by itself. This was the plutonium reactor, a remnant of Earth's weapons technology. On the far end of the station was the docking station for supply ships and shuttles. The Administration area sat atop the docking module, a windowed blister on the spider-shaped docking port.

Most of the station was in micro gravity, like Angkor's lab. Here and there were areas that had up to .9 g, created by spinning arms or rotating wheels. Angkor avoided these areas; it was quicker to swim around these areas than to transit through.

He closed the hatch into the Admin pod behind him. Sergeant Betty Hodges, Earth Defense Forces, sat at the reception desk. "Hey, Ang," she greeted him, "in the main conference room." She pointed a stylus over her shoulder.

Ryder Finn sat at the table, hands folded on the synthetic wood. He was restrained to the chair by thigh clamps. Angkor sat, clamped the restraint and placed his hands on the table. "I greet you, Doctor Angkor, son of Tenzing, chairman of the Earth Council," the blue skinned humanoid said in his clipped accent.

"I greet you, Ryder Finn of Mithranderar, friend and advisor to my father," responded Angkor. Then he hesitated. What would bring his father's closest friend and advisor all the way out here? "I trust my father is well?"

"Very well, yes," answered Ryder. "Your wife? She has adjusted to this place, yes?"

Angkor nodded.

Ryder pulled a small box from his pocket. He set it on the table between them and pressed the top. "Your Sergeant Hodges is one of my agents," he said." We will not be disturbed or recorded."

They sat for several awkward moments. Finally, Ryder said, "I suppose you are curious about my visit here. Your father sent me. His plans have come to fruition. You recall your last face to face conversation with him, yes? You conceded that a monarchy would best serve Earth and mankind best. The Council has decided; your father will be named the Monarch of Earth in three months.

There are two immediate issues at hand. You and your brother. The Council agreed to a hierarchal passing of the leadership at the death of the king. By tradition, this would currently be Suishin. He is unsuitable at best. Your father has enemies who will kill him, convinced they can control your brother. They have already infiltrated Suishin's inner circle, with drugs and sexual perversions." Ryder spat the last statement as though he was trying to rid his mouth of a foul taste.

"What do you want of me?" queried Angkor. "I have no interest in politics. I have all I could want here - my wife, my job, my research."

"There is more to the universe than your test tubes and beakers," Ryder shot back. "I speak of the greater good."

"I am fulfilling my contribution here to the greater good," argued the scientist, "and any question of me succeeding my father is a moot point anyway. Suishin is the elder; it falls to him to replace my father."

"By tradition, yes," Ryder said. "But we are in a new age, Angkor. The old ways must be swept aside for the new order. If the best available heir to your father is your brother, then the factions allied against your father could sweep in and fill the vacuum your brother is sure to create. There would be resistance, civil war. Right now, your species could not survive a civil war."

"So, your implication is that I am some kind of a savior?" asked Angkor.

Ryder steepled his fingers and stared at Angkor for a long minute. "What I am saying is your father and I have been making plans since before you were born. We are approaching a point that will either create the great dream Tenzing and I have fostered for over forty years, or Earth will fracture again and forces you cannot imagine will ensure the extinction of your species.

"Your father has taken the dream nearly as far as he can, although he doesn't understand this yet. What you decide will determine if our dream succeeds or fails."

"I have everything I want here," repeated Angkor. "My wife, my job, my friends. Can't you find someone else be your savior? Perhaps you can turn Suishin, make him this leader you desire."

"There is no time," Ryder clasped his hands together. "Suishin is lost; his passing will be regrettable. You must replace your father. You will found the line that will lead your people across the cosmos, provided you build on the foundation your father will leave for you.

"You will be a legend."

"I do not want to be a legend," Angkor stressed. "I am a scientist. I am a husband. I am a scholar. That is all I want, that is all I will be."

"Yes, you are all those things. And more." Ryder answered. "And legends rarely want to be legendary. Indeed, when your story is told in the future, you will scarcely resemble it save for your name and perhaps your appearance.

Your Empire, though. Your Empire will last for more than ten thousand years and bring order and prosperity for all your citizens...and subjects."

Ryder Finn released his leg restraints and drifted upwards. "The next shuttle will be here in seven days. When it departs, you must be on it. Bring your wife or leave her behind; she will be but a footnote in all of this anyway. Seven days, Angkor."

"I have a mission to collect samples on Enceladus," argued Angkor. "I will not be here in seven days."

"Seven days," stated Ryder, "Your friends can go to Saturn for their samples. I need you on Earth in two weeks."

"I must speak with my wife..." began Angkor.

"Bring her or leave her. Seven days." Ryder floated out of the room.

The shuttle sped silently away from Ganymede Station. It disappeared behind the moon for several minutes before appearing on the far side of Ganymede, a sparkling snow flake drifting across the angry face of Jupiter.

Sophia stood at his side, her arms wrapped tightly around his waist. She had said little when Angkor told her of Ryder Finn's visit, except, "Wherever you go, Husband, I shall be there beside you."

"But I don't want to go," he wept. "I have all I want here."

"The gods have determined you have a higher calling," she countered as she brushed an errant lock of his hair off his face. "Who are you to question the will of the universe?"

They had discussed Sophia returning to Earth with him. Angkor talked with the station manager and arranged for her to stay on Ganymede Station indefinitely. "It will be safer for you," Angkor had argued. "I don't know what I am getting into and I don't want you to walk into a trap with me."

"My place is by your side," she said in her calmest manner. "Where you go, I shall be there beside you."

"There will be great danger," he pleaded. "I want you to be safe."

"There is no safer place for me than by your side, Husband," was her answer. "I will not leave you to the dangers of the world. I will be by your side, every step of the way. Now, enough, it is time for bed. Put out the light."

But where am I taking you to, my love? He pondered, *how can I keep you safe if I don't know where am I going?*

The week had passed quickly enough. They hadn't accumulated much in their ten years of marriage and what little that had collected was packed away in a few boxes. Angkor's research was dispersed amongst the other scientists. On the morning of the departure, he sat in his silent lab for hours, watching Jupiter through his window.

She drifted in through the door in the last hour. The shuttle had gravity, so today she was wearing the fuchsia sari she knew he loved. She settled onto his lap, his arms instinctively wrapping around her.

They watched the boiling of the clouds, stirred by winds hundreds of miles an hour or more. Fanciful lighting arced and danced. The tumult reflected the turmoil Angkor felt, his own thoughts churning and racing. Yet, on his lap reposed the calming center that of his world. He nuzzled Sophia's neck she purred appreciatively and wriggled against him.

"Doctor Angkor, Sophia Marshall," the call came over the tannoy, "Your shuttle is prepared for departure."

She raised her arms and rotated, her body pressed against her husband. "It is time, my love," she said, kissing him.

"It occurs to me," he whispered, "This is the one place I have been closest to you on the whole of this station and it is the one place where we never made love."

They giggled. "Well, there is no time for that now," Sophia said with regret. She winked and tipped her head. "But I am sure we can find somewhere on the shuttle."

Angkor's heart tugged and stretched to the station as it faded from his view. His vocation, his dream, his perceived life's work grew dimmer and dimmer until it faded from view entirely, swallowed by the angry god.

Chapter 9

December 3043

They settled near the Occident city of Seattle.

Ryder Finn, of course, was furious. "I did not bring you back
from across the solar system to settle on the other side of the world!"
he said, his clipped accent tinged with anger. "How can you fulfill
your duties to your father if you are half a world away!"

They had started in Zurich, the traditional capital of the Earth
Government since the collapse of the old United States some six
hundred standard years before. The region was nice enough, the
couple agreed. But the weather was harsh to Sophia; she disliked the
cold in the winter.

Angkor found he missed the peace and quiet he had enjoyed
both in temple and Ganymede station, so Sophia had explored the
various provinces of Earth. She had a sister who had long since
moved to Cascadia and often told Sophia of the seemingly magic
area. Cascadia had avoided much of the strife during the North
American collapse of the twenty-third century. It had risen slowly as
the old countries collapsed and new countries formed. It was the
largest of the Occident Free states, stretching along the mountain
range from which it drew its name, from Prince Rupert in the old
northwest territories to Port Orford along its southern coast.

Sophia had found their home in a tiny community called
Indianola, just west of the city. A tiny cabin, it was nestled in tall
firs, looking toward the city across the Puget Sound. She and

Angkor could sit on their deck and watch the wildlife scurry across their tiny, rocky beach or enjoy secluded walks in their green, misty forest.

"It is a ten-minute journey via air car to Boeing Field," Angkor argued. "A three-hour flight to either Zurich or my father's Keep. This is my choice, Ryder. Mine and Sophia's. Or are the words in the new order's laws about free choice only words?"

"As long as you are fulfilling your duties," Ryder had finally conceded.

Angkor was rarely in Zurich, anyway. Much of his time was spent traveling across the fifteen worlds of the Terran Union. He would bring Sophia along during the missions outside the Sol system. The couple thrilled to visit the exoplanets. From the vast, rich forests of Vespa to the ocean world of Mer, they delighted in exploring of the cultures of the colonists and the natives of the burgeoning Terran Union.

"I could have never imagined such a life," Sophia told Angkor one evening as they cuddled in their favorite chaise at home in Indianola. "Had I known the sights I would see, the adventures we would have together," her voice trailed off. Then, impishly, she said, "The little tea girl would not have wandered off so quickly that first day. Of course, my wiles seemed to have worked on you, Husband."

They had discussed children. Angkor had extracted eggs from his wife and examined them at the university in Seattle.

Combined with his sperm, he could see no reason he and Sophia could not have children, using a surrogate.

When he broached the idea to his wife, Sophia grew silent. She listened to his argument, then responded, "Yes, Angkor, we could do all these things. I want nothing more than to bear you a child. But, I can't, I can't do this. I…" she rushed from the room holding back her tears and slammed the door to their room. His heart ached with every choked sob he heard behind their bedroom door. In the morning, she unlocked the door and hurried for their tiny bathroom to wash her face. She was silent and withdrawn for a week. Bit by bit, she came out of her mood. But the sorrow seemed to hover in their home, just out of reach.

Her sister visited one weekend, heavy with her third child. The sisters sat for hours, chatting and laughing while painting one another with henna. Sophia insisted Angkor drive them to the Great Temple in Belfair, near the city, where the sisters entered the temple for hours, leaving Angkor outside to fend for himself. They returned home, the women happy but tired. Sophia snuggled closely to Angkor that evening, whispering about the prayer ceremony the women held for her soon to be born niece. "Imagine, my little sister, being a mother for a third time!" Sophia said happily. Soon, her face was buried in Angkor's chest, weeping uncontrollably.

Tenzing had insisted both his sons learn the inner workings of the government. Hours and days and weeks of monotonous reading of reports. Angkor was determined not to bring his work to his home. But there was just so much to learn.

Suishin seemed not to have this problem. Indeed, it was hard not to notice his brother, as often as he was on the newsfeeds, dating the daughter of this wealthy patron or vacationing with that handsome industrialist. His irrepressible grin, his exotic queue, and his striking physique shown proudly with his trademark vest and tight breeches made good vid copy. There were rumors, of course, of scandalous transgressions being hushed up, but what public figure didn't have a skeleton or two in his closet?

The press largely ignored Angkor, the younger brother. For that, he was extremely grateful. At the end of his work week, he and Sophia would race to their transport and make the three-hour trip home. Angkor's air car would be waiting. There would be a quick stop at the market in their tidy town for supplies, then to their cozy home. Often, they would entertain friends is the evenings. Close friends might be invited for the weekend.

Dawlish accepted Angkor's winter invitation, provided he left his uniforms at home. A windstorm lashed the bungalow, the lights flickering on occasion. Angkor had built a cheery fire and the trio spent a grand evening singing, telling stories and jokes. Sophia was pleased to see Angkor so relaxed; he was working so hard lately! Half past midnight, the long day caught up with the couple. They bade Dawlish good night and went to bed.

The Turk sat for staring at the dying fire and listening to the whistling winds. He envied his old friend, a lovely wife and a beautiful home. He had chosen his path and regretted it for not a second. But evenings like this…

Bah! He was being too maudlin. And in the morning, he had a mission to accomplish. The bed in the guest room looked inviting.

The bed was indeed comfortable. General Dawlish Zoltan could hardly remember such a night since he had joined the Turkman Army. A tap at the door woke him.

"Hey, Dawlish, are you awake?" Angkor whispered.

"I am now, my friend. What's up?"

"The storm has broken and blown through," Angkor said. "I've made us some coffee. Come on, let's go catch the sunrise!"

'Will Sophia be joining us?"

"She's still asleep."

Dawlish pulled on his boots and robe. The cabin's deck was screened for the winter, though there was a chill in the air. Angkor handed him a heavy mug of Arabica, the beans grown for centuries in the gardens back at his father's Keep. He settled into a chaise and sipped the brew with a contented sigh.

Heavy winter clouds hung in patches in the early gloom, illuminated by the still invisible sun. Fiery rays began to spike their way across the sky, seemingly igniting coals in the cloud banks racing swiftly northward. Clothed in a ruby robe, Sol finally made his majestic appearance and claimed the heavens once more.

A gull flew along the shoreline calling *cree-cree-cree* as it searched for a scrap of food along the shoreline. Across the misty bay, a boat's engine rumbled.

"Beautiful, friend Angkor," Dawlish sipped his cup. "I can see why you and your wife settled here."

"It is a blessing for the both of us," agreed Angkor, "but that is not why you came to see me, friend Dawlish."

"No," Dawlish stiffened to attention and steepled his fingers. "It seems politics has sharpened your senses. What do you know of augmentation?"

"I have heard of it, of course," admitted Angkor. "The use of prosthetics for injury or birth defect has been around for centuries. Augmenting soldiers through the use of combat suits is one of the business's Xaid is involved with, yes?"

"Yes," Dawlish acknowledged. "There is a new line of research. It involves grafting these components directly to a human body and adding a computer processor hard wired into the brain. It is thought augmenting a soldier or a worker to operate at a level far beyond human capacity is the next step in human evolution.

"Horrifying!" exclaimed Angkor, "Turning man into machine! Does my father know of this?"

"I do not believe so," Dawlish replied, "though I think your brother is involved. Further, the project has gone into the prototype phase."

"No! On human subjects?" pressed Angkor.

Dawlish stood. "I need you to join me on Luna station this week," he said. "I will arrange discrete transportation for you. After the trip, you and I can discuss our next step."

Crime had exploded in the twenty second century. Prisons were filled beyond capacity, resulting in riots, which added to the carnage. In Occident, one such riot broke free of the walls and resulted in a small town being destroyed, women and children violated, the men tortured horribly to death. The local militia was overrun by the former prisoners. Finally, the governor sent armed jets to bomb the rioters into submission. Capital punishment was ineffective. So many convicts ended up on death row, executions resembled assembly line slaughter.

The introduction of electromagnetic drive and rail accelerators made lifting of cargo and humans into earth orbit efficient and profitable. Convicts would be loaded into shuttle hulks and lifted into orbit. When they rioted, the airlocks were opened and the all the convicts in the hulk would be executed through spacing. Later, penal facilities were introduced on many asteroids as a cheap work force for mining.

Luna was chosen to house a research facility that offered long term inmates an option. Their sentences would be reduced if they consented to experimentation. Most of these experiments involved radiation treatment and vaccines to counter any number of viruses and diseases they encountered on extosystems.

Few of the diseases were benign. Most of the subject's bodies were ultimately sealed in cargo pods and launched into the sun.

Angkor and General Dawlish met Doctor Jhon Weir, Director of the Luna Research Facility. Hairless save for a small grey soul patch, his eyes were eager and his smile easy. "I'm so pleased to see the government take such an interest in my research,"

105

he bubbled. "Once this technology becomes proven, we will be able to take hardened, career criminals and make them useful tools for society. Not only can we send them into environments that would kill humans, we can replace human soldiers with my augmented men and they will succeed brilliantly! Imagine, using a battalion of my super soldiers to replace an ordinary human division. Imagine the ease with which we will move across the universe. And at a fraction of the cost!"

"Show us your…augmented men," ordered Dawlish.

The room was white, with all smooth edges and shiny plastic. Moments after they arrived, the far wall slid into the ceiling, exposing a nude man secured to an angled table. Plates and flat boxes were affixed across his body and extremities, joined by tubes and wire bundles. A hexagonal fixture dominated the top third of his head. With a start, Angkor saw his eyes had been replaced with a camera and sensor cluster. He looked closer. The thing's chest wasn't moving. Instead, Angkor heard the whisper of an air pump.

"The unit has electronic and hydraulic servos assisting its legs and arms," explained Doctor Weir. "Most of its internal organs have been replaced with mechanical components which are more hearty and durable than organic.

"The brain is our proudest accomplishment. We repurposed much of the tissue, as the human brain has an astounding number of neural connections. The attachment is a prototype microprocessor, using the human tissue as a storage medium. It can access information at a much greater rate. Since it receives more and higher quality information faster than a silly old brain, it can analyze much faster and react far quicker than any ordinary human. Further, the microprocessor also maintains a record of the activity so we can review the actions and some of the thought processes the augment uses to arrive at it decisions and actions."

"You can read its mind?" Dawlish gripped his fists tight.

"Yes. It is a critical element of the augment control. Without it, we would be reduced to guesswork for any adjustments needed to the neural net," explained Doctor Weir.

"Show me the brain schematics," ordered Angkor. A panel slid open, revealing a view screen. He studied it for several minutes, his hand on his chin, hmmming and making comments to himself. "I see you have removed portions of the cerebrum," he commented.

"Yes."

Angkor pointed to several areas. "Memory here and here. This section, the moral seat. Nearly gone." Angkor glared at Doctor Weir. "You have loosened the moral restrictions inherent to humans."

"Unit Delta Thirty-Seven, access personal memory," the Doctor said, returning Angkor's glare.

"Working," came a mechanical reply. "I am Steven Raab, from Kansas City, Missouri."

"Details of your convictions, please."

"Murder; first degree, Fahad Corbin, guilty. Murder; first degree, Bomana Zultan, guilty. Murder; first degree, Herman Bowfin, guilty. Murder..."

"Enough, Unit Delta Thirty-Seven. Summarize, how many counts of murder were you convicted of?" asked Dawlish.

"Murder of the first degree, eight convictions. Murder of the second degree, thirteen convictions." the metallic voice replied.

"Indeed," Dawlish squinted. "You are programmed to obey all orders without question?"

"Yes, sir."

Dawlish set a drinking glass before the augmented man. "Crush this glass with your left hand," he ordered.

"Yes, sir." There was a crunch and the glass fragments spilled onto the table. The augment's hand dripped blood beside the remains of the glass.

Dawlish unholstered his sidearm and set it on the table. "Unit Delta Thirty-Seven, pick up the weapon. Point it at Doctor Weir and kill him with it."

The augment stared at the gun, then looked at Dawlish. "Why?" he asked.

Dawlish moved too swift to see. He snatched his weapon from the table and fired five rounds into the head of the augmented man. Blood and solid components erupted as the head exploded from the penetration of the heavy bolts passing through its skull, brain tissue and processor. What remained dribbled from the remnants of Thirty-Seven's skull as his body pitched forward.

Doctor Weir fell back against his chair. "Wha...Wha...What, why did you do this?" he demanded.

"Two reasons," Dawlish holstered his weapon and beckoned to Angkor. "I gave your machine an order. According to your claim, he should have taken the weapon and tried to kill you. Your morality program should have made sure of that. I have examined the records for this experiment. This is the indication that shows the programing and memories are already beginning to interact and conflict. Your own reports are disturbingly accurate in describing this process, Doctor. I believe the result is the augment becomes insane and homicidal. It would have to be destroyed, anyway." At the door, Dawlish stopped, glared at the bleeding pile of metal and flesh. "The second reason was more personal. Bomana Zultan was my sister."

Plasma burned with a pink glow outside the window as the shuttle fell planetward. Angkor noted Dawlish's quivering hands and clenched jaw.

"There is something more, my old friend," Angkor said, "something you haven't told me." The muscles at the corners of Dawlish's eyes blanched in scowl as he struggled for control. "There is much I must tell you, friend Angkor." He rubbed his face and breathed heavily. "I needed for you to see this...perversion. This is the nature of the enemy we face."

"What enemy are you talking about, Dawlish?" queried Angkor.

"The enemy that controls your brother," seethed the Turk. "Angkor, friend...brother. Suishin must not succeed your father. If he does, you are dead, Sophia is dead, I am dead…Millions will die. Suishin is the puppet of terrible men and women who will sell mankind to the highest bidder in the galaxy. With the Terran Union already declaring your father monarch, it is only a matter of time before they order Suishin to kill him and assume his throne."

"You have evidence of this?"

"I showed you only a small piece of what we have found," declared Dawlish. "We have much more we will show you. And we have a plan."

"You said 'we,'" Angkor noted. "Who are these 'we?'"

Dawlish leaned forward, intense. "Those who would see you as the next leader," he said. "Those of us who know you and know what is possible if you lead us."

"You seem very confident in my abilities," Angkor snorted.

We have every confidence in your abilities," Dawlish settled back. "We only need you to agree."

"Who are these 'we?'?" Angkor repeated.

Dawlish smiled for the first time that day. "We are on our way to meet them," he said.

Chapter 10

The great airship lifted regally into the sapphire night sky. Unlike its ancient ancestors, no crews on the ground scurried about like ants. The ship released itself from its tethers and silent fans hoisted it into the night. Angkor and Dawlish watched Jerusalem fade into a field of lights from the window at the bar. When it was but a smear, it was joined by illuminated strands to other indecipherable blobs of light as the airship climbed.

At the top of the airship was a plain, white, and formless room, much like the laboratory on Luna. Fifteen men and women turned as Angkor and Dawlish entered. Two came forward, their arms extended.

Angkor greeted his old friends. "Xaid, Salaam. I suppose I should have known."

"Sit, please," Xaid gestured. Sixteen comfortable looking chairs rose from the floor, constructed of the same, plastic appearing material of the room. One rose higher than the others; Dawlish led Angkor to it. Angkor was visibly surprised to find the chair was as sitting on a warm, firm cushion. Several of the group suppressed giggles.

"Very nice," commented Angkor, his hand stroking the smooth arm on his chair. "Perhaps I missed my calling in school. I could certainly force myself to live so luxuriously." The room now shared a laugh. "Well, on to business…" Angkor began.

A servitor rolled in with a tray of fruit juices. Angkor took an orange colored beverage and watched with amusement as an end table silently rose from the floor to the perfect height to hold his glass.

"I want to know what is going on," Angkor said. "What is this meeting about, why all the secrecy and security?"

"This place is my personal ship," Xaid's voice was silk. "I live here much of my days. It is also the most secure facility we have. The crew are my men. If I ordered any one of them to leap from the ship, a dozen would volunteer to do so. In this place, we are safe to discuss what needs to be done."

"These men and women," Dawlish swept his arm to the assembly, "have sworn their lives to you. We are soldiers and businessmen. Government officials and private citizens. For years, we have been watching your brother and the cabal who have lured him in. The obscenity I showed you today is not the worst they have to offer.

"Angkor, as I told you on the shuttle, your brother's cabal doesn't look to the future of our species; they look forward to their own accumulation of wealth and power. It is not too late. The enemy knows you. They don't consider you a threat. You are seen as weak, ineffective.

"They know nothing about us. This has worked to our advantage. We are poised to strike, eliminate their leaders and expose the rest. You will add the degree of legitimacy we need and be this committee's public face. With you, we are positioned to seize control of the Union and ensure safety and survival of our species."

What am I to do? Angkor asked himself.

He felt the presence within him. *Listen,* it told him. *What do you hear?*

The water, Master. The fountain at the glade.

Then place your stone, young Pitth, and listen to what the fountain tells you.

"Tell me of our enemies," directed Angkor.

A pedestal rose before Xaid. He touched its face and a holo formed inside the circle. "Alexis Shurkorov, Russian Federation," he said.

The image was of a short, corpulent man in an expensive suit. His hair was long and stringy; an uneven beard circled his chin and jowls. He was holding a glass of sparkling, a dazzling woman on his arm. He laughed at an unheard joke, his jowls flapping like a swimming jellyfish.

"Age seventy-three. CEO and President of Shurkorov Enterprises. His company is the largest producer and exporter of energy in the entire Earth Union," explained Xaid. "With his net wealth, he could buy each of the next five largest companies outright and still have enough to buy controlling interests in the next five. There have been rumors for years about his politics. Our research has revealed he has become very interested in your brother."

The next holo was a tall, severe yet handsome woman. "Ameranda Whitestone, Lakota Nation, Occident," Xaid reported.

"Age fifty-seven. Senior Vice President of the Lakota Nation and Chief Resources Officer. A lawyer who shows a great business sense combined with much guile. Under her stewardship, the Lakota have gained control of much of Occident and the Nation has holdings on thirteen worlds in the Union. She infamously has a string of men she calls upon when she desires. Your brother is one of them."

The image shifted again. Angkor recognized the short, bald doctor from Luna.

"Doctor Jhon Weir, Luna." Xaid looked up from his pedestal, "Age forty-five. Director and head researcher of human studies at the Luna Penitentiary. Doctor Weir is married but has no children. His line of research, as you saw today, is human cyborg integration. Indeed, he is the leading researcher in this field. Funding for his research come largely through Shurkorov Industries. Doctor Weir was introduced to Shurkorov through your brother."

"I am seeing a pattern here," interrupted Angkor. "Tell me, how many richer industrialists, lawyers and scientists are on this list?"

"My sources have identified fifteen in Shurkorov's inner circle," Xaid's pedestal sunk into the floor and appeared before Salaam. He tapped it and a series of beings appeared within the holo circle. "Another forty who advises him directly. But these three are the most important."

"What is their plan?" Angkor pressed.

"It must be understood; they are not yet ready to move against your father," Dawlish explained. "Your brother still hasn't consolidated enough power to confront your father directly. A year, perhaps two, then he will strike. I imagine he will assassinate your father and assume his position by the laws of the Khalkha tribe and the Terran Union Council. He is convinced you are not going to oppose him. When the time comes, he will have us rounded up and executed as a threat to his regime."

"And our plan?" queried Angkor.

"Understand, friend Angkor, that you cannot be part of the execution of our plan," Salaam stated. "I have the assets in place to chop the head off the serpent, as it were. When the time is right and you are ready, they will all die within hours of each other."

"All of them?"

"Yes," replied the Egyptian man. "In my service to my government, I have acquired sufficient tools to make this happen. All I need is your order and the top traitors in your father's regime will die."

"The others are mine," resumed Xaid. "I have collected enough information on the forty. When the order is given, the worst of the traitors will be exposed. My assets will ensure most end up in prison, or worse. The rest will either join us or be ruined."

Angkor watched as figure after figure appeared on the holo. Eleven showed themselves to be more grist to the horror mill into which his life had been thrust. Product to be ground up and fed to the Empire his father had started and a crown he was be soon forced to wear.

Very well.

"You plan is approved," Angkor stated. "Save one. My brother. He is mine. You are not to touch him; I will be the object of his demise. Understood?"

They all nodded. "The order is given." Dawlish announced. "The operation begins in ninety-six hours."

Chapter 11

The *Potemkin* sat in a comfortable orbit. It was easily the largest yacht in the Earth Union as befit its owner, Alexis Shurkorov. Nearly as long as a destroyer, its design had its roots from a time when designers still thought of space vessels as flying things. Hence, it had wide, curved wings sprouting from a flattened hull. White and chromium paint decorated the graceful ship; priceless gold filigree lent an elegant opulence.

Inside, the ship was spotless from stem to stern. Alexis was rumored to have once flogged a cabin girl to death because of an errant thumb print on a crystal glass at one of his parties, then to beat her supervisor half to death because the foolish girl had the bad manners to bleed, vomit and die on the carpet for which he had paid 2000 credits a square foot!

The ship wasn't perfect enough for Shurkorov. Faster than light sleds were too expensive, even for a man as wealthy as Alexis Shurkorov. But when he wanted to travel outside the home system, his wealth and power always assured his vessel a prime location on a sled at a very good price, especially since he wanted no other ship parked adjacent to his. His wealth ensured he would have an unobstructed view.

Today's journey wouldn't be quite so exciting, though. Shurkorov was showing off to some of his business partners today. Just a quick jaunt to the Kuiper Belt and back, with lunch. Many of these partners had been his friends for years and had been on plenty of these trips. Most of these business partners were now part of the Shurkorov cabal.

Pavel crawled on his hands and knees, scanning the bottom of hydrogen tank number seven with a rag and his bottle of cleaner. While it was doubtful Mister Shurkorov would tour down here today, there was the unspoken acknowledgement amongst the crew that it was better to assume he would than he wouldn't. Woe be to a crewman who made the erroneous decision and then have Mister Shurkorov show up to find any discrepancy. At the very least, one would surely lose their job. At worst...

Pavel was examining the myriad of pipes under the fuel cell when he spotted the small bulge. To be more precise, he spotted the thin thread hanging from the bulge on the pipe. He knitted his brow, certain he had never seen that before. The alarms weren't going off, so it wasn't an issue with the integrity of the pipe. The thread was securely attached to the bulge, that was certain. With the ever-present knife from his pocket, he probed the edge of the bulge carefully, looking for a way to pry it off. Mister Shurkorov would certainly notice this anomaly if he inspected this area. He thought of the cabin girl and probed with more intensity.

His knife caught an edge. Pavel pried with a twist and pushed the knife in just a bit deeper for yet another twist.

Salaam watched the sunrise from the deck of his home on the plains of Luxor, overlooking the ageless Nile. The hot winds off the desert were starting as Ra-Horakhty of ancient times ascended into the sky. The execution of the plan was set to begin shortly. He sipped his tea with a satisfied sigh.

His father had enrolled him in the *hashashin* as a young boy. It was a family tradition going back more than a millennium. He had enjoyed the training and worked hard to please his masters. Today, the brotherhood had fallen on hard times. The rigid doctrine that the elders had written in the sixteenth century no longer had an effect on the young men it once had. So the elders had rewritten the laws. Less fire and damnation. More glorification of the rewards for success. The mullahs demanded obedience and were lavish with the gifts supplied by their benefactors. The training was harsh, the price for failure high. Wherever there was a training camp, a well-hidden graveyard was nearby.

Today, the modern *hashashin* was poised execute its greatest strike ever. Salaam would achieve legendary status amongst all the brotherhood for all time.

A flash, high in the sky, was brighter than the sun. Lovely to see, a blossom of silver-tinged light hung high above the clouds for several seconds until it faded into the morning sky.

He checked his chronometer and frowned. The bombing was twenty-seven minutes early. While it wouldn't affect the rest of the mission, it spoke to poor planning or sloppy execution.

He checked his pad for the boarding manifest on the *Potemkin*. Ten names, including Alexis Shurkorov, were confirmed on the yacht. Their names could be crossed off now. There were still five left to die today. Along with Suishin.

Salaam finished his tea and went to his bath to prepare for the day. It would certainly be busy.

The prairie wind swept across the timeless ocean of grass. It had been hot this summer, so the rustling of the dried grass took on a crackle as it waved. Painted, gossamer clouds floated high in the sky, the gods' water colors decorating the heavens as the sun went down.

It was the poet in him. During his training, the masters had warned him about becoming distracted. The *hashashin* had to focus at the task on hand, for the task was all. Great dishonor and horrid death awaited the *hashashin* who failed, not to mention eternal damnation.

Still, it was a pretty sky. He wondered if the target would notice this as she died. For her sake and the sake of her soul, he certainly hoped so.

His ship was well hidden in a hollow five miles away. Doubtlessly as soon as she fell, her security forces would be here to see what happened. It would take him hours to retreat, stealthy, to his ship.

He would not be captured. His training would prevent that. And should Allah not favor him this evening, the explosives in his chest and equipment would protect the brotherhood. His ship would destroy itself as well.

His auditory nerve tingled. *"Execute your mission."* He acknowledged the order by touching his tongue to the nerve cluster inside his mouth. The microwatt transmitter was an innovation of the brotherhood, nerve impulses transmitted and received directly from his own body.

Many of the modern *hashashin* held an affection for the ancient tools of their trade. Not Salaam; he used the latest and best weapons available. The weapon was a mag-sniper. Three thin rails attached to the power supply and computer site. The weapon was so precise, so accurate that anyone could hit a target from a thousand yards.

His target would be riding an air-cycle at low altitude and high speed. It would be a difficult shot at best, so he challenged himself and made the distance three thousand yards. It would make the shot nearly impossible.

It would also add two thousand yards to his escape.

His auditory nerve tingled. *"She has departed, Master."* He acknowledged and listened for her approach.

Doctor Jhon Weir said "lights" as he entered his apartment. The illumination rose to a comfortable level. "View," he called.

The pressure door over his window raised, exposing it to the Fermi Highlands on the so-called dark side of the moon. His apartment, as befitting a director, overlooked the Tsiolkovskiy Crater, bathed in sunlight. He recalled the words of the American astronaut - "Magnificent desolation." Doctor Weir couldn't agree more.

He fixed himself a drink and settled on his couch watching the moonscape. The rugged vista never failed to calm him. Certainly, given the events of the last few days, he needed to be calm. The destruction of his Delta unit was a major problem. His team had scarcely started to test the unit before that double-damned general had shot it. And in the processor! It was doubtful whether there would be any useful information now.

He heard a sudden, unfamiliar *tick* sound. A small dot, immediately surrounded by frost had appeared in the center of his window. Doctor Weir sighed. A micrometeorite. While not uncommon, it was a tiny bit odd it would hit a window. He took a patch from the emergency repair kit and slapped a patch over the noisy leak. He would have to call maintenance to come tomorrow to perform a permanent repair.

There was an odd crackling noise. He looked at the leak again. The hole had enlarged to the size of a stylus and a web of cracks was snaking out from it. Doctor Weir huffed. "Huh." He thumbed the comm unit and called. "Maintenance."

A weathered face with long dark hair appeared. "Daniel Abdo, duty engineer," came the reply. "How can I help you this evening?'

"Mister Abdo, this is Director Weir," Jhon called out. "I seem to have a micrometeorite strike on my main window."

"Have you applied a patch, sir?" Abdo asked.

"I have," Weir answered, "but the size of the hole is increasing and the window is starting to crack."

"Hmmm, well that's odd," the engineer was nonplussed. "The self-sealing feature, along with the patch, should have stopped the hole from growing and prevent any crack propagation. I'll send a crew out immediately, Director. In the meantime, I suggest you close your pressure door, just in case the hole gets any larger. Worst case scenario, we'll have to change the window. The repair crew will be there shortly."

"Thank you Engineer Abdo." Weir closed the channel. He pressed the pad that would close the door over his window.

It didn't budge.

There was another cracking noise. Doctor Weir examined the window again. The hole was nearly double its size again and more cracks were expanding. The patch bulged ominously into the hole. The hole expanded to half an inch in diameter. Doctor Weir now saw there was a yellow stain inside the hole. *Acid!* He realized. The patch began to disintegrate.

He slapped the emergency switch next to the window. Instead of dropping the shutter, the window gave another loud crack. Holding down on his panic, he opened an emergency panel next to the window and pulled the handle down.

The hatch still didn't budge.

The patch failed and a loud whistling scream came from the hole as the atmosphere in his apartment streamed out into the lunar landscape. An alarm went off, screaming, "Integrity breech! Evacuate immediately! Security has been alerted! Integrity breech! Evacuate immediately! Security has been notified!"

Jhon Weir raced to his door. It didn't open. He hit the latch, then the emergency release. The portal was frozen, unmoving as any edifice. He pounded on the door, screaming, and crying "HELP!"

Another crack and the whistling became a whoosh. The retreating air tugged at his shirt now. He turned and saw a salvage team outside his window, working with grim desperation as the window was fracturing. The hole was enormous now, three times its original size, his original patch gone and the temporary patch the salvage crew had installed blowing up like a pallid moon.

They suddenly turned and raced away. "Dear god, no," whispered Doctor Jhon Weir as the window cracked a final time and launched everything in the room across the Tsiolkovskiy Crater.

Her air cycle was fueled and ready to go. Ameranda Whitestone's chief of staff was standing beside it to warn her as he did every time she took off on a midnight ride on just how foolish she was being. As always, she would brush him off and roar into the night.

"Miss Vice President." He handed her the helmet. "Will you at least wear this tonight? She laughed; this was a new part to the familiar routine.

Come now, Rabbit," she scolded. "You've tried riding with me before. If I wipe out, do you really think this is going to do me the slightest amount of good?"

Clint "Rabbit" Nuiman shook his head. "No, I suppose not," he said. "It's just…I have a funny feeling about tonight. You're sure I can't talk you out of tonight's ride?"

"Oooooooo, spooky!" she wiggled a gloved hand at her aide. "Come on, Rabbit, you can do better than that! See you in a couple of hours." She lowered her goggles and roared into the night.

As soon as her taillights faded into the dark, Nuiman tonged the nerve cluster in his mouth. *"She has departed, Master."*

The prairie air flowed over her leather clad body like the grip of a lover in passion. Ameranda's pony tail was a fluttering pendent behind her. A rictus grin preceded her, from the force of the two hundred mile an hour wind.

Oh, it was the greatest feeling since…she pondered. She was going to tell herself the greatest thing since sex. But she had been disappointed as late. She had eschewed many of her playthings since Alexis had delivered Suishin to her. The foolish boy was no match for her charm and drugs. Oh, his body was as magnificent as always, maybe even better as he physically matured and thickened in just the right places.

But he had become addicted to the dauderign. An expensive narcotic from a spiny fish native to Mer, she had used it to seduce him, then to make him her eager plaything. Once he was under her control, it was an easy thing to have Alexis manipulate the poor fool to follow their directions.

They would kill him, of course, when he was of no more value to them. But that was a conversation for another day. In the meantime, there were still any number of tasks to accomplish.

Especially Angkor. They would have to do something about him. Alexis scoffed at the second son of Tenzing, mocking him as a "worthless academic barely worth even the time to consider if we should consider." Ameranda wasn't so sure. True, her spies had found nothing yet. Still, perhaps she should have him eliminated, just in case.

"She has departed, Master."

It wouldn't be long. He breathed evenly, ear microphones straining to hear the sound of the cycle. It appeared precisely where he expected. He touched the targeting stud and placed the cursor on the intersection of her body and her shoulder. The red light went steady and he could feel the targeting servos holding the rails in line with the target.

He listened to his heartbeat, then pulled the trigger on the slight gap in his cardiac rhythm. The weapon was silent as the round accelerated through the magnetic rail, popping slightly as it passed through the sound barrier. Tiny guidance fins extended from the round as it left its rails. At 7000 feet per second, it had struck Ameranda at the top of her left collarbone before his heart made the next motion of its beat.

126

The round was a malleable metal, designed to hold shape as it raced to its target, but expand as soon as it hit anything solid. As it struck the leather, it began to grow in its predesigned form, intent on doing as much damage as possible. The actual impact pulverized her collar bone and shoulder. A shock waved formed ahead of the round, exploding her ribs and vaporizing her heart and lungs. The soft mass of digestive tract absorbed much of the energy, so by the time the missile reached her spine, it merely shattered vertebrae before exiting and flying nearly a mile beyond.

It buried itself in a long narrow trench and would be hidden for two hundred years until a treasure hunter from Cassini Four found it while looking for arrowheads from ancient savages said to have fought mighty battles here. It lay in the Museum of Terran History on that world for many centuries beyond that before becoming lost for all time.

Ameranda tried to gasp as the sledgehammer blow knocked her from her air cycle, but she no longer had lungs. Her body hit the turf messily and tumbled for a hundred yards before she came to a stop. Her last conscious thought was, *Silly girl, perhaps you should have worn that helmet...*

Chapter 12

June 3044 A.D.

Suishin stormed through the halls of the Keep toward his chambers. *The fools, the damnable fools!* He had returned from Zurich following the Council meeting and it had not gone well for the eldest son of Tenzing. He did not fathom how they couldn't understand the simple logic of diverting funds from agriculture into military research.

He had laid out the plan exactly as Alexis and Ameranda had shown him. It made such sense; how could they not see the plan's value? That Alexis and Ameranda would profit significantly was of no importance. It was for the good of mankind

Well, the Union Council's opposition would soon be a moot point. He had decided to insist they move the plan forward. His father hadn't voiced support for Suishin for the last time. It was time to remove the doddering old fool and his filthy alien sidekick. It was time to remove all the aliens from Earth and start his campaign through the stars.

Oh, it would be glorious! Suishin's eyes would tear up when he saw the Empire he was to create. Humans, spread across the sky, on every world. Oh, he'd be magnanimous, allowing enough of the aliens to live and serve their human masters.

He smacked his lips. His mouth was dry, the first indication that the dauderign was wearing off. The headache would start soon, along with the pain in his stomach.

He didn't need the dauderign, of course. He could stop taking it any time he wanted. He'd be sick for a few days but the effects would clear up and he'd be fine.

But, damn it, he loved how powerful it made him feel. Since the first time Ameranda had shown him how to use the inhaler as a teenager, he'd enjoyed the confidence, the strength, the superiority the drug enhanced in him.

With it, he imagined, he could not only challenge his father, but defeat him. Perhaps he could even defeat Alexis Shurkorov.

He resisted the urge to kick his chamber door open. He could feel the madness at the edges of his mind, behind the headache burning its way into his brain. Trembling hands opened the drawer on his nightstand. He found the mask and clamped it over his face and inhaled deeply. It clicked once.

Empty! He threw it to the side. It had been half full this morning, he was sure of it. Trembling, he swept his hand along the shelf in his closet. The spare wasn't there, and the headache was searing into the core of his head. He gripped his skull and groaned. He didn't want to go through this again. Early on, just once, he defied Ameranda and she withheld the dauderign. He had wanted to die. He'd rather die than face this pain again.

The bathroom! He kept one in the bathroom! Under the sink! He staggered across his apartment, tripping over the ornate

129

rug in the middle of the room. He bounced once, getting to his hands and knees, crawling like a beast. Clawing at the door of the vanity tore it from its hinges and he dug through the towels and bottles, certain the flask was there. When the cabinet was empty, the pile of debris mocked him as he tore open boxes, shook out towels, the madness in his brain screaming. The dauderign wasn't there!

Suishin sat on his bathroom floor, sobbing. Gods, his stomach was starting to twist. He retched and vomited into the toilet. Shaking and sweating, he staggered back into the main chamber, wracking his brain to remember where he had hidden his emergency inhaler.

"Is this what you are looking for, Brother?" Angkor stood in the window adjacent to his balcony, the coveted canister of dauderign in his hand.

"Brother, please," Suishin begged. "I'm sick. Give me my medicine."

Angkor shook his head. "Brother, I am a doctor," he said. "I know what this is. It explains much. Please, Suishin, let me help you."

"You want to help me, give me my medicine," demanded Suishin.

"You'll thank me one day, Brother," Angkor replied. "Perhaps you'll regain your sanity when your body throws off the effects of this poison. When you regain your senses, then I will use you in my government."

"Your government?" Suishin's stomach rolled again and he growled. "What government would that be, Brother? Your test tubes and beakers? Pah!" He hacked and gagged, trying to spit at his brother. Alas, his mouth was as dry as the desert outside his window.

"Nevertheless, you will not be replacing Father," Angkor was calm. "We discovered your cabal, Suishin. Your masters are dead now. Your power is broken. I am the only reason you are alive today."

Dead? Ameranda? Alexis? How could his whelp of a brother do this? "I don't believe you, you're lying," Suishin groaned.

"No, he is not lying."

The brothers turned at the words from their father, who strode into the room followed by Ryder Finn.

'Give that here," Tenzing ordered. Angkor handed his father the dauderign canister. Tenzing held it with two fingers, the odious and filthy thing. He flicked it to Suishin.

Suishin clamped the mask over his face and breathed deeply. Ah, the briny dust filled his lungs and cleared his head. He seemed to grow several inches as he straightened and flexed his massive chest. Fulfilled, he removed the mask and tossed it on his bed. "That's better," he groaned as he stretched, "I feel human, more than human. I feel like a god again. Thank you, Father."

"Do not thank me, vile creature," snarled Tenzing. "Either of you. I am ashamed of both of you! Suishin for allowing yourself to

131

be taken in by such vermin. And you," his accusing finger pointed long at Angkor, "for presuming! Everything that was happening with your brother was what I had planned. Now you have killed potential allies and placed agents of mine in harm's way! Further, you have forced my hand. Now, tonight, in this place, one of you must die."

"Fair enough, Father," Suishin cracked his knuckles. "Are you ready to meet the gods, little Pitth?"

"Why are we fi…" was all Angkor got out before Suishin leapt at him, his massive arms spread wide. Angkor ducked and his brother crashed into the doorjamb. Suishin roared to his feet and swung a fist at Angkor's head. He connected, throwing his brother across the room. He followed Angkor closely, gathered him in his arms and raced to the wall across the room, releasing him a fraction of a second before Angkor hit it, crushed between his brother and the unyielding stone.

Angkor slumped to the floor, trying to breathe. Suishin, a placid look on his face, raised his fists and pounded down on his brother, bam, bam, bam. He grabbed Angkor by the collar to lift him just as Angkor's fist shot out and connected with Suishin's groin. Gasping and groaning followed as the elder brother fell to a knee. Angkor, still grasping for breath, swung wildly, punching Suishin in the face three times.

They both staggered to their feet. Suishin dropped his right arm, then launched a looping haymaker aimed for Angkor's chin- and missed. Angkor jumped on his brother's exposed back and latched his arm across Suishin's throat. "Surrender, Brother," he hissed in his brother's ear.

"Never!" came the strangled reply. Suishin repeated the method he used moments before, this time with Angkor on his back. It worked again and Angkor was crushed between Suishin and the wall and he lost his grip. Both combatants fell to the floor.

A statue had fallen from Suishin's nightstand. Angkor grabbed it and crawled to his brother who was stirring. He used the statue as a club, pounding over and over until the larger man lay unconscious.

"Finish him." The order came from Tenzing, a look of disgust on his face.

Angkor leaned back against the wall. "No, I will not murder my own brother."

There was a sliding click noise. Tenzing was pointing his personal needle gun at Angkor. "Finish him," he ordered, "or I will. Ryder will be my witness that you assaulted us both, intent on killing your brother so you would be the next leader. Remember, the punishment for murder of a Khalkha brother is long and painful."

Angkor stared at his father for a long minute, then crawled to Suishin. All the years of bitter anger and resentment boiled to the surface. The insults, Suishin's shameful actions. He gripped Suishin's throat and began to squeeze, constricting his brother's airway. Leaning forward, he placed his full body weight on Suishin's throat. Already semi-conscious, Suishin could only grunt and feebly attempt to push Angkor away.

133

Time passed slowly, feeling like hours instead of the five minutes it took for Suishin to die. Angkor's rage started to subside as his brother's struggles became weaker and weaker, finally ceased. Suishin's last breath rattled from his ruined throat and it was over.

Tenzing grabbed Angkor by the collar and threw him to the side. He pried open Suishin's eyes, examining them for the spark of life. He nodded. "Ryder, my friend," he said, "not exactly how we planned it, but it's done." He stood and the two men embraced. "I shall miss you, my friend."

"As shall I," replied the blue-skinned man.

"You know what to do," Tenzing said, rubbing his eyes. Ryder nodded, picked up Suishin and carried him out onto the balcony. He raised the body over his head and threw it over the rail. There was the messy sound of a body hitting the stone courtyard below.

"You will go to your quarters and stay there," Tenzing ordered Angkor. "When the inquisitors come to question you in the morning, you will say you entered your brother's room in time to see the alien throw poor Suishin over the rail. I, in turn, will order the deportation of every alien on Earth, with the orders to shoot Ryder on sight when he's spotted."

Angkor painfully stood. "Why, Father?" he asked. Tenzing backhanded his son, knocking him to the floor.

"Because I am the leader and this must be done," he snarled. "There can be only one leader, one Khan. And I need you, your reputation intact, to be that leader." He spun on a heel and left the room, Ryder Finn at his side.

There was outrage at the murder of Suishin, son of Tenzing. Cries for justice and vengeance spread across the planet. Aliens of every sort were attacked on sight by mobs, seeking to extract any measure of revenge for the murder of the tall, powerful heir to Tenzing.

Lost in the news was the mysterious explosion on Alexis Shurkorovs yacht and the untimely death of Ameranda Whitestone in a motorcycle accident.

Ryder Finn had disappeared. Two days after the murder, Tenzing reluctantly agreed with the Council and ordered all aliens to leave Earth. "It is clear that so long as one alien of our dear Earth is allowed to roam freely, then no citizen of our precious world is safe," stated a grieving Tenzing. "As such, I state that no alien shall ever set foot on Earth again!"

The planet roared its approval. Scenes were shown on every media of aliens of every sort being forced onto shuttles and lifted off the planet. There were riots in several cities where the perception was that the government wasn't moving fast enough. Nearly one hundred beings, human or otherwise, died in one such riot.

Interesting, thought Angkor. *Am I the only one to notice Father issued a statement, not a declaration? And that the Council hasn't taken the statement under consideration and made my father's statement a law? Just what are you up to, Father?*

Security had installed a ballistic curtain over his balcony, so his view of the valley was obscured. A guard waited outside his door, politely but firmly keeping Angkor in his chambers.

So he sat and meditated.

He missed Sophia terribly. After the meeting on Xaid's airship, Dawlish had taken her away and hidden her for her safety at Angkor's insistence. He didn't regret sending her away. He had rushed into this situation without considering her safety, only remembering her after Salaam's team had started the killing. For that, he felt terrible guilt. Still, she was safe. He prayed he'd see her once more before...

Father's plan. Angkor had been so frightened at what his brother would do, he never considered his father might have a plan. When Dawlish and his friends had presented their plan he rushed forward without considering the consequence. Now Sophia was in hiding and his brother was dead by his hand, himself locked away in his father's Keep.

Still, Father had said he needed Angkor safe and with his reputation intact. Clearly, Tenzing had a plan within the plan.

Five days after Suishin's murder came his funeral. The Keep's bonzes had ritually cleaned his body and cremated him. The white box with pictographs of prayers and glyphs sat on the altar. Angkor had donned his robes from Temple Angkor wat, watching the ritual from the side. The bonzes sang the long prayers and burned incense to help Suishin's soul find its way in the next life.

136

The tottering eldest bonze lift the remains from the altar, holding the box with shaking, bony hands. He shuffled to Tenzing, mumbling in a high-pitched voice. Tenzing accepted his son's box with a bow. Spying Angkor from the corner of his eye, he whispered an order to an aide before leaving the temple.

"Your father orders you to change into traveling clothing and meet him at the mountain portal," the aide stated. "Your guard will show you the way."

The clothing was waiting in his chambers. Not the ceremonial breeches and jerkin he had worn in another time and place but rougher, hardier. The boots were stiffer, durable. At the mountain portal, his father waited with two ponies.

They traveled silently into the mountains. The summer scrub was dry and brown. Only along the numerous streams was there color, pillows of moss clinging to the rock, beds of wildflowers nodding in the sun. Insects snapped and buzzed, flying to and fro amongst the tufted stalks of grass and summer flowers. There was food to eat, nests to build, eggs to care for. The passing of the two men wasn't enough to disturb the cycle of life.

Dusk came. They camped in the lee of a cliff. Tenzing produced a portable thermal and their camp had a cheery glow in the dark mountain night. After eating, father and son lay under the wide sky, each lost in his own thoughts. The thermal shut down after an hour, plunging their campsite into the darkness of the deep mountains.

Above them, the sweep of the universe was in stark relief to the ground beneath them. Tenzing considered the cost of the plan he had set in motion. It was proceeding as it needed. But the cost…Dear Gods, the cost.

Angkor searched the pinpoints of light, straining to locate Jupiter and Ganymede Station. What he would give to be back there, Sophia at his side amongst his scanners and notes. Tonight could be movie night, an ancient tradition a thousand years old. Groups of the residents would gather in each other's homes, watching old movies and eating. There would be laughing and joking, friends enjoying each other's company.

Sophia. He missed her terribly. The days since the assassinations had begun were the longest they had been separated since the night before he had confronted the old tea merchant. He drifted off to sleep, weeping silently. He swore he would never send her away like this again.

The next morning, they traveled deeper into the Khangai Mountains. Cresting a hillock, they saw a wide grass covered slope descending the mountain, dotted with summer flowers waving lazy in the slight breeze. Beyond, mountains stood sentinel to the far side of the vale.

"Here," Tenzing said.

They dismounted and unstrapped the shovels from their saddles. Each stopped from time to time to admire the view. Suishin, spoiled in life, nevertheless had a spectacular vista for his eternal sleep. Tenzing, his eyes red and watery, placed his eldest in

138

the hole. He pulled the dirt in the hole with his hands and patted the mound.

He sat next to the grave and sighed. "I imagine in the first days, the Gods themselves sat here and admired their work," Tenzing said. "Perhaps, should they find themselves back on this hilltop, they could pause and say something kind for your brother.

"I'm glad it is you who are here with me today, Angkor," his father said. "This is how the plan said it would be, although today I would give anything for it not to be so.

"There will be war, Angkor. We thought our victory over the Solarians would finally convince the Galactic Council of our worthiness. We hoped we would at last be allowed to grow. But the Galactic Council fears us, hates us. Ryder and I have spent the last forty years trying to prepare Earth for the next war. But it is a lost cause, my son. When the Solarian war was over, we returned to our petty divisions and arguments. Our fleet never recovered from that last battle and is now old and obsolete.

"I ordered the aliens off Earth so when the war comes, we aren't killing innocent beings. Perhaps the colonies will be left alone and the humans there can survive.

"But here, on Earth, we are doomed."

Chapter 13

June 3044 A.D.

"But here, on earth, we are doomed."

His father's words weighed heavily on Angkor's heart.

Doomed.

Following the burial of Suishin, they returned to the Keep. The return trip was busy with conversation as Tenzing and Angkor discussed the impending war. Tenzing had invested heavily in spies to see if they could find who and when the Council would attack. Ryder had directed the spy web; as an off-worlder, alien beings were more likely to respond to him than any average human.

Now, of course, every species in the Sagittarius Arm knew he had murdered the son of Earth's leader. Tenzing expected Earth's greatest enemies on the Council would fall over themselves to curry his favor.

Suishin had pushed to increase spending to the fleet. "Except if we spend every credit in the budget," Tenzing stated, "we will still fall far too short to the necessary upgrades the fleet. No, we need a new fleet, a modern fleet. Unfortunately, a modern fleet will take decades to build even if we had the funds.

And time," Tenzing sighed heavily. "I'm certain we just don't have the time."

"Then we need to find another way to fight the war, Father," Angkor insisted. "What of an insurgent war?"

"Again, our enemy is time," explained his father. "If we have a patient enemy, insurgency might work. But at what cost? And suppose we face an enemy who has no patience? At the first hint of insurgency, I would pull my troops and bomb the planet into submission…or extinction."

Arriving at the Keep, Tenzing beckoned to Angkor. "I have something for you, my son," he said. "Perhaps the most important thing I can give you."

Deep in the Keep, they arrived at a heavy wood door, strapped with silver bands and gold rivets. "Within is the greatest treasure of the Khalkha people, my son." Tenzing's tone was hushed, reverent.

The door opened smooth, silent. The room beyond was dark but as they entered, hidden illumination brightened. The walls were tall rectangles, each the size of a crypt. In fact, each rectangle was a crypt.

"My father, Moi," Tenzing pointed, "my grandfather, Raaune, My great-grandfather Tsao…" On and on Tenzing went, naming five centuries of ancestors.

"Each was headsman of our tribe. All were leaders of our nation, Mongolia, in one fashion or another," explained Tenzing. He indicated the last sepulcher. "Here is where I will wait for eternity.

"There will be no more headmen of the Khalkha buried here after me. I will be the last of that line.

"You and I will journey tomorrow to Ulaan Baatar. There, I will declare you headman of the Khalkha. Further, I will demand the restoration of the ancient title Khan, the God-King of Mongolia. I will retain the Earth Council. Perhaps together we will find a way that will allow some of our people to survive."

"I must fetch my wife first, Father," protested Angkor.

"No. It is not yet safe enough for her to return." Tenzing clapped his son on the shoulder. "Take it from me, boy, after fifty years of marriage; enjoy the respite from your wives, as brief a time as it will be. I know I do."

"I only have one wife," said Angkor. "She is all I need."

"Truly?" wondered Tenzing aloud. "How odd."

The tribal leaders of the Kurultai Council protested the new Headman of the Khalkha. That he would claim the title of Khan was too much for many.

"Why are we resurrecting a title a thousand years past?" thundered an Oirat representative. "What are you trying to pull, Son of Moi? Are we going to dissolve the Kurultai also, so to feed your hubris?"

"I resurrect the title because it is time to bring back the title," Tenzing roared back. "Brothers, Sisters! We all have seen the reports, and we all know what Earth faces. As leaders of the Union, it falls to us to lead! When the enemy inevitably strikes, we will be the ones humans will look to."

"But with what will we lead?" came a question. "The fleet is in disrepair. We have only recently been able to get all the nations to join the Union and follow us. Our army has pretty uniforms but wouldn't stand up to a strong breeze."

"And you give us an ancient and useless title as though the enemy will shirk from that," another scoffed.

Angkor stood, arms crossed, peering down his nose. "This Council is wise to have questioned the course my father has set," he said, then raised his voice. "But you are being foolish. Yes, we are not ready for war with the Galactic Council. Not now. But we must start preparing right now, this very moment. The title Khan is ancient and honored not just amongst our people, but all the nations of Pan Asia and Europe. The mention of our ancestral Khans invoked terror and respect in our enemies. Today, we shall use that title to rally our people, then the whole of the Union.

"And if our enemies wait too long," Angkor lowered his head, his brow furrowed, his eyes blazing, a cruel grin adorning his face. "Then they will learn why the ancient Khans were so feared."

The vote was overwhelming. Minutes after his speech, Angkor son of Tenzing, became Angkor Khan of the New Mongolian Empire. Tenzing himself produced the furred, brimmed cap and crowned his son.

Exactly as he had planned.

The new Khan wasted no time in contacting the nations of Pan Asia and demanding a war Council to start the planning for the defense of their world. Representatives from Africa, Occident and

Europe attended to observe the Khan and report to their governments.

What they all found was a quiet, studious man, used to carefully gleaning over data. He was everywhere in his palace in Ulaan Baatar where the War Council was taking place. He would quietly enter committee meetings, take copious notes and leave equally quiet. Soon, each committee would receive a missive from the Khan with observations, questions and demands that the committees move along and, for the god's sake, make decisions!

General Dawlish Zoltan of the Army of Persia stood on the plaza of the Imperial Palace of Angkor Khan. Once known as the Governor's House, it was an unpretentious building in spite of its lofty name, much like the Angkor Dawlish knew from the heady days of their youth in Delhi.

It was a low, three-story building, with a sandstone façade to mimic the rest of the city. The square building had narrow windows and a flat roof. Dawlish noted immediately the dozens of soldiers guarding the palace. His practiced eye also spied the concealed weapons and disguised shield generators around the square.

The guards showed proper respect as he approached, saluting sharply. There was no need to announce himself; the staff knew who Dawlish was and escorted him directly to the office of the Khan. It was what he would have expected of Angkor. A dozen secretaries outside the portal, busy entering data, checking records and speaking in low, hushed tones on comm's.

The doors were already open, aides moving in and out with efficiency. Into the office through the left door, out through the right. The room itself was large, dominated by Angkor seated behind an oaken desk. Aides stood at attention before the Khan while he reviewed their reports. Dawlish noted Angkor reviewed each page a single time, then acted decisively. The report was either signed and approved or sent away for corrections.

His escort cleared his throat. "My Khan," he announced, "General Zoltan, as you requested."

"Friend Dawlish!" the Khan rose from his desk and wrapped his arms around his old friend. "I am so pleased to see you! Come, sit. Have some tea with me." He led them to the setting outside the French doors behind his desk. The waiting aides left the office, closing the doors behind them.

Angkor poured the tea, adding sugar to Dawlish's and a pat of butter to his own. Dawlish shuddered as his friend sipped from his cup. "Gah, Angkor, how do you stomach that?" he exclaimed.

The Khan smiled. "It is an acquired taste," he admitted.

Dawlish settled back in the comfortable chair. "I should say you've done very well for yourself," he said, "though I don't know whether I should call you Angkor or my Khan."

His friend snorted. "Angkor, please my old friend," replied Angkor. "I swear, some days they all traipse in and out with my Khan this and my Khan that. It's nice for someone to remember I have a name."

"I take it Sophia hasn't returned yet?"

145

"My father and I discussed that topic this morning," Angkor said with regret. "Soon, he says. I can fetch her soon.

"My father. I asked you to come here today on his bequest. Dawlish, we are reorganizing the Union Army. The officers running the Army now are political appointees. Career officers, who know the right things to say and the right decisions for the good of their own careers. Not the officers we need to create our Army."

"I know many of your officers," Dawlish spoke carefully. "Fine officers, one and all."

"Yes," agreed Angkor. "Not a scoundrel among them."

"No," Dawlish admitted. "Why am I here, Angkor?"

"My father and I agree. We need you to organize the Army," Angkor stated. "You will be the Chief of Staff."

"What, not Field Marshall?" Dawlish asked mockingly.

"We both know you can get more done as Chief of Staff than as a uniformed peacock," Angkor grinned. "What do you say?"

"I will have your ear?" Dawlish demanded. "I won't do this if I have to answer to a damned committee or present a song and dance for a general who wants to flex his stars."

"Only my father and me," promised Angkor. "Anyone else will find themselves scrubbing vent ports on a garbage scow out on the Kuiper Belt."

Dawlish smiled and raised his tea cup. "My Khan," he said.

Chapter 14

September 3044 to August 3045 A.D.

In the early twenty-first century, all of Earth was charmed to see a dark feature, heart-shaped, on the first clear images of Pluto. Later analysis found the feature to be a frozen lake of nitrogen. *A region so cold as to freeze nitrogen,* mused Angkor, *so cold, so dark. Just the sort of place Sophia would hate.* As the shuttle approached the world named for the ancient lord of the underworld, Angkor smiled and sighed.

She was there. Waiting patiently for him. She had spent ten longsuffering months for him to come fetch her as he had promised.

Today was the day. His father had given him a long-range shuttle for the five-day journey. He slept little the entire journey. If only the ship were faster.

They swept over the frozen fields while they descended, revealing the details of the tiny world. Pluto Station, located near the equator, was the command center for both commercial operations and outer system defense. Out this far, there was little sunlight. Pluto Station relied on its plutonium reactor, a byproduct of nuclear weapons developed back in the twentieth century.

Angkor bounced on his toes, waiting for the docking portal to equalize. Sophia was only yards away, separated from him by a pair of airlock doors. A blue light flashed. The door slid open with a bang. Before he could step forward, the station door slid open with its own crash.

A vision in sea green, the day in the market a dozen years and a hundred million miles past. Her hands were clasped anxiously, her mouth opened in a slight "o". Her brow relaxed when she saw him across the airlock. Even in the low gravity, her long blonde hair swept down her back. Her sparkling blue eyes flashed before she lowered her gaze, a faint smile blushed on her lips.

He raced across the chasm between them, sweeping her up in his arms. They clung to each other. "My wife," Angkor breathed into the wisps that framed her beloved face, "I have come to fetch you home."

"Yes, husband," cooed Sophia. "I have been waiting here for so long."

Into the station they ambled, hand in hand, their joy evident to every bystander. A line of officials was there to greet him, but he scarcely paid attention. Director So and So, Doctor Such and Such. Angkor nodded politely, shook the proffered hand and moved to the next official, while Sophia smiled regally, as if she had been a Khan's wife for fifty years

The ordeal came to an end at the end of the line. "Ladies, gentlemen of Pluto Station, my thanks for your warm greeting and hospitality." Angkor said. "But it has been a long journey and even longer months since I have seen my wife. We will see you this evening for supper. Until then."

She led him to her rooms. A guard in an unfamiliar uniform straightened and saluted as the couple passed through the door. It closed and locked with an audible click.

Since he had first seen Sophia in a sari, Angkor had admired how the elegantly simple bolt of cloth, carefully wrapped about his wife, and enhanced her and her beauty without overly revealing much.

He also admired the way she would unwind the garment and reveal herself to him. Her breasts, firm and high in the lighter gravity. The gentle flare of her hips he had so admired years ago as she walked away on that magic day in the market. The hint of a swell that was her firm belly, her long graceful legs. Her head with its loosened cascade of gold seemed at once to grow too heavy for her slender neck, and threatened to follow sea green silk to the floor. "Husband?" she whispered.

Angkor gathered his wife and carried her to the bed chamber.

They nuzzled in the tangled bedsheets. "Whew, dear wife," he gulped, "perhaps I should send you away more often if this is how I am to be greeted!"

She slapped him playfully. "Don't you dare," she scolded. "Ten months is far too long to be away from you. Especially in this place. I swear, Angkor, why is it we always seem to go to such cold places?"

"Because then we get to go to bed and warm each other up, my love." He nibbled on her neck.

She giggled and cooed at his ministrations. "I should suppose so," Sophia breathed, then sat up suddenly. "Angkor, stop. Look at the time. We have supper to attend to!"

"Let them wait," he grumbled. "Surely they'll understand. It has been ten months, Sophia."

"And if you had your way, we'd make them wait ten more months," she replied, leaping from the bed. "Hurry, hurry. We have time enough for a quick shower."

"Oh?" Angkor sat up, "Together?"

Sophia let out an exasperated shout. "Stop thinking with your little head, Husband," she called as she raced into the bathroom. "I'll be a few minutes, then your turn."

He heard the sonics running as his wife cleaned herself. She emerged minutes later, wiping herself with a large disposable towel, applying pleasant scent to her entire body. "Hurry, lazybones," she chided. "I left a manly scent for you on the towel rack." She began to brush the love tangles from her long, golden locks.

Grumbling, Angkor climbed out of bed.

The room exploded with applause as the Khan led his wife into the banquet. Angkor wore a tan, high collared suit. He had allowed Sophia to brush his hair back into what she called a civilized tail. He pointed out that, as a Khalkha warrior, he would not wear his hair bound so. She pointed out she was his wife and she would not allow him to appear in public like a barbarian.

She wore a flowing fuchsia sari with a filigreed white blouse, adorned luxuriously with gold necklaces and earrings. Angkor was bursting with pride with her on his arm. *Wait until Father and all the ministers back home see my stunning wife.*

The dinner was set under the main dome of Pluto Station, a mile in diameter and two hundred feet high. Because of the heat produced by the industries and laboratories in the station, the plastisteel remained clear, allowing stunning views of the star field outside the dwarf planet's thin atmosphere.

White linen, fine silver and imported china, not what one would expect so far from the more civilized interior worlds. Yet, most of the residents were employed by Terran corporations, so it only stood to reason they would insist on their creature comforts.

Dozens of officials awaited introductions to the young Khan. Sated, Angkor paid closer attention now as Sophia introduced officials and officers of the station and various nearby outposts. "Husband, may I introduce Samson Beagoodfellow. Samson is the Union leader for the Kuiper Belt miners."

Angkor shook the paw Beagoodfellow extended. He was a massive man, six and a half feet tall and nearly as wide at the shoulders. His obsidian eyes were only shades darker than his smooth shaved head. "Mister Beagoodfellow…" he began.

In a voice that sounded as though it came from the depths of a black hole, the miner replied, "Samson, please Doctor Angkor. Or is it Doctor Khan?"

"Samson. Then it should be Angkor, please," He liked this giant and flashed a wide, brilliant smile and a musical laugh.

"It is a pleasure to meet you, Angkor," rumbled Samson. "Your wife has been a delight to all of us here on the frozen frontier. I should hope you journey this way again and you bring her with you."

"It would be my pleasure, Samson," responded Angkor. "Perhaps you'll come visit us in Ulaan Baatar when you are earthside?"

Sophia was tugging on his arm. He nodded to Samson and followed his wife.

"Angkor, this is my special friend I wished for you to meet. Kassidy, this is Angkor. Angkor, Kassidy Jones, my closest friend." Sophia made the introduction.

Kassidy extended a slender, dark hand. "Honored, sir," she said in an Occident accent. The heavyset black woman was wearing an indistinct uniform without badges.

"Kassidy was assigned by our…friends to be my personal bodyguard," explained Sophia, nearly whispering. "In the ten months I have been here, we have become fast friends."

"Then the honor is mine, meeting my wife's special friend." Angkor gave Kassidy a slight bow.

He caught Sophia mouthing Kassidy a message. "Later." Later, what?

The dinner was accompanied by several speeches. New to politics, Angkor nonetheless deduced the residents were currying favor of the future leader of the Terran Union. He listened politely, but anxiously. He wanted to return to their chamber and get a good night's sleep before the two-day trip home. He begged off making a speech, pointing out it had been a long journey out to Pluto Station and they had to leave early in the morning. The couple returned to their quarters and disrobed.

Their sex was slow and gentle, the lovemaking of practiced lovers, each in tune with the body of the other. Afterwards they spooned, Angkor's arms wrapped around his wife.

"Husband, I have been thinking," Sophia whispered.

"Yes, of what, my love?"

"I have been small and petty," she confessed. "I have used my affliction to bring harm to you. I am sorry, my husband."

"What are you talking about, my love?" Angkor kissed her shoulder, "What affliction are you worried about? You have always been a perfect wife. The harm has been mine sending you away."

"The separation has given me time to think," She said, "My sterility has caused me sorrow, not being able to give you a child. Now you are leader of our people and there must be an heir."

"We have discussed this already, my love," he answered. "You cannot bear a child and I will not take a second wife. Especially just for an heir."

Sophia rolled onto her back and kissed her husband. "You have no idea how much this pleases me, Husband," she said. "My heart can hardly contain the joy these words give me.

Tell me, Angkor, what do you think of my friend, Kassidy Jones?"

"She is a nice woman, I suppose," he replied. "She must have good sense, as you have taken to her so. Why do you ask?"

"She is a lesbian," Sophia whispered conspiratorially. "She is not interested in having a family of her own right now. But she has incurred debt in her service and her company is threatening her if she cannot pay. She has agreed to carry our child as a surrogate if we would help her to eliminate her debt. Please, Angkor, you said you could combine my eggs with your seed, so the child would purely be ours."

"What has brought about this change, Sophia?" he asked. "A year ago this was unthinkable to you."

"A year ago, yes," she told him. "A year ago, you were not Khan. And a year ago, I had not been separated from you. For you, I want to give you the heir you need. For myself," she kissed him softly, "I will always have someone to remind me of you."

They spent weeks discussing their child. A boy, they decided, with Sophia's blue eyes and Angkor's dark hair. Sophia didn't realize there was so much to discuss about their son, height, build, inherent talents. She wanted him to be honest, hardworking and artistic. He wanted intelligent, athletic and charismatic. In the end, Angkor was able to design the child they both wanted.

Guide me, Master, he prayed quietly as he combined their egg and sperm, then spent two weeks rewriting the child's DNA. He had done this a hundred times in his career. This was different. The child would be their gift to the future. In meditation, he studied the stone he was placing in his fountain. When it was perfect, he inserted the egg into growth medium. The cells divided, then divided again. He called Sophia and Kassidy to the clinic in the palace and five minutes later, Kassidy was pregnant.

As Khan, Angkor was expected to live and work in Ulaan Baatar. The palace was certainly nice enough, having housed the leaders of Mongolia for two hundred years. Tenzing's Keep was also nearby. But the winters would be cold and there was now painful memory for Angkor at the Keep. They both longed for their home in Indianola amongst the pines, on the shore of the Salish Sea.

Whenever they could, Angkor commandeered a sub-orbital and made the three-hour trip to their home. Kassidy would join them; Sophia was convinced her son could feel the warm *Te* of their tiny home.

The new Khan quickly became a popular leader, first in Pan Asia, through all of Earth, then among the citizens of the Terran Union. It was he, in a magnificent speech that suggested they change the name of the planet.

"When we began," he said before a crowd gathered in a stadium in Munich, "we were a single, small world in a magnificent universe. One by one, nation by nation, we stepped off our fragile world. We joined together in brotherly and harmonious missions and pushed outwards, to Luna, to Mars and beyond. We invented the Space Fold sleds and moved ourselves into the heavens.

Centauri first, then Vespa and Tantalus. Today we are a dozen worlds around a dozen stars.

We came from our common background, our beloved Earth. But today, we are more than just children of Earth. We are more than just humans. Our ancestors called our world *Terra Firma*. Today I say, we are children of Terra, Terrans one and all. And we live under the banner of our new state, the Union of Terra!"

The Union Council held a *pro forma* debate. In the end, the decision was made by proclamation.

As the new World leader, Tenzing leaned heavily on Angkor as his closest advisor. They talked daily for hours and met frequently to discuss plans, actions. The elder admired his son's ability to go through data swiftly and accurately, then decide based on the data, not just his emotion.

Their decision to appoint Dawlish as Chief of Staff, for instance. Angkor had fired many of the generals and officers in the Union Army when he arrived. He promoted hungry young officers eager to serve him and the Union. He scrapped useless contracts and held conferences to determine just what the mission of the Army was to be. Then he selected a youthful naval captain, Thomas Schurenburg, and promoted him to Admiral of the Terran Fleet. The old ships left over from the Solarian War were used extensively for training of the nascent new fleet. To be sure, there were a few new cutters and the call had gone out for a new fighter design.

Tenzing and the Council demanded a new class of destroyer. Schurenburg and his officers huddled together and came up with designs for the new ships. The hull of the first, the *Quarrel*, was christened within the year.

Late summer found Angkor suddenly summoned from Zurich back to the Keep. Kassidy Jones had gone into labor and Sophia demanded he come to witness their son's arrival into the world.

His wife refused to allow their son to be born in a yurt, as the child's ancestors had. Angkor and the dozen of his friends - Khalkha, Oirats and Buryats he had known from his childhood - along with contemporaries he had met serving with the Kurultai, stood and sat on the open balcony outside the suite where his son was to be borne. They sipped on buttered tea and laughed as Angkor waited nervously for word.

There was shouting from Kassidy's room, then a tiny wail. The baby was dipped in ice cold water, then cleaned. Although he had designed the child, Angkor's heart leaped when Qui, his mother, opened the door and cried out, "Angkor Khan, son of Tenzing, son of Moi. Come, meet your new son!"

They had discretely wheeled Kassidy out of the room to a suite of her own. Sophia sat in a rocking chair holding the squalling child in her arms. "Husband," she quoted the ritual, "I give you a new Khalkha warrior."

Angkor lifted his son and examined the noisy beast. How small, how wrinkled and…purple? But he had the thin wisp of dark hair and he certainly had the lungs of a warrior.

"I greet you and welcome you to the world, young Buru, son of Angkor," he whispered to his boy. He carried the babe to his friends gathered on the balcony. "My son!" he cried with delight.

Two months later, a full moon had risen over the Hentiyn Nuruu Mountains to the west of the Keep, bathing the fortress and the valley outside Angkor's balcony in an ethereal blue light. Angkor paused, admiring the sharp contrast; features exposed to the light of the moon were sharp, defined, while the shadows were long and hidden in the darkness. The Keep was quiet this time of the evening, though the odors from the evening meal hung lightly through the halls.

Angkor and Tenzing were dressed casually for the evening, the day's toils mostly forgotten. A carafe of honey wine sat on the low table between them.

The tiny child, Buru, stared at his mustachioed grandfather. Tenzing clucked and cooed at the new scion of his line.

"Father, I have been thinking," Angkor said, staring into his goblet.

Tenzing sighed. "Work this evening?" grumbled the old man. "You have a new son here. Relax, let's enjoy the moment, shall we?"

"It is because of my son that I am thinking," Angkor said. "Along with our people and our small union, I am thinking about all of our future. I may have a plan."

"Oh?"

"Yes. We currently have fifteen Space Fold sleds. Ten are used commercially, five held for the military. We have five more being built and another five are planned," Angkor recited.

"Using current technology, we can suspend a human for fifty years before we see signs of mental instability. After one hundred years, viability drops another fifty percent. On hundred years beyond that, we are not sure.

"We have no artificial womb protocol that works for now. However, we can freeze human embryos for centuries. What I propose is, we send several Space Fold sleds Spinward and beyond. Through the galactic center and to the far reaches of our galaxy. Each ship will carry frozen embryos and suspended staff to care for them. As time passes, we reanimate members of the crew to give birth to their replacements, train them and die. When a habitable world is found, they can reanimate more staff to give birth. They will study the world and design the ultimate human to inhabit the world and eventually conquer it. The ship would then move on to find another world."

"What keeps them loyal to us? To Terra?"

We program that deep into the DNA," explained Angkor, "into the very base sequences. To adapt them to the environments they inhabit will change them into creatures we may scarcely recognize. But, we will have the advantage, their programmed loyalty. Indeed, we can imprint them to seek us out. Imagine, a ready-made Empire for us as we spread across the galaxy."

"Your plan is ambitious, my son," stated Tenzing. "Perhaps too ambitious. Perhaps we should study it closer before committing to it."

"Of course, Father," Angkor agreed. "We may yet have time before the Galactic Council moves against us."

"And we have many enemies right here on Terra." His father's voice was flat. "I propose we address these enemies first, obliterating the enemy within before we address the enemy without."

"Of course, Father."

"You friend? The fat one? He will agree to our plan?" queried Tenzing.

"Yes. I have carefully fed him the information to him." explained Angkor. "I believe he will fit our needs nicely. And as I believe he will see profit for himself, he will be even easier to manipulate when we bring him in to discuss our plan. He may even have a tactic we haven't considered."

"Very good. Summon him to Zurich. I wish to get the next phase underway as soon as possible." He sniffed and handed his grandson to Angkor. "Buru needs to see his father," he stated.

"Thank you, Father." Angkor took his fragrant son and held him at arm's length while calling for the nursemaid.

I have set this stone, he thought. *Let's hear how the fountain pour sounds for now.*

Chapter 15

April 3055 A.D.

Xaid Singh despised Zurich.

If the truth were told, he hated walking anywhere on the surface of Terra. He had been raised in Calcutta, the steamy, seething pit of humanity teeming with the underclass and diseased. Father had insisted on demonstrating charity toward the lesser fortunate. Xaid would obey, but when they returned home from handing out envelopes of rupees and baskets of food he would go to the bathhouse and spend hours scrubbing their stink from every inch of his body.

On one such trip, he had heard a curious buzzing noise aloft. A great airship floating placidly above the city. The significance was not lost on him. Up there, high above the city, beyond the sewer of populace. Freely passing through the clouds, up in the clean, fresh air.

That would be his future, he determined then and there. High above the cesspit of the cities, looking down on the rubbish from a clean, sterile home.

But business required, from time to time, that he descend from his citadel to the surface. He did so with the utmost reluctance and trepidation. He learned to be prepared, conduct as much negotiation as possible prior to arrival, and then conclude the deal as swiftly as could be done, so he could return to his refuge.

Then home and hours cleaning the stink of the worms who lived on the surface.

He had tried going into space once. The prepackaged air and close quarters of the ships, not to mention the stomach-churning motion sickness, left him fleeing back to Earth.

And he hated Zurich. The air was thin, the city untidy, disorganized. The government quarter was built along Lake Lucerne. Poets had written couplets to the lake, lauding its beauty. Artists had wandered it shores and rendered it in every medium, trying to capture the alpine lake in its finery. Xaid saw none of this. The lake looked cold, its shoreline teeming with unexploited forests or haphazard construction.

What bothered him most about this trip to Zurich was that his old college friend, Angkor, had summoned him to appear here before Tenzing's Council. Summoned him. As if Xaid were a servant or of low caste. He considered ignoring or politely declining the order. No, his company, *Akash Industiech,* did too much business with the Union government. For him to ignore such a summons would surely have an adverse effect on his business. So he had graciously accepted, as though he had decided to attend at his own suffrage. A government air car (and not a new one, he noted) delivered him from the airport directly to government house.

He was wearing an expensive white suit, to impress the government insects here of his wealth and importance. While not infirmed, he had taken up some years ago to carrying a cane. For two reasons. One, he felt it added an air of panache to his wealthy presence. The other was the small needle gun hidden in the cane.

Unfortunately, the scanners in the government house were quite efficient. Polite guards in the new uniform of the *Terran* Army stopped him and relieved him of his cane. "Weapons are not permitted to visitors of Government House," he was informed. He was handed a simple composite cane, quite efficient for someone who might need it. "Pah!" barked Xaid, throwing the plain stick back at the officer. He straightened his back and confidently followed his escort to the Council chamber.

He was not announced. The tall double doors were opened and his escort beckoned him to enter. The room was smaller, less grand than he would have expected. Efficient was the word that came to mind. The opposite wall was a large series of windows overlooking Lake Lucerne. A curved, real-wood table dominated the room, a terminal and monitor at each position.

A chair faced the raised table. It must be his - all the chairs behind the table were occupied. Tenzing, leader of the Terran Union, sat at the center. To his left were a dozen men in suits, although none as fine as Xaid's. To his right sat another dozen men, these dressed in uniforms of the new Terran Army and Navy. Save one.

Angkor. He sat at his father's right, wearing a plain dark suit.

One of the minions at Tenzing's left stood. "Xaid Singh, you have been summoned to this informal Council at the behest of the

Leader and his son, the Khan. While you may decline to answer any question, it is requested you answer honestly and completely. There will be no recording of this meeting nor any sanction for what is discussed or decided here. You are not liable for the decisions made today. Will you accept the invitation by this Council to this meeting?"

"Certainly."

An officer stood. "You are President and owner of *Akash Industiech*, is that correct?"

"Yes."

"Your offices are located in Delhi, correct?"

"Again, yes."

"At last accounting, you are the third wealthiest individual in the Terran Union."

"That is not correct," Xaid responded. "As of the open of the markets this morning, my personal wealth, along with my holdings in my company, make me the fifth wealthiest being in the Union."

Another minion to his right stood. "Interesting. Would you inform us as to who are wealthier than you?"

"That is fairly simple. The individuals who are wealthier than I am are the four oldest children of the late Alexis Shurkorov. When he tragically died five years ago, his fortune was divided amongst his twelve children. While all twelve-owned equal share after their father's death, the four eldest had manipulated those shares into a powerful block which has made them extraordinarily rich."

"So the Shurkorov family is wealthier than you?" Another minion rose and asked.

"No, that is not accurate," explained Xaid, "The Shurkorov Corporation is the largest corporation in the Union. Its stock was initially held strictly by his children. Two years ago, the company went public. The way the individual members treated their shares increased or decreased their value accordingly. Shurkorov is an excellent investment; I hold several billion in shares myself."

Another officer to his left stood. "Please tell us, Sir, what would be the effect on the Shurkorov Corporation should an investor start short selling its stock?"

"Why should anyone want to do that? As I said, they are an excellent investment," Xaid stated.

"Please, answer the question."

"It would sell quickly, without a doubt," Xaid answered. "Although speculators would be curious as to the devalued sale. The market would get nervous and the general price of the stock would fall."

"And if another significant investor should suddenly sell at an even more depressed price?" the officer asked.

Xaid stared at the woman for a minute. "It would add to the speculation of the value of the stock," he predicted. "More stockholders would become nervous and perhaps start a downward trend on Shurkorov stock."

"Devaluing the company."

"Oh, most certainly."

"And a third short sale and subsequent devaluation?"

Xaid sat back in his chair and steepled his fingers. "You want to bankrupt the Shurkorov family," he said.

"No," Xaid was surprised to hear Angkor speak, "we're not concerned about their personal wealth in the least. What we want are their holdings."

"Their holdings?" asked Xaid.

"Laboratories. Weapons and propulsion mostly," recited Angkor. "Graving docks. Space stations. Industrial equipment."

Xaid stroked his chin. "An ambitious plan, to be sure. Very well, if I become your partner in this, what's in it for me?"

"Beyond the potential of becoming the wealthiest man in the Terran Union?" Angkor handed a stack of papers to the officer on his right, who delivered them to Xaid. "An exclusive manufacture contract with our government for the next five hundred years. The government will be responsible for research and development, *Akash Industiech* will do the mass production at a fair market value."

"And what of the dear, late lamented Shurkorov Industries?" Xaid asked.

"We will retain seventy-five per cent." Angkor said.

Xaid straightened. "My partners and I will want forty percent."

Angkor's eyes narrowed, "We will retain seventy-eight per cent."

Xaid shook his head. "You don't understand, Angkor. You say seventy-five, I counter with forty. Now you come back with

166

seventy and I come back with thirty-five. You lower what you will take and I lower what I want. That's how it works."

Angkor chuckled. "You're right, my old friend. Eighty."

"I can leave right now," Xaid stood.

"Yes, you can," Angkor said, "And tomorrow, we start a run on your stock with the help of the Shurkorov family. Then you end up penniless and it will take us that much longer to achieve our goals of taking over their holdings. Now, what is your price to be?"

"Fifteen per cent."

"Agreed."

Xaid was thrilled to get fifteen per cent. It was nearly double what the front man to the hostile takeover would receive.

Xaid stood, "I assume you gentlemen want me to start right away," he said. "Once I have formed my team, I will contact you about your money in this game." With a low, sweeping bow, he indicated each member of the panel. "Success, my friends." He whirled and left.

It wasn't until he was back aboard his own ship that he realized Tenzing had never said a word.

Three months later, a small block of investors representing a pension fund for the Occident city of Des Moines divested itself of Shurkorov stocks. The price was a shocking three centicredits below the market price. The stocks were purchased immediately.

A week later, the University of Birmingham in England sold a considerable lump of their Shurkorov holdings. This time, the price was a stunning fifteen centicredits below the last quoted price. While the stocks sold quickly, a number of other investors grew nervous and relieved themselves of a portion of their holdings, all below market value.

Financial news programs mentioned the sudden small devaluation of the stock in passing. The move was small, hardly worth mentioning. Still, two devalued sales in seven days was curious.

On Friday of the following week came a hammer blow. The primary Bank of Tantalus released all of their Shurkorov stock for sale at the unheard-of price of one credit fifty below market price. While the Bank only held three percent of the publicly held stock, it sent a shudder throughout the entire banking industry. Complicating matters, the Bank of Tantalus offered the sale late on Terra's Friday, with the markets closed over the recognized week-end. Much of the stock had been purchased at the extraordinary price before the market closed.

Investors and brokers waited nervously over the weekend. Rumors abounded. The Shurkorovs were devaluing their own stock to lower the price for a general repurchase of the public shares. The Securities Exchange Commission was preparing charges against the Shurkorovs. Alien influences were attacking the Shurkorov interests in preparation for an economic war against Terra, to be followed by invasion. Each rumor was substantiated by enough fact to appear real.

When the market opened Monday, the Shurkorov stock plummeted. The family had enough cash to purchase a significant amount of the public offering. Still, at the end of the week, it was nearly twenty percent below its value only a month prior.

The marketed quieted for two months. Shurkorov stock began to recover its lost value.

Then it happened again. The city of Johannesburg in Afrique-Sud sold its stock in Shurkorov, citing poor market performance and return. They devalued the stock by half a credit a share. The results staggered the market. Across the global whole of the markets, prices plunged. Many brokers panicked, dumping Shurkorov stocks at prices unimaginable just a year previously.

Clementina Shurkorov, the eldest of the clan, personally appealed to Tenzing, Leader of the Terran Union, for relief. The Council acted quickly, purchasing space docks and laboratories from the devastated company. The cash infusion slowed, then stopped the plunge in the market.

For a week. *Akash Industiech*, a heavy investor in the Shurkorov, demanded the Shurkorovs purchase the stock *Akash* held. The family was out of cash and there was no way they could maintain their holdings. Again, Clementina Shurkorov appealed to Tenzing.

In the end, not even the Terran government could stop the collapse. Clementina Shurkorov signed the last of her family's holdings over to the Terran Council, personally handing the documents to Angkor Khan in Zurich. She and the rest of her family boarded the last remaining Shurkorov yacht and were transported via Space Fold rail to the Rim.

It was believed they would never heard from again.

Chapter 16

January 3053 A.D.

The large ground car pulled as close as possible to the bulbous Hecht vessel that landed on the tarmac at the fringe of Ulaan Baatar airport. It parked in that manner out of concern for security, yes, but mostly because the Hecht abhorred the cold. Winter on the high plateau was unpleasant for most life forms. For the lizard-like Hecht, it was intolerable.

The Hecht visitor was briefly exposed to the biting cold. Grrrscnk hissed her displeasure as she moved from the warm airlock, across the carpet the monkeys laid on the ground between the vessels. *A thoughtful gesture,* she thought. *Uncommon for monkeys.* The ground car wasn't fancy, but it had a powerful heater.

The trip to the government house was short and treacherous. The ground car was heavy, traveling on paving stones that had a thick glaze of ice. It jerked and slid on the slippery surface. Grrrscnk scrambled in the back as she was tossed from side to side. Her crest flared in fear and irritation; she hissed and croaked irascibly. An inflated chamber had been erected at the entrance to government house. The ground car entered and the chamber was sealed. Grrrscnk's annoyance eased as she crossed the balmy tunnel into the building, walking again on the red cloth the Terrans had laid down for her. *Curious.* Angkor waited in the foyer. They hadn't seen each other in twenty-five years.

171

The fur on his head was longer than she remembered. He had fattened up, thicker in the chest and belly. His face was lined, speaking of responsibilities. She wondered idly at the taste of the older Terran.

"Grrrscnk," he said, bowing.

"Friend Angkor, it has been so long." She lowered her head, they rubbed cheeks.

"Shall we?" He extended his hand, they walked together to his office, chatting.

"How is your…mate? Friend Sophia?" she asked.

"She and our son are well," he reported. "They are in Seattle, visiting our surrogate and her partner. Buru started school two years ago. The temple reports he is studying hard and his grades are acceptable. Kassidy is close to delivering, hers and her wife's child. Sophia wants to be there to help."

Grrrscnk shook her head. "You monkeys are so odd," she stated. "You are bi-gender, but you allow this…this…" she waved her arms in frustration. "I cannot find the words. We do not have such a thing amongst the Hecht."

"And yet, it works for us. And there are other species who have three or more genders," Angkor argued. Grrrscnk shook her head.

"And you," he queried. "How are your children and your mate?"

"My children are well. My eldest daughter is preparing to enter secondary school," she answered. "My mate is an adequate hunter. He is minding our nest while I am here."

In his office, Angkor had already arranged cushions for Grrrscnk to settle while he sat on the couch. There was a teapot on the low table between them and a covered bowl. He lifted the lid, saying, "I had this lamb freshly slaughtered for you this morning. You enjoy lamb, as I recall."

She dipped a claw into the bowl, extracted a dripping cube of the savory meat and into her razor-toothed maw it disappeared. She chewed noisily and swallowed the tidbit. "Yes, I remember," Grrrscnk purred. "Delicious. And an excellent metaphor to today's meeting."

"Oh?"

She selected another morsel, ate it and stated, "I am pleased you agreed to see me today. With your father's law regarding alien presence on this world, I was not certain you could agree to this meeting."

"There are always ways around laws…Technicalities, you could say."

She pondered, then nodded. "Ah, the cloths on the ground. Not protection from the cold or honorific," she said.

Angkor smiled. "Exactly. Technically, one could say you haven't actually touched the planet, therefore you are not on the planet."

"A niggly detail," and her jaw snapped in amusement.

173

"But an effective one. So, tell me why you have asked for this meeting?" Angkor inquired.

"As you are aware, there was never a formal treaty after your war with the Solarians," Grrrscnk stated. "You defeated them and as a result, they were expelled from the Galactic Council. There were more pressing issues for the Council to deal with following their expulsion; the issue of your world was tabled.

"I have been serving my government for ten years on the Galactic Council. I am a member of the Committee of Assets, studying and determining the disposition of worlds rich in resources. After many years, Earth…"

"Terra," Angkor interrupted, "We have gone back to the ancient title of Terra."

"Well, it doesn't matter," Grrrscnk stated, waving an arm dismissively. "The topic of this world was considered by the committee. I was called to testify on your behalf. I didn't lie, Angkor, I spoke truthfully to the committee about my experiences here.

"All facts were taken into consideration. We voted and it was unanimously decided.
You are a violent, destructive race. You prey upon yourselves and the species around you. You are capable of the most horrific acts upon sentient and non-sentient life forms the committee has ever been forced to witness. Even the Bougartd were sickened by the cruelty your species exhibits.

'Since there has never been a treaty between our governments, the need to declare war is not necessary. Your case will be presented before the whole of the Council in a month's time. We have already recommended an executor for your world. She has selected the race that will secure your planet and the bonds for the resources of this planet."

"By 'she,' am I to assume I know who this executor is?"

Grrrscnk selected another tidbit. "I will assume that position after the Council agrees. As I have spent the most time on your world, I am the most suitable for the task." She said. The meat disappeared into her mouth.

"And this is supposed to please me?" Angkor growled.

"Friend Angkor, it doesn't matter whether you are pleased or not," Grrrscnk said. "The decision has been made. Your people are who they are. It is sad, but you have been found unfit for civilized society. If we don't take this action now, the probability of war with your species is certain."

"So as long as we were good little monkeys and stayed in our tree, your kind had no issues with us," Angkor shouted. "But now, since our curiosity has liberated us from our planet and we have begun to explore the stars, you have arbitrarily decided to eliminate us!"

"Eliminate?" said the surprised Hecht. "No, no, no, Angkor, you misunderstand. You race isn't to be driven to extinction. What do you think we are, barbarians? The governance of your world is to

175

be taken away, yes, and the other worlds you have squatted upon will be taken back for the committee to decide.

"You are a young race, immature. For all your high ideals, it is impossible for you to be anything more than what we have observed. So, you will be cared for. It is a poor shepherd that allows harm to come to her flock. After this planet is secured, the races I have sold your resources to will establish the mines and farms. We will need workers, of course; your species will serve as these workers. The Hecht has a great deal of experience in this process. You and your kind will live in the blissful happiness of being cared for and supplied good, honest hard work and all its benefits."

"You mean slavery."

"I mean you are beasts who will be bent to conform to our will. On a personal level, I have already slated you and your family to come under my personal supervision." She leaned closely. "I had a portion of human once when I was a child. A street person, a vagabond who strayed into our encampment outside Delhi. He was delicious. I have spent years wondering what you taste like, friend Angkor. You will comply or I will feast on your wife and child first before I consume you."

"We will defy you," Angkor vowed. "Even at the cost of my family."

"Of course you will," Grrrscnk cooed. "That is to be expected. And in the end, we will be victorious and I will eat your suckling child at my victory feast."

"So you will be leading the assault yourself?"

"Oh, no," she condescended. "There is no need to risk valuable Hecht lives on this trivial matter. We have contracted the Vinithri to secure this planet. They live in colonies underground anyway, so they are natural miners. In exchange for your mineral rights, they have agreed to perform the invasion. Should you choose to resist."

"In a month?" asked Angkor. "We can expect the invasion to start then?"

"Well, no, these things take time," Grrrscnk explained. "If you had only studied contract law on our level, Angkor, you would understand there are procedures that must be followed, strict guideline to be observed. I believe the contracts will be signed and the permits issued in a year, if all goes well."

She stood and gathered the bowl of lamb. "I may keep this, yes?" Angkor nodded.

When Grrrscnk reached the door, he stopped her. "So you understand, there will be war," he told her. "We will not lie down and willingly allow you to do this. We will resist and we will prevail. And should it take ten thousand years, we will exact our vengeance for every Terran you kill."

"Yes. Yes, I'm sure you will, little monkey," she replied and was gone.

After his guard informed him Grrrscnk's ship had left, he placed a call to his father. "She confirmed what Ryder reported," he recounted to Tenzing. "We have as much as a year."

"That will not be enough time," Tenzing answered sadly. "Nevertheless, we must try. I am assembling the War Council tomorrow in my Keep. Be there."

"Yes, Father."

Chapter 17

The War Council of the Terran Union was solemn as Angkor finished his report.

The dozen officers from the Army and the nascent Fleet looked about at each other. Invasion, the very thing they had feared for the one hundred years, since their predecessors had driven off and defeated the Solarians. Now the nightmare was returning.

Ryder Finn stood. Angkor was mildly surprised to see the blue-skinned alien, but glad to see his father's oldest friend and dearest advisor.

"Mithranderer feels the Hecht will support the Vinithri invasion more than what Angkor was told," he reported. "The Vinithri are not a warrior race, nor is there a history of their species engaging in a great many battles. She feels the Hecht will bombard Terra before having the Vinithri soldiers and workers land on the planet.

"The Vinithri are a hive insect race. They have a single queen who lays all the eggs. The only males are produced strictly to fertilize the eggs. When finished, they are put to death, as they have no role in Vinithri society. Ninety-five percent of the Vinithri are workers, four and a half percent are warriors and the remaining half percent are their leaders and scientists.

When the queen dies, eight eggs are selected to receive the special nutrition needed to create a new queen, just as the rest of their society is fed the appropriate food for their chosen roles.

Mithranderar has no record of there ever being more than one Queen. We are not sure what the significance of the remaining seven eggs are." Ryder Finn sat.

"State of our fleet?" Tenzing asked Admiral Schulenburg.

"The *Quarrel* and the *Boxer* are on patrol along the Union border," the admiral reported. "They will be recalled at once, of course. The *Fisticuffs* is on his shakedown cruise; he should be operational within the month. None of the rest of the destroyers will be anywhere near cruise capable within the next eighteen months."

"Can they stand up to a Hecht war cruiser?" asked one of the Generals.

"They will fight valiantly," promised Schulenburg, "but in the end, we simply don't have the assets to face a Hecht fleet. My apologies."

General Zoltan was resplendent in his green Army uniform, gold braid at his shoulders, the collars bearing the ring of five stars. His dark hair was slicked back, his pencil moustache perfectly centered and squared beneath his proud nose. Dark eyes flashed as he reported, "We are recalling every fighter from the Union, since they intend to attack Terra first. Every native-born soldier we have will be emplaced by the year's deadline. I have already drawn up a list of strategic locations we cannot allow to fall. At the conclusion of today's meeting, we will start a training program for any Terran citizen who wishes to join their local militia."

Tenzing stood and motioned General Zoltan to sit. "My friends," he said, "the time has come for us to face facts and make hard decisions. We are outgunned and the Galactic Council holds the high ground. Not even the honor and fearlessness of our greatest warriors can save us. But in our own hopelessness, we have the spark needed to prevail. While they may kill millions of us, we will kill billions of them. Let the screams of their dead fill the ears across empty space to their mighty Council. Let our world's resources be forever stained by the blood of their warriors we kill. I, for one, vow to kill one hundred before I succumb."

They all stood and cheered, save for Angkor. Silent, he left the Keep.

He wandered outside and down a path. In the summer months, the village of his mother's people would camp here, their cattle grazing on the steppe. He continued past the frozen campground to the river.

It was nearly frozen over. Only a narrow channel in the swiftest part of the river flowed, edged with shiny, lacy ice. Closer to the beach, thick white frost covered the river and the beach. It was near here, so many years ago, he and Sui had made tiny boats of sticks and leaves, racing them down the river by pushing them with sticks. He smiled, recalling the warm, sunny day, falling in the mud and laughing, throwing clumps of muddy grass at his brother.

Angkor kicked at some rocks frozen to the river bank. A few skittered loose and he gathered them thoughtlessly. He couldn't skip the rocks as he and Sui had done as boys: the ice would make it too easy. He recalled a trick Sui had shown him. Rather than throw across the river and make the rock skip, his brother threw it high in the air, so the rock came down nearly vertical. Rather than make a big splash when it hit, the rock striking the water would make an odd *phhudt* noise. That was the trick, to make the odd noise.

Angkor heaved one rock high in the air. His aim was true; it landed in the middle of the free-flowing water with the desired *phhudt*. He was pleased to see his aim was so true. With the next rock, his aim was slightly off. Instead of hitting the water, it punctured the thin ice a few feet from the water's edge with a less than satisfactory *craunch*. He huffed; his aim was better than that. Prepared to execute a third and perfect throw, a thought struck him. He looked at the stone still in his hand and his eyes grew wide.

"Gods below!" he whispered, whirling to run back to the Keep while screaming to Tenzing over the comm.

"Father! I have it! I know what to do! Recall the Council! Find someone who can get Samson Beagoodfellow to Terra!"

"We will win this war!"

Chapter 18

July 3053 A.D.

Six billion years before, in the nebula that would one day be known as the Pillars of Heaven, an eddy knot formed in the streams of gas. As the gas coalesced, it heated. More gases were absorbed as the mass in the gravity well grew. Heat increased. More gas and solid matter increased the density of the new proto-star. Heavier elements were drawn into the whirlpool and swirled into their own small gravity wells.

A fateful day arrived. Heat and compression fused hydrogen atoms which then split, creating more heat. The elements were further compressed, fusion transforming them into heavier elements that were thrown clear by the massive energies being released. There was a sudden flash, the star Endari 43 was ignited and fed on the colossal amount of hydrogen it had gathered.

It illuminated a vast nimbus of dust and heavy elements. The smaller whirlpools that now orbited Endari 43 gathered the heavy elements and the inner, rocky planets formed. Further out, the dust and gas coalesced into cooler gas giants. The formation of the new planets didn't capture all the debris. Vast bands of dust and debris would continue to orbit Endari 43 throughout its lifetime.

The region acquired as many names as there are spacefaring species. To the Bougartd, it was *gesNapt,* "the place of garbage."

To the Solarians, *Awoos,* where they believed departed souls went while awaiting passage to the life beyond.

To Joe Campbell and Jackson Avaya, it was a place to make money. Back in the Terran system, the debris belt was a wide band, the Kuiper Belt, from Mars to out to beyond Pluto, where a strong man with a little intelligence could make a stake and mine the skies for elements a growing Terran Union needed. He would start working for one of the companies on an asteroid, wearing a cheap, company-owned suit, praying that the radiation coating still worked.

When enough credits were saved, he'd buy his own suit, then try and hook on with one of the Rock Hounds, the tiny two and three man ships that went scouring the smaller stellar bodies in search of the rare, most valuable elements. It might take years. Truthfully, only a handful ever found gold, or industrial grade carbon that could be pressed into diamond. Rarer still were the crews that lasted more than a few years.

Their ship, the *Leaky Tiki,* was the end result of Joe and Jackson's partnership. The *Leaky Tiki* was a fairly common rock hound ship. Three hundred feet long, two hundred fifty feet wide, it had two hexagonal decks and an engine cluster on the stern that looked like it had been thrown on as an afterthought.

The upper deck was where the crew lived and navigated the ship. Sensors and controls dominated its forward third. Amidships and aft were the main computer, the eating area and toilet (although not next to each other) and the sleeping closets. Along the rear area was a gymnasium. Staying fit was an issue on a mine ship as there was no gravity generator for budget considerations. A three-foot-wide rotating track that established a low gravity area, was designed to provide the crew some gravity and act as a treadmill.

A row of windows completed the upper deck. One of the designers had thought it would be a nice feature and help the miners spot the asteroids they were hunting. Jackson had pictures of his children and drawings they had made for him, while Joe had racy pictures of women on his side.

The second deck was largely kept unpressurized. It held the airlock, pressure suits and tools of a rock hunter, along with the engine/computer units they would affix to their finds and send the minerals on their way to the process stations. The assay lab was there on Deck 2 as well as the cargo hold.

Joe and Jackson were an odd couple and a perfect complement to one another. Joe was short, thin and nervous. He was a whiz with computers and sensors. There wasn't a single component on *Leaky Tiki* he hadn't torn apart and rebuilt. Jackson was a tall, powerful black man from southeast Occident. He had the luck about him, able to find just enough salable minerals to keep them in the black. While never finding the mother lode, they were considered solid, steady miners who made enough to keep their ship in good shape.

So, naturally, Samson Beagoodfellow had recruited them for the big government job.

They weren't given a lot of details. They didn't need them. Samson had told them there was an opportunity for more credits than a motherlode. It would mean going out of system, but the government was fronting all the cost.

"An' I won't bullshit any of you boys," Samson had told the thirty select crews. "It's gonna be dangerous. Mighty damned dangerous. That's why the government is paying you all so much. And for those of you who have…ah, legal issues, well, that's gonna be forgiven, too."

"What's this all about, Sam?" The grizzled captain of one of the older ships had asked. "Sure as hell the government ain't shellin' out all this scratch without a good reason." Other crews agreed and cat-called the question.

"Let's just say there is some aliens out there who mean some bad intentions for us," Samson said, "and the government has decided to sell them some rocks. Special delivery."

Samson had chosen wisely. All thirty crews signed on. Their ships were loaded on three-fold rail ships and departed Charon Station hurriedly.

The job was simple enough. Each ship would go and find rocks that were greater than fifteen metric tons of iron or nickel. They'd strap guidance computers and sub-light motors to them and look for another. Each ship carried ten motor/computer modules. Samson's ship carried another three hundred.

"Ya gotta be *quiet,* boys," Samson had stressed. "Nobody knows we're here and we wanna keep it that way. No tearing around with your sub-lights. Idea is to be *delicate*-like." That got a roaring laugh. No one would ever confuse miners with anything delicate.

There would be a hefty bonus to the crew that assembled the most asteroids and another for who found the largest. And they had only two weeks to complete the job.

The *Leaky Tiki* had already mounted its first ten packages. They had taken on ten more units and were out searching the debris cloud for still more. They hadn't been greedy about the ten rocks they'd mounted; soon as they had one that met the criteria, they'd suited up and strapped the package aboard.

The radio squawked. "Hey, *Tiki,* this is *Seabrook.* You there, Joe?"

Joe keyed the comm. "Yeah, Sal, it's me. What's up?"

"You guys wrap up your first trip yet?"

"Yup. Heading out with our second set. You?" Joe asked.

"Heading in. We got a unit with a fault," Sal answered. "We'll pick up a load and head back out." The hiss of space filled the comm for several moments, then Sal continued. "We found a pretty good field of rocks. Want the co-ordinates?"

"Sure. Save us some time."

They were quiet for several more moments, then Sal asked, "Hey, Joe?"

"Yeah?"

"This is all really something, isn't it?"

"Yeah. Who'd a thought the future of mankind would come down to a bunch of rock hounds," Joe mused.

"You really think it's that big?" Sal asked.

"Can't believe they'd send us all this way if'n it wasn't," Joe replied. "Kinda funny though. Rock hounds to the rescue."

"Yeah. Well, here's them coordinates. Good hunting, Joe," Sal signed off.

"You too, Sal. See ya in a week."

A soft scent awakened the First Daughter of the Vinithri. Third Aide Daughter was outside her sleeping cell, her neck ganglion exposed politely and correctly. "First Daughter, there is a communication from Home world. It is the Mother." She had conveyed the message in perfect fashion, her use of pheromone-speak was exquisite. First Daughter would let her live.

It would be undignified to scramble out of her cell, even if Mother was calling. "I obey, of course," she told Third Aide. "Tell Mother I am on my way." She crawled from her cell and groomed. No time to clean herself fully; she wiped the sleep from her antennae and polished her mandibles. Erect, on her mid and hind legs, the First Daughter stood nearly six feet tall. Her bulbous abdomen added another five feet to her total length. She was the high caste yellow, with the gold-brown streaks of the royalty and emerald green eyes further denoted her high station among the Royalty of the Vinithri. She wove the vestment of office around her thorax and moved as befitting a noble to the command center.

Her ship had no name. There was no need. It was one of ten Vinithri colony ship moving in an elegant fashion, in convoy to occupy Earth. Each oval ship was a mile long with its engines mounted as graceful tapers from the front of the ship. Inside each ship, a million worker and warrior class slept in their cells, arranged in an efficient honeycomb-like structure that filled the interior. They would sleep until the Royals and leaders awoke them.

The convoy's escort was a dozen Vinithri warships, silver/white starbursts dancing around their charges. The Hecht fleet of solid dreadnaughts led them through otherspace.

All the center's crew bowed as she entered the chamber. "I await the message from Mother," she audibled to the comm officer. The crew were not Royals, not worthy of pheromone-speak, so she vibrated the remains of her vestigial wings together to communicate.

The otherspace message began, the holo emitter shimmering the majestic form of the Mother of the Vinithri. Her head and thorax were as tall as her First Daughter; however her abdomen was swollen and fifty feet long, laying the billions of eggs of the Vinithri race. Her shell was the mottled gold and brown, reserved for the Mother. Emerald eyes glowed as her daughter bowed, exposing her neck and nerve ganglion.

"I greet you, my Mother and Mother of us all." First Daughter released the correct pheromones in the most respectful manner. The repeater transmitted her scent to the Mother's repeater.

"I greet My First Daughter," her mother answered, the pheromone words coming from the repeater. "I have dreadful news. The war is over. We have lost. We are all dead."

The First Daughter staggered. "Dead, Mother?" she asked, "How? I don't understand."

"Scientist Daughter Twelve detected movement in our system's debris field fifteen minutes ago," Mother explained. "Her colleagues verified that six hundred rocks are inbound as we speak. They will devastate Home World and all of our colonies within half an hour.

"We have several dozen ships available. I have ordered every single egg, fertilized or not, to be loaded and evacuated. I have also ordered every bit of royal jellies and worker/warrior food also be loaded. Still, it will not be enough to save us.

"I have failed you all, Daughter. I was to have years to serve you, my children. I had not produced enough Queen jelly to grow a new queen. As such, there will be no more Queens. I shall be the last."

The First Daughter's legs collapsed. "Mother!" she begged. "You must escape! Make your way to a ship and get away. We cannot go on without you!"

"It is over, First Daughter," Mother's scent was pure anguish. "I am dead. You will now lead an extinct people. I can offer one small bit of hope. You must go to the Terrans and surrender. Make any treaty with them you can. They are clever, these Terrans. Perhaps they can find a solution to save us. Otherwise, you will be the last First Daughter."

"Mother," the First Daughter replied, "I cannot…"

"You must, Daughter." The image shook. "Ah, the first strike. It seems we do not have the half hour. It will be over soon.

Remember my orders, First Daughter. Farewell." Mother raised her forelimbs in salute as the image danced and shimmered.

Then she was gone.

Chapter 19

July 3053 to October 3053 A.D.

"My friends, I bring momentous news!" announced Tenzing on
every vid, every news source and every media. He explained to
joyous Terrans of their salvation from the evil hordes of the Galactic
Council with a plan conceived by his brilliant son and carried out by
brave miners.

On Terra, Angkor and Sophia appeared on the balcony of the
Union Parliament in Zurich and received the accolades of the throng
that assembled there. Planetwide, adoration reigned for the young
leader and his bold plan that saved mankind.

The big blow-out happened under the main dome on Mars
Station. The miners had returned on the otherspace rail ships to
hundreds of vessels, from tiny private cutters to the Terran Navy
Destroyers *Quarrel, Boxer* and the newest ship, *Fisticuffs.* The
Navy launched Kanata fighters to escort the thirty ships and keep the
enthusiastic revelers at a safe distance.

The governor of Mars greeted the heroes and presented them
the keys to the colony. Every whim the miners could imagine was
made available. Tables were laid out on the central square, fairly
groaning under the weight of food and drink. Women and men
flocked to the heroes, offering their bodies…and more.

For Joe Campbell, it was the debauch to end all debauches.
He arrived at the big blow-out in a Saville Row suit from the outlet

in Mars City. On his arms were a pair of beautiful women. He had drunk, drugged, danced and partied since the moment he left the *Leaky Tiki*. He was being held up by buxom women and stims and would crash soon, he knew. But for now, he was going to squeeze every bit while he could still stand.

Jackson Ayana had left the ship and gone straight home to his wife and children. Having survived months in space normally, he thought the relatively short mission to the Vinithri home world wouldn't have a significant impact on him. But seeing his family waiting at the door of their home, and considering the impact of his mission…Jackson wrapped his burly arms around his wife and two children, tears flowing freely in gratitude they would live another day.

Something, he knew, the Vinithri children would not.

Jackson and his wife arrived at the party shortly after Joe's grand entrance. They found their seats with the rest of the married miners. His old friend, Curtis Frunnel, captain of the *Misty Mae,* leaned to Jackson and yelled, "Your boy Joe is in fine form tonight. Wanna bet how much longer he lasts?"

Joe was trying to climb on the main table. From other nights in the seedier parts of Mars Dome and a dozen other ports, Jackson was certain what would come next. For that matter, nearly all the miners and their spouses knew what was coming next. "No bet," Jackson yelled back. "I just hope he passes out before the cops show up."

"The police wouldn't arrest him at this party, would they?" asked a starry-eyed girl. She was newly wed to a crewman on *Emma Louise*.

"You haven't seen Joe's show," her husband, Paul, told her. "Oh, he's made it on the table. Here we go!"

The bleary-eyed crewman wavered. "Gentlemen!" Joe slurred. "Ladies! Your hizzonor Guvnor! I give you a bit of culture with poetry I wrote for this occaizh…this occaizh…for this party! If I may, yerhizzoner…" He bowed to the Governor, nearly spilling from the table. He placed his hand to his chest and raised the other, dramatically cleared his throat and began:

"There was a young doxie from Mars,
Who chased after rock hounds in bars.
She'd take them to bed,
An' give them some head,
Then cry when they went back to the stars!"

The reactions were boozy cheers and groans. Joe bowed and bowed again. Someone threw a buttered roll at the impromptu stage. It was followed by drinks and more food. Joe stood tall and shook his head. "Very well then, ye heathens!" he hollered. "Ye asked for it, ye get it!" He let out a yell and began singing an unintelligible chanty. Others in the crowd joined in. Empowered by the adulation, Joe danced about on the table, stripping off his soiled and sodden suit.

Amelia, Jackson's wife, patted his arm. "It's time we ladies left," she told him. "Don't get too faced, Luv. After Joe's done and you get him to bed, you have your husbandly duties to attend to." The other wives excused themselves and hurried out.

Joe was down to his boxers. He wriggled and writhed, eliciting more catcalls and hoots. He spied the governor and his wife sitting dumbfounded at the head table. "Yerhizzoner!" Joe cried. He stepped toward the shocked hosts, tripped over the centerpiece and fell slowly in the three-quarter gravity, landing squarely in a platter of canapes and creamed spreads. On his knees and crawling forward, he stumbled into a gaily decorated cake, face first. "Cake anyone?" he belched, and passed out.

"Party's over," Jackson announced. He and Frunnel gathered Joe up as knots of miners saluted Joe and went back to the party. As they carried Joe away, Frunnel remarked, "Is it any wonder we never get invited back anywhere?"

Tenzing dispatched Angkor and Sophia on a grand victory tour throughout the dozen worlds and stations of the Terran Union. "This is an opportunity, my son," explained his father. "You are extremely popular for the moment. We have circulated a, ah, more romantic story of you and your wife amongst the colonies. Polls are showing the people are clamoring to see more of the both of you."

Since the collapse of the Shurkorov family, the government had its choice of any of their opulent yachts. Both Sophia and

Angkor would have been happy on a cutter or even a mining vessel, but Tenzing would hear none of their dissension. "You are representing the Union as well as our line," he admonished the couple. "The people want to see you as successful, powerful and beautiful leaders. To appear in anything less…well, Ryder and I agree, this is the only ship that is suitable."

The yacht was the *Siene,* sister ship to the late, lamented *Pomptenkin.* The crew had been replaced by agents known loyal to the Tenzing and the government. On the tour, the *Siene* was joined on the fold rail ship by *Fisticuffs,* the Union's newest destroyer.

It was a spectacular tour for the Union. Angkor and Sophia were an attractive, cosmopolitan couple. She wore a variety of saris at each stop. Soon, the fashion houses across the Union were clamoring for silks and fabrics to fashion the chic garment. Whole stores sold out of Sophia's new glamorous look and jewelry in hours.

Tumultuous cheering would erupt when the couple would step from the ground car to the adoring crowds. Sophia would shyly acknowledge the cheers while Angkor would step to the microphone and announce, "For those of you who don't know me, I am Angkor Khan, son of Tenzing, the man lucky to accompany Sophia Khan to your world."

Angkor was proud to have his beautiful wife on his arm and amused to see the excitement she created. He dressed conservatively in brown or blue suits and gave masterful speeches written by his father's best writers. He was a welcome guest on each world's news programs, speaking little of the battle, instead speaking of his vision of the Terran Union.

"There should be a common set of laws," he would explain, "common sense laws unburdened by excessive explanation and niggardly detail. Simple enough for school children to learn so when they become adults, all of us know what is expected, what is allowed and what is not. The law should be strict of course, punishment swift and severe. In this way, we will have a secure, prosperous people and Union."

The speeches were received with great enthusiasm. The people worshipped the handsome young man who shared his vision for each of them. A news feed on Vespa questioned the new law, asking what the punishments might be. After all, Vespa had one of the most forward thinking reformatory policies in the Union and recidivism was low. They pointed out the Khalkha punishment for stealing could be as severe as being tortured to death, depending on the enormity of the crime. One day after the editorial, the news feed offices were burned to the ground and the writer of the article was found in the great forest, half consumed by a deadly *Vearchka* cat.

For Angkor and Sophia, it was a chance to travel and spend time together. The tour was tightly scheduled, and each day saw them as slaves to the careful plan laid out by their handlers. Nevertheless, for all the speeches and dinners, receptions and tours of various wonders, they were *together*. From time to time, they were able to snatch a quiet moment alone. That Sophia was at his side gave Angkor great comfort. Even in a teeming crowd of shouting well-wishers, he could escape for a moment, ignoring everything and everyone around him, focusing on the most important person in his life.

The placement of the stone that is Sophia was incredibly harmonious, he often thought. *No matter the flow of the rest of my fountain, she is the single, purest note.*

The twin suns of Tantalus IV were bright and inviting as Angkor stepped from the air car delivering him to the convention center. He closed his eyes and warmed his face for a moment in the welcome sunlight. Tantalus IV was an agricultural world, suppling needed foodstuffs to the Union. While a majority of people's diets were of protein algae grown on nearly every world, Tantalus supplied hard to grow vegetables and fruits, highly prized throughout the Union.

Sophia was off visiting schools while he gave his speech to local farmers and businessmen. He thanked them for their support of the Union and laid out his plan for the future of them all.

The lunch was *bolindia* medallions with local vegetables. Angkor relished visiting Tantalus; he and Sophia had never eaten so well since leaving Terra. Doubtlessly she was eating the local version of a cafeteria lunch and acting as if she were being fed a feast. Her adaptability to any situation on this trip, her warmth and grace had the crowds clamoring for more.

His speech was well received. The audience laughed at the appropriate times, stood and cheered at his bullet points and finished

198

with the accustomed ovation. Angkor waved to the crowd and returned to his seat.

Or tried to. An Army officer had stepped out onto the stage with a pair of guards in battle gear. "Please, sir," the officer insisted, "you need to come with us."

"What is the meaning of this?" exclaimed Angkor.

"Sir, I can't say. You just need to come with us," insisted the officer. He grabbed Angkor's arm.

The room gave a low rumble. Farmers are a protective lot. To see anyone grabbed by an armed group was sure to draw their ire. "Here, now, what's all this then?" A tall, rawboned farmer stood. He was Tomas Engle, a respected farmer on this world. The emblem of his farm, a stylized lion, was inked on his forearm.

The soldiers eyed Tomas warily. "Sirs, there is a situation," the officer explained. "The Khan is urgently needed back on his ship. If you would excuse us?" He hustled Angkor to the door.

"My wife, where is my wife?" Angkor demanded.

"She is being handled by another team," explained the officer. "Now if you'll come with me, please?"

"No." Angkor shrugged off the grip of the officer. "Not another step until you tell me where is my wife?"

The officer glared, then his face softened. "Of course, sir," he answered. He touched his headset. "Control, team one," he stated. "Sawbones wants to know about Goldilocks? Says he won't move unless.... Yes sir, I will tell him." He released the headset. "She is safe, sir," he reported. "On her way to the *Siene* we speak.

199

Somewhere I need to get you to immediately, sir." He grabbed Angkor's arm again, hustled him into the street and deposited him unceremoniously into a waiting ground car.

They had landed a shuttle in an athletic field near the meeting center. The car nearly hit the ship, the door yanked open and Angkor found himself pulled from the car and into the ship. Even before the ramp closed, the shuttle was streaking to the heavens.

Angkor was seated in a lounge and handed a warm towel. He spied another army officer and asked, "What is going on, Lieutenant? Where is my wife? Are we going to her?"

"Your wife is secure on your ship, sir," he was told. "The commodore needs to see you on the *Fisticuffs* pronto. We're heading there now. You just sit back and enjoy the ride, y'hear?"

Southwest Occident, Angkor thought. *Many of my finest officers come from Occident.* He dismissed the thought and waited, focusing on what he knew as opposed to what he didn't.

The *Fisticuffs* came into view. This newest of the modern Terran Navy, he was one thousand yards long at the cigar shaped primary hull and two hundred fifty yards in diameter. Two additional barbettes, nearly as long as the hull, added another two hundred yards to each side. Inside the barbettes were the engineering and primary weapons. The *Fisticuffs'* primary weapon was a pair of newly developed meson rifles, one to each side. Several turrets blistered his hull, containing mainly close range lasers. In its black and grey tactical paint, Angkor shuddered for the poor aliens who would have to face the *Fisticuffs*

They approached the belly of the destroyer. Angkor could see the heavy clamps that held *Fisticuffs* and his brothers to the fold rail for interstellar trips. Between them was the shuttle bay. The shuttle shuddered and banged as it climbed up into the middle of the destroyer. Angkor was pleased to see both ships survived the encounter, though the pilot apologized profusely: "Sir, the auto docking system for *Fisticuffs* clearly has calibration issues."

"Nevertheless, we are here, more or less safely. Thank you, pilot."

Commodore Ridgely was resplendent in his white naval uniform, his rail thin body at stiff attention as Angkor entered the wardroom. *He's sweating,* noted Angkor. *They're all sweating. This must be some very bad news, indeed.*

He instinctively took the head seat at the table. The Commodore hesitated, then sat to Angkor's right. His hands fumbled on the tabletop and his eyes shifted nervously before settling on the young man. He took a deep breath, blowing it out forcefully. His voice broke as he said, "Sir, I have news that is not only dreadful for our Terran Union, but will be tragic for you personally." He glanced around the room, then nervously took Angkor's hand in his own and said, "Sir, I regret to inform you that your father is dead."

Chapter 20

November 3053 A.D.

The streets of Ulaan Baatar were quiet. The noises of a bustling city were unusually muted. The whole of the city and its inhabitants were in silent contemplation.

Tenzing had been quite detailed in his will. The grand state funeral for the leader of the Terran Union had been held in the main square in Zurich. His body had then been flown to the capitol of the Mongolian Empire for a funeral befitting a Headman.

He had resided in state at the government house for three days as tradition demanded. He was magnificent, wearing the traditional jerkin, trousers and boots of a Mongolian warrior. His cap was the flat, black furred hat of the Khan. Seated on a simple wooden throne, he held a bow in one hand, a whip in the other. Mourners knelt, touched their foreheads to the floor and chanted, "I offer my life to you, my Khan, in this world and the next."

Tenzing's wives were on the left-hand side of his throne, each wearing sackcloth, covered in ashes and wailing. Their mournful chorus was the only sound on the square, save for the low murmuring as each citizen knelt before his leader.

Angkor stood to the right of the Khan's throne as tradition demanded of the heir. He noted without emotion which of the ministers and officers honored his father by following the tradition in its strictest sense. There were those few who merely bowed or failed to swear the eternal fealty. Those he filed away in his head. There would be time for them later.

On the third day, Tenzing's eight most honored companions mounted poles to the throne and carried it to the main temple of Ulaan Baatar. Ryder Finn was not present. The Mithrandian was still being sought for the murder of Suishin.

The Temple prayer ceremony was mercifully short. Incense was burned, prayers offered and incantations chanted. The Khan's throne was borne up again. As the will specified, the journey to his Keep, one hundred twenty miles away, was to be as in the ancient times. Mongolian soldiers would carry the throne and march the whole of the distance to the cadence of a solitary drum.

The people lined the ancient highway, kneeling as their leader passed on the way to his eternal rest. Garlands of flowers were tossed along the whole route. Local priests chanted prayers, their multicolored robes adding color along the dreary journey. Ordinary citizens cried their laments or bowed and swore their fealty as the upper crust of Mongolian society had done, back in the city.

Sophia insisted her exhausted husband take rest during the week-long parade. He had not slept well since Tenzing's death. He was insistent that he view the events of his father's death, during the speech in Buenos Aires. Tenzing was magnificent on the sunny day in the stunning port city. The crowds chanted his name and cheered wildly as he waved and shook their hands. He ascended the dais and was giving a marvelous speech, spreading his arms wide and basking in the cheers of the excited crowd.

Then the clutch to his chest. His eyes going wide, his mouth gasping. He dropped to a knee, then toppled over, convulsing. Aides and soldiers surrounding their fallen leader. A shuttle appeared. Tenzing was loaded ungracefully while the crowd milled and cried out, trying to understand what they had just seen.

The announcement came an hour later. Toni Rebeyessa, his willowy Press Secretary from Luna appear at the hospital doors where an anxious crowd had gathered. Her eyes were red and teary, her voice quavered. "Tenzing Khan, son of Moi," she announced, "has suffered a massive coronary event. Despite the efforts of the splendid staff of Saint Maria's hospital, our leader has died. Excuse me, please." She broke down completely, burying her face in her hands and weeping uncontrollably.

The news flashed across Terra and throughout the Union. Black bordered images were displayed on every form of media; posters appeared immediately on most walls and public forum.

Tenzing had warned him they had enemies. *Which, Father?* He wondered. *Those without? Or those within?* He would need to move carefully. But duty first.

The funeral procession arrived at the Keep. Bonzes led them into the depths to the crypt of the headmen of the Khalkha. Tenzing, still seated on his throne, was placed within his tomb with gentle care. His wives and advisors hung garlands of marigolds on the body and throne, then kissed him on the cheek.

Angkor was the last to enter. He draped his garland around his father's neck and leaned close. "I do not believe you died of a simple heart attack, Father," he whispered. "I shall avenge you and complete your dream."

Strong masons pushed the onerous stone door into place, grinding stone on stone until the door dropped into the channel cut in the floor with a hollow thud. Steel screeched in the silent tomb as the heavy hasps were closed. Angkor donned heavy gloves and was handed the signet. Ministers threaded six seals in the hasps, holding them taught as Angkor sealed his father's tomb.

"It is finished," Angkor announced. "Thank you for honoring my father. Now, please leave, I wish to spend time alone with him before this ossuary is closed." Silently the priests and ministers left Angkor to his meditations.

Sophia embraced her husband, kissing him softly on his cheek. "I will be in our apartment, Husband," she told him. "When you are ready, I will be waiting." The door closed behind her. Angkor sat in lotus, cleared his mind and began to reflect.

A soft footfall approached. "I was sure you would show for his interment at the very least, Ryder," Angkor stated without surprise. "Come into the light and join me in my reflection."

Ryder Finn stepped into the dim yellow pool of light. Gnarled hands, spotted with purple age spots and raised violet veins pulled back his hood. His blue face was more lined than Angkor recalled. The old Mithranderer placed a shaking hand on the door of the vault and pressed his head against it. Angkor watched as he murmured unintelligible entreaties, then straightened, sniffling and wiping his nose.

"Thank you for that, Angkor. I was hoping you would let me say goodbye to my oldest friend."

"Honor would demand no less. And I owe you a debt I can never repay."

Ryder pursed his lips. "So you have come to accept your destiny."

"It would seem I have no choice."

"No," was Ryder's regretful response.

"Tell me why my father forced me to murder my brother," Angkor asked. "And why did you accept the blame for his death?"

Ryder slid to the floor, his back against the crypt, exhaling. "We, your father and I, had to know if you could do the unthinkable," he said. "Mithranderer told your great grandfather that your line will lead your people to godhood one day."

He smiled and winked. "Mithranderer would never admit it, but she can be wrong from time to time. Still, having examined your records, I could find no error in her reasoning.

"Nevertheless, we had to be sure. We had sent you away to receive the best education we could provide. Suishin squandered his gifts and education and corrupted his body with drugs, bringing dishonor to his family through his perversions.

"Had you failed to kill your brother, I would have killed him, anyway. You would have been accused of the murder, but we would have made sure you were acquitted. Your dishonor would have set our plans back twenty years, but you would still prevail as the Leader, albeit much later."

"It seems fortuitous that you and my father were correct," commented Angkor, "given my solution to the Galactic Council and their lackeys, the Vinithri."

"Ah, the Vinithri," Ryder brightened. "I spoke with Mithranderer after your war. She is most insistent that you, yourself, intervene in the negotiations. She says they are an unexpected but necessary factor to your line's godhood."

They sat in silence, each lost in his own thoughts. Finally, Angkor said, "I am the leader now. I can grant you a pardon for my brother's death. There will be questions, but none will dare disobey my edict. You could sit by my side as my advisor as you did for my father. We could even become...friends."

"Thank you, Angkor," Ryder responded, genuinely touched, "but I must decline. I am one hundred ninety, old for either of our races. I find myself longing to return home and retire into quiet communion with Mithranderer. Soon, my body will fail and I will be embraced to the bosom of She Who Holds Us All.

"I am sure you understand now that you cannot trust any of your friends. Your father..."

"Was murdered, yes," Angkor answered in a flat voice. "I watched the vid. I suspect a needle gun."

Ryder reached into his jacket and withdrew a data stick. "This file contains the real autopsy," he said, tossing it to the younger man. "You are correct. A mag-rail weapon, specifically designed for this kind of killing. It is a military weapon, but I have received reports there is an ancient criminal organization which has obtained a several of these weapons. They call themselves the *hashashin.*"

Angkor's face remained stoic as his brain screamed, *"SALAAM SARKIS!"* He had never officially known Salaam's role in the murders of Alexis Shurkorov or Ameranda Whitestone. His own agents had reported the leader of the terrorist organization was buried in the Egyptian government. Which could only mean Dawlish Zoltan and Xaid Singh were involved as well.

He stared at the three stones in the fountain. What he thought had harmony was revealed to be discordant, foul, obscene. He gagged at the masque. "What am I to do?" he thought, his rage straining against the ropes of his control. He wanted to grab the stones and fling them as far as he could.

"But to what end?" His Center sat in lotus next to the fountain. "If you throw the stones, you only have to go find them later," his center inculcated. "Rather, if you leave them in place, you can adjust them back into accordance."

"So I should just ignore them?"

"Of course not! Keep a close eye on them. Adjust them carefully." His Center grinned, baring his teeth. "Then, when the time is right, you gather them and smash them to dust."

Returning from reverie, Angkor stood and helped Ryder to his feet. "It is time. You and Father prepared this burden for me; it is time I take the odious thing up," he said. "I know who did this. I swear to you; they will be made to pay for this sin." Angkor embraced the old man.

"I haven't the words, my friend. My father loved you. You and your people will be honored by my descendants long after we walk amongst the stars as gods."

"Then, until that day," Ryder said, "I take my leave. My Lord." His deep, silent bow swore lifelong fealty.

"You should declare yourself Emperor." Dawlish stated before the War Council.

"To what ends, General?" asked Angkor, "My father, dead less than six months and you want me to claim such a lofty status?"

"To the ends that you are a splendid example for our people now," explained his chief of staff. "To stand before the Union Council and declare yourself Emperor…" he rubbed his chin and continued. "The people worship you now. Were you to declare yourself Emperor, they would revere you as a god."

"By your Mongol tradition, you are already a god," chimed a minister. "When your father named you headman of the Khalkha, you technically became the Crown Prince. In the ancient times, such a declaration ascended you to godhood. Therefore, claiming the Empire is the next logical step."

So you say," acceded Angkor. "That means my son, Buru, will replace me as Crown Prince. Does this mean he also becomes a god?"

"Your son is not part of this discussion," snapped Dawlish.

"But he is," Angkor pointed out. "As my son, he is heir as headman of my tribe. When I die, he replaces me as leader. So says the law laid down by my father and the Council."

Dawlish Zoltan's eyes narrowed. "Your son is not of age," he answered. "When he is, then we will discuss his role. For now, we need you. You are a powerful symbol, Angkor. As Emperor, you will be the public face of this Council. Our enemies will be forced to acknowledge this. To stand against you would be political suicide."

"We need it to be more than political suicide," thundered Angkor. "To stand against me shall be unthinkable. To do so shall be not only death for you, it shall also mean death to your family." He stood, crossed his arms and peered down his nose at his Council. "I will not be a symbol," he declared. "I will agree to become Emperor only when I have the loyalty and obedience of this Council. For both me and my descendants. Including my son."

"This is a discussion for another day." Dawlish bit off each word. "We have a more important consideration. Will you appear before the Union Council and declare yourself Emperor?"

The men glared at each other. Finally, Angkor set his jaw. "My son succeeds me in this office," he declared. "There will be no further discussion. Call the Union Council. I will appear before them tomorrow. There, I will make the declaration you seek."

"Majesty," A female Army General stood and bowed. "Might I suggest we recess? A short break after such a decision would be prudent."

Angkor nodded. "One hour," he declared.

Majesty," called Dawlish. "May I have a moment of your time? Privately? "

" My office," agreed Angkor, "Fifteen minutes." He strolled from the chamber as if he had not a care in the world.

Chapter 21

December 3053 to February 3054 A.D.

The office of the Leader of the Terran Union in the Keep was an expansive, airy room, its balcony overlooking the Gobi Desert from the western slopes of the Khangai Mountains. Tenzing had decorated it with bookshelves of texts from all across the Terran Union, including writings from worlds outside the Union. Busts of classic Terran leaders, paintings from the affiliated colonies were scattered throughout the office. On a shelf, firestones from the Great Vent, a volcano located deep in the oceans of Mer, the ocean world. A garden box from Tantalus IV stood next to the doorway to his balcony.

Angkor could not bring himself to use his father's workplace.

Instead, he continued to use his nearby, more modest office. There was no window. He would have been happy with just his desk and a computer terminal, but Sophia had thought otherwise. She painted the room in a pale white and added dark wainscoting. A curio cabinet fashioned of *poota* wood was a gift from the Archbishop of Vespa. He was building a school, with the lofty hope of it becoming a University one day. The gift was a subtle indulgence to garner the Khan's favor. Within it, small figurines, and souvenirs from twenty years and millions of miles of marriage. A comfortable, overstuffed leather couch was on the opposite wall.

(Angkor became fond of the couch in short order; it was perfect for a quick afternoon nap).

His desk was modest, the computer terminal built in to save space. Each item on the desk was set in perfect symmetry; pad square to the edges, pens and pencils aligned perfectly against them. Angkor maintained a neat, orderly mind, reflected by the order of his desk.

A plain wooden chair was for visitors. It sat slightly lower than the Khan's. Visitors invited to appear before the Khan often felt they were being inspected by their headmaster. On a credenza behind his desk sat the same self-heating teapot his mother had used all the years he lived with her on the steppe.

A gilt-framed picture faced Angkor from the left side of his desk. Dawlish lifted it and inspected the image. Brightly smiling, youthful Angkor and Sophia looked back at him. Her young face was bruised and swollen. *Ah,* he thought, *their wedding day. I wonder why he didn't have the marking the old tea seller left on her face removed from the image.*

He replaced the picture as he heard the rattle of the washroom door. Angkor emerged, wiping his hands on a towel. He poured tea for himself and sat behind his desk.

"So, Dawlish, what did you want to speak to me about?" queried Angkor. He frowned and adjusted the wedding image on his desk a fraction.

He did not offer his old friend the chair.

"You will not address me in that tone is a Council meeting again," Dawlish was controlled but furious. "I am the Chief of Staff of the Army, not some underling. Further, I am a Turkman. You will address me in an appropriate manner of respect befitting of my station."

"Of your station," mused Angkor. "I would remind you who I am. Khan of the Mongolian Empire, Leader of the Terran Union. I should think you would be cognizant of my station."

Dawlish seated himself in the chair across from Angkor. "Yes, your station," he sighed. "Leader of the Terran Union. I remind you who placed you on that throne, Leader." His voice dripped sarcasm.

"My father placed me here," answered Angkor. "His dream, his life's work. All led to me being exactly where I am today." He tapped the desktop forcefully. "I earned this through the hard work Tenzing demanded of me. I have been forged by his lessons, prepared since I was a child. Today I sit here at the bequest of my father."

"You sit there because I seated you there," Dawlish said. "Your father may have provided for you to become Leader. But it was my friends and I who actually placed you there." He leaned back and steepled his fingers. "Never forget, oh great leader, that you sit there at others' indulgence. Should you ever forget who is truly in charge, it shall be easy enough to demonstrate who the real leaders are.

"I have already executed one nearly bloodless coup. Do not think for a second that I would be unwilling to execute a second. You will go before the Terran Council. You will declare the new Terran Empire with yourself as Emperor. You will make certain everyone knows you are Leader." Dawlish settled back comfortably in the wooden chair. "You will do this and comply with my orders."

"And if I do not?" Angkor responded. "Suppose I refuse? Or perhaps I should expose you?"

Dawlish rubbed his hands together, stretched and placed them behind his head. "It should be easy enough for you to understand. Refusal? Your family could pay for your disobedience. Exposure? Should I get a hint that you are trying to expose our arrangement, then we will see a new Khan behind that desk. I wonder how compliant your young son would be under my tutelage."

Angkor knew he had been outmaneuvered. For now. "What are your orders, General?" His anger was barely contained.

"Come now, Angkor, no need for any hostility," Dawlish said. "You will go to Zurich tomorrow, as I ordered. My speech writers will have your pronouncement ready. You may have a coronation if you wish.

"Then I want you to finish the damned Vinithri negotiations. I cannot fathom why it has taken so long…"

"Because we cannot agree on a suitable planet for their survivors to settle on," interjected Angkor.

"Then find one!" Dawlish demanded. "It should not be so difficult."

"They surrendered to us, offering much but asking for little," Angkor explained. "With the death of their Queen, what they really need is a facility to see if they can replicate their Queen Jelly…"

"I don't care," Dawlish cut him off. "Whatever it takes, make it happen." He rose from the chair. "I need you to be productive," he stated. "The Empire cannot grow, much less survive with an ineffective leader like your father on the throne. I expect results, Leader. I will have them."

"…We have vanquished the enemies the Galactic Council has sent against us. Indeed, the Vinithri are now a subjugated people and the Solarians cower in fear and refuse to leave their world, lest we visit them again and rain our fury on them once more. We have sought out treaties with our neighbors and they flock to us, seeking our wisdom and protection.

"Our enemies cower before us. The Galactic Council fears us. We are a new force in this sector of the Sagittarius Arm, a force to be reckoned with. We do not seek war. But for those who would wish us ill, I point to our defeated foes and say 'You hold no power over us! We will not cower and whimper, begging for our lives!! We will stand by our friends and together, rout our enemies! See what we have done. Fear us and tremblely obey!'"

(Wild applause and cheering)

"My father and I spoke often of the nature of government. He believed, as do I, that all beings, human or otherwise, wish to live in safety and security. They want prosperity and the knowledge that their children will have the same opportunity at happiness and success that their parents had. All wish for fair, just laws that protect us all from those who would prey on the weak and misfortunate.

"We believed, my father and I, that such a government was possible, such a society was inevitable. The time for such a government is now, here, in this place.

"As your leader, it falls to me to create and establish this society. Today, here and now, I declare the Terran Union has fulfilled its purpose. It has grown to the maximum of its potential. It is time for us to fondly send it into history and move forward. It is time for us to stand and declare in a loud voice who we are today and forever.

"We are the Terran Empire."

(More wild applause and cheering)

"As your leader, it is incumbent upon me to assume the title of Emperor of the Terran Empire. I do so in the utmost humility. I have served the last fifteen years as Khan of my beloved Mongolian Empire on Terra. Today, I add to my responsibilities by declaring myself Emperor Angkor Khan, of the Terran Empire...."

-From the speech by the Emperor Angkor Khan to the Terran Council, 1 June 3061

My husband is certainly listless tonight.

"Angkor?" Sophia's touch was feather light. "Husband, are you awake?"

"Yes, my love."

"I want you to know, that was a very fine speech you gave."

"Thank you."

"I would have never imagined such a thing," she stated matter-of-factly." A poor tea seller such as myself marries a fine doctor, goes to the stars with him and returns to a life in which he becomes Emperor." She shook her head, wonderment on her countenance. "No, I could never have imagined such a thing."

He rolled to face her and took her in his arms. "You know, this makes you an Empress," he told her.

She stiffened. "I had not thought of that," she admitted. "Truly, this is even more amazing. Do I have to wear a crown?"

"I don't know."

"Well, surely you will. It would be most befitting of your station."

His sigh was heavy. "I should suppose," he said. "Though it would seem pretentious. Perhaps I should just continue to wear my hat of the Khan."

"No," she answered. "That will fall to Buru when he achieves his maturity." She thought for several minutes.

"Husband?"

"Yes, my love?"

"Would you like me to design your crown?" she asked.

"I would prefer not to wear a crown at all," he said.

"Unfortunately for you, it is not an option," she countered. "When you assumed the mantle of leadership, you assumed all it entailed. Even," she flashed her cheery smile, "the silly hat of that position."

"You will not make me look silly."

"Of course not!" she chided. "It will reflect the iron needed to be a firm leader, yet the humility a strong, wise leader needs."

"You have already given this thought, I see."

She kissed his nose. "Of course!" she exclaimed. "It is my duty as your wife to think of all those things you are too busy to think of. That is the secret my mother told me of having a harmonious house and marriage."

"Oh?" he asked, "And what else did she tell you of making a harmonious marriage?" He reached under her gown.

She chuckled naughtily. "There are a few things I learned on my own," as she slid her hand into his pajamas.

True to her word, Sophia designed an unpretentious, but powerful crown for the new Empire.

They were to appear before the Terran Council in Zurich, a month after Angkor's speech declaring the new Empire. Today, he was to receive the blessing of the Council. Then, it would dissolve itself at the pleasure of the new Emperor.

"I spent time researching both crowns and the rainbow robe your mother purchased for you on your naming day," Sophia explained. "The robe is similar to what was worn by the last of the Chin Emperors. The golden color reflects the image of the sun. The dragon and the horse were powerful creatures in Chin lore. And the colored stripes represented the legions of people their Emperor would rule over."

She handed him the simple, elegant crown. It was a buffed and polished steel ring, a pair of hoops passing over the top secured by a single rivet at the intersection. A thin strip of ermine graced the bottom of the ring, into which a blue cap was fitted. "I chose steel, for it has been forged to strength as well as flexibility, two attributes the Emperor should have. The ermine is traditional for the ruler to wear, but I kept it modestly small for your humility. The blue cap is to represent Terra, though I had many other color caps made so you may change it as you wish."

"And the hoop?" he asked,

She giggled. "Because it looks so handsome on you with those hoops."

She donned the diadem she had designed for herself. A thin gold band, with an upswept peak at her forehead. As with his new crown, elegant, simple, modest.

They entered the Council chamber, Angkor in his brilliant new rainbow robe, breeches and boots, Sophia wearing a golden sari streaked with rainbow threads. A set of unadorned thrones sat on a low dais before the Union Council. Angkor escorted Sophia to the dais; they sat together on the new chairs.

"Majesty. My Lady," Dawlish bowed before them. "Today, the Union Council wishes to express its gratitude that you have agreed to assume the mantel of leadership that our new Empire so richly deserves. Today, this Council has agreed to dissolve, leaving the leaderships and rule to your divine majesty."

Angkor stood and returned the bow of General Zoltan, then bowed to the Council. "My thanks to you all," he said. "Your toils have been long and arduous to reach this point. And I have no doubt in my mind the task before us will be equally challenging.

And I understand all too well, having been amongst your number for all these years, that no one man or woman will ever have the ability to solely run our Empire alone. Therefore, while I discharge you of your duties as the Terran Union Council, I reinstate each of you to my Imperial Council."

He lifted the crown from his head and set it on the throne. "This will serve to remind you, when I am not present, you are still operating under my authority. My rule. My law. As your Emperor and Khan, I demand of each of you to serve me and serve for the greater good of my Empire!"

The room erupted in raucous cheers. Angkor took Sophia's hand and escorted her down the central aisle of the Council chamber. Out of the corner of his eye, he watched General Zoltan seething.

Chapter 22

May 3055 A.D.

Angkor reflected on the vista before him. The wind was cold, not bitterly, but enough for him to pull his shawl tighter. The sun was rising behind him; soon he would need to discard the wrap, anyway.

The pot began to bubble. He lifted the self-boiling crockery from the grass and poured his tea. Ah, he could feel the warmth of the morning sun strike his back. He sipped the drink as its first rays swept across the glade and valley below him. A brush of light banished the vestiges of night and replaced it with yellow and green grasses, lumps of lichen, splotched grey stone and splashes of color from the midsummer wildflowers. The morning wind rolled over the ridge behind Angkor, bathing him in the sweet odors of the grasses that grew in the valley beyond.

The whoosh and buzz of an air car came from his left. Minutes later, a muffled *tclick-tclick-tclick* of measured footfall not of this Earth greeted his ears, accompanied by the soft footfall of his guards.

"Master, it…she is here," the guard nearly whispered. He had that effect on people. They felt the need to bow and lower their voice. He would use that advantage soon enough. But first, he had this negotiation to finish.

A click of mandible with a sickly-sweet odor. A mechanical voice from her translator stated, "I greet you, Emperor Angkor Khan of Terra."

She was taller than he thought, standing on her mid and aft legs, her forelegs curled under her thorax and head. Her lowered head exposed the black fibers of her main nerve ganglion between her head and thorax segments, and her antennae lay flat. She was a dirty yellow and green color and smelled earthy. Jeweled emerald eyes studied him.

"I greet you, First Daughter of the Vinithri." He motioned to a blanket laying on the grass, "Please, sit. Make yourself comfortable."

She maneuvered carefully, then lowered herself on the quilt. She waved a leg, the tip covered with a cotton boot. "A curious requirement, Emperor," she stated. "You guards would not let me leave my ship until I had donned these. Now you wish me to sit on this covering?"

"A legacy of my father," explained Angkor. "He declared no alien foot should ever touch Terra. Inconvenient, yes. This is a concession to my supporters." He produced a jar and loosened the top. "A gift from me to you. The hives this came from have been in my family for generations."

The First Daughter accepted the gift, removing the lid and extending her slender tongue. Her antennae vibrated. "Magnificent!" she exclaimed, lapping at the golden honey again. "I shall be sure my diplomats begin a new round of negotiations for trade, provided Terra puts this on the list to trade!"

"I am pleased you enjoy my gift," answered Angkor. "Now to business."

"Yes," she put the jar aside with reluctance. "I would like to thank you personally on behalf of my people for your concession on Falleron. It is a close approximation for our lost world."

"You have been equally gracious on the terms of the mining concessions, First Daughter," he answered. "And allowing Terra to exploit the Kuiper belt is also very generous."

"I believe we have learned our lesson on that topic," the First Daughter's antennae lay flat again, the Vinithri symbol of sorrow.

"I am curious," The First Daughter continued. "I understood the negotiations were complete. I was to meet you on Luna to sign the treaty between us. Now, I have been asked to come here for one more meeting before we sign this treaty?"

He handed her the cylinder. The Vinithri had no written language; the cylinder had recorded the odors their language used to record the treaty. The First Daughter read the odors, her head suddenly turning to Angkor.

"This is non-negotiable," he told her firmly. "Though, as you can see, we both have reason for keeping it secret between just you and me. Should you decline, I will cancel this afternoon's ceremony and we will once again be at war. Unfortunately for you, this is a war that will mean your end, as you are now an endangered species with no way to reproduce."

224

"This is an outrage, monkey!" she responded. "This will keep my people slave to Terra for all eternity!"

"This is your only chance. Yes, your new queen and her offspring will be genetically predisposed to obedience to Terra. But this will ensure that not just both our peoples survive, but fundamentally alter the balance of power in the entire Sagittarius Arm.

"Imagine, First Daughter. If you agree to this, not only will you will ensure the future of both our races, but you will be instrumental in bringing order to the Sagittarius Arm. Terra will do this with or without you. Our success, though, will be greatly enhanced with the Vinithri at our side, rather than as a footnote to history.

"Already we have found the possible solution for your queen jelly. With your scientists and ours working together, we will soon be able to deliver the savior queen to your people. And potentially, the savior for mine."

"So," he asked, "am I leaving to go to Luna and complete our agreement or should I return home, destroy what we have found of your queen jelly and plan with my allies for Terra's future?"

The terms were simple enough. Ten thousand Vinithri would be quietly transported to Angkor's Keep in the Khangai Mountains. They would tunnel deep into the ribs and roots of the stone, creating a vast living area and laboratory. The egg that would be the new queen would be transported there, along with the finest geneticists from both Terra and the Vinithri. The queen's DNA would be subtly

225

altered to ensure that she and her progeny would be unfailingly loyal to Terra.

The new queen would be transported to Falleron, the new home of the Vinithri. Already tens of thousands of workers on the Vinithri colony ships originally planned for Terra were being awakened to start the new royal nest for her arrival. There was sufficient male seed to create the first generation of males and workers. Within ten years, the Vinithri people would be vital and robust once again.

Back on Terra, once the new queen had left for Falleron, the real work would begin. Twenty-Four Vinithri eggs would be turned over to Terra. The blueprint of the zygotes implanted in these eggs would be designed by a committee of Terrans, aided by their insect colleagues. Their goal was to create eight children, who would compete to be the next leader of the Terran/Vinithri alliance. Each generation, twenty-four eggs would be turned over, eight more children produced to begin the competition again.

Most of the scientists of the first generation assumed the genetic material would be supplied by Terra's greatest soldiers, scientists and athletes.

They were wrong. Only Angkor and his closest allies knew the source of the supplied material. For the sake of the future Empire, only one source would be used.

Emperor Angkor Khan and his wife, the Empress Sophia.

Mare Traquilltatis has long held historic significance to Terran history. In the mid twentieth century, it was the location of the first-time humans stepped on a celestial body other than Earth. In the twenty-first century, the first outpost on another world was established, Luna Prime. It was also the first colony destroyed in war. Luna Colony was rebuilt in time to be used for the Solarian War, larger and more advanced.

The signing of the formal peace treaty between the Terran Empire and the Vinithri was the latest in a long line of history making events. As with any treaty ending a war, it was largely supported by the majority of the Empire, though there was dissent, mainly among the hawkish citizenry. Their news services branded the Emperor a traitor and vowed to fight the peace.

The first raids were in Atlanta at the New Confederacy Eagle news service. The offices were attacked by Imperial Intelligence agents in black combat uniforms. Computer terminals and servers were destroyed, data cubes confiscated and the offices burned. Editors and reporters were arrested in their homes and turned over to I.I. for questioning. The owner was arrested and disappeared. Charges were filed against many of the editors and reporters, but few came to trial. Special Courts were held in the monolithic Imperial Intelligence office in New York. The guilty were never seen again. Those who were released refused to speak of their experiences while in custody. Most applied for visas off world.

The events in Atlanta were repeated across the Empire a half dozen times. Rapidly, word spread. Dissention against the Empire or the Emperor was not tolerated.

When reports of the raids were acknowledged by the government, the general opinion across the Empire was; *"Tsk-tsk, they got what they deserved. How could anyone hate this Emperor? He's made us safe, after all. And prosperous!"*

Nine of the Vinithri ships arrived at the Falleron system. Located twenty light years from Terra, the system had five habitable worlds and three gas giants. The Vinithri started on the second world, a heavily forested planet with vast mineral deposits of gold, silver, rubidium, cal-selenium and other rare elements. The planet was blanketed with flowering foliage from the ground to high in the trees, hundreds of feet in the air.

The foremen set the workers to their tasks as soon as the shuttles touched the surface of their new home. Orbital scans had found a particular plateau suitable for tunneling. There was an underground grotto that could serve as the Grand Hall until a proper facility was excavated. Ten separate entrances were dug to the grotto, then another dozen tunnels branched down and outward. A mile below the grotto, the queen's chamber was burrowed, a wide chamber with a soaring cathedral arch. Service tunnels came next, leading to the mammoth egg chambers, where the billions of eggs laid by the future queen would be allowed to mature.

The workers were of low intelligence, focusing only on their work. They had no time to consider or hope the scientists would be able to create the new queen. A burrower found a large crack along the path of the tunnel she was digging. Since it wasn't in her plan and there was the possibility of a cave in, she stopped and signaled for a supervisor. The supervisor's conclusion was that, while there was a danger, it was worth the risk to continue. It was a ruinous mistake. The crack expanded and the new tunnel collapsed, killing fifty workers. Guardians arrived quickly, cut the head off the supervisor and dragged her body to the recycle burrow. A new supervisor arrived, inspected the cave in and directed the workers on the new routing of the tunnel. The dead worker's bodies were recovered and joined their supervisor in recycling.

Around the new nest, planners and workers created the spaces needed to store and manufacture the food that would sustain it. Others assembled simple machines, which in turn created larger machines, creating the industry needed for the Vinithri civilization. As their laboratories became available, scientists were awakened on the colony ships and moved to the expanding nest.

The Elder Sisters made the journey down into the nest once the Grand Hall was declared ready. First Daughter had been insistent and detailed. The nest must be built. It must be ready. She asserted the monkeys would find the solution and rescue their race.

And if they didn't, the Vinithri would die in their own home.

Chapter 23

August 3062 A.D.

The Imperial shuttle circled the ancient temple complex of Angkor wat. The Emperor sighed. It had been too many years since he had visited the hallowed campus where he had learned so much. Indeed, his gratitude ran so deep that Angkor had taken the name of the temple for his own on his naming day.

Buru would celebrate his own naming day in a few weeks. While tradition said Angkor and his son wouldn't meet prior to the ceremony, he hoped they could find a few minutes to visit after his meeting today.

The shuttle flared and landed so gentle as to not even create a ripple in Angkor's tea. As it should. After all, the pilot was transporting the Emperor.

His escorts framed the ramp leading to the landing pad, wearing polished combat uniforms and severe weapons. Their moves were precise, mechanical, another reflection of the pride and professionalism demanded by General Zoltan. Angkor tried to remember when the two of them sat and chatted, as they had when they were students. It had been too many years, he decided.

Angkor missed the lively talks.

As the ramp of his shuttle lowered, Angkor saw his former master, Nom Ng, standing with the bonzes awaiting the Emperors arrival. "Master Nom!" he cried, foregoing formality to rush down the incline. Master and student embraced, Angkor's heart nearly bursting from his chest with the joy of seeing his proctor.

"I see you have earned a promotion," Angkor stated. Ng now wore the sash and headpiece of a master.

"As have you, young Pitth." Ng said.

"Master Tok?" queried the Emperor.

"Awaiting you at Fountain Glade," Ng said. "He is head of our order now. He thought meeting there would be most auspicious.

"We are most grateful for the honor you showed the Temple, Emperor," Ng continued. "Daily, we receive inquiries about class availability. Many, from both inside the Empire and from without, are eager to have their children learn at the institution that trained an Emperor."

They passed through the familiar portal, where Tok sat placidly on a mat, his eyes closed. Ng and Angkor joined their ancient master on the grass. It was all as he remembered, save for the mat. The gentle fall of the water in the fountain relaxed and cheered Angkor for a moment, though it wasn't as he remembered. It was changed, discordant.

"Yes, Student, you have been quite busy, haven't you?" Master Tok sounded disappointed.

"Master?"

"Look to the fountain, young Pitth," admonished the old man. "It has changed much since you left us, yes? I swear, some of your stones have been spun about like tops. Are you not listening when you meditate?"

"Master, I try…" began Angkor

"Try? Try!" the master was angry. "What did I teach you? Did I teach you to try? No. You were not taught try! You were taught better than this, young Pitth. You were taught to consider and act. This…" he pointed to the fountain, "shows strong indication of responding, not consideration and action. You were not trained to let others to decide for you, but even a simpleton such as yourself can see that is precisely what has happened. As a result, you are confused, out of harmony."

"What should I do, Master?" The conversation was not what he expected.

Tok heaved a sigh. "Tell me of this request you have. Ng has told me much; I want to hear it directly from you."

The Keep, now Angkor's, was ready. The vast facility beneath the temple was excavated and most of the furnishings for the vast laboratories were in place. Two separate wings had been quarried, one for the resurrection of the Vinithri Queen. The other waited for the eggs the new Queen would deliver to produce Angkor's heirs.

There was only the transfer of the project from Mars to the safety of his fortress to accomplish.

Progress on Mars Station was going well. Doctor Lungrun reported the sequencing for the new queen was nearly complete. The Vinithri queen jelly they sought was still eluding them. The etymologists were exploring every option. Doctor Lungrun was confident they would soon have the answer. Now that the Keep was ready, the entire team, including the Vinithri, were to transfer to Terra to integrate the code into a Vinithri egg and wait for the hatching of the new queen.

"The replacement of the queen will be the completion of just the first phase of my plan," Angkor explained. "Phase two will be the creation of the child who will succeed me. As Ng explained, I consider the bonzes of our order to be the most qualified for the new Khan's design and education."

"How long do you expect this project of yours to last?" asked Tok.

"Master, you can clearly see my plan. This will not be for just my grandson, it will be for all my descendants," explained Angkor. "I should like to leave the future of the Empire in your hands by teaching my heirs as you have taught me."

"And will you follow our decisions?" challenged Tok. "Will your children follow our decisions? What guarantee do you hold that your plan will bind the future of your heirs and the Empire to our ministrations?"

"Only my law, Master," Angkor replied. "The law of the Emperor will be sacrosanct and obeyed."

"Oh?" asked Tok, "Why do I meditate in your presence on this mat, foolish one, if your law is so powerful?"

"I…I don't know, Master," the confused Angkor answered.

"I was not born of this world," revealed Tok. "I am originally from Vespa. My order sent me here to study. I have grown to love this world and elected to stay and run this order. But by your father's law, I am not allowed to touch the earth here, as I am technically an alien."

"But you are Terran," protested Angkor.

"No," answered Tok, "I am Vespan, although I have lived most of my life here. How can you claim the force of your law for my order if your father's law holds this unintended consequence?"

"I can change the law."

"So can your descendants."

Angkor pondered for several minutes, studying the fountain. He spied a stone near the base of the fountain, nearly covered with moss. He dug the stone out, wiping the dirt off, but leaving the moss in place. He set it reverently in the upper font of the fountain. He listened to the fountain, adjusted the stone and nodded, satisfied.

"Master," he said, "This is the most ancient stone of the foundation of the fountain. It is clear the mason set this stone with care, from around it springs the younger stones. For centuries, this humble stone has been the base for the other stones, which in turn has been the base for the fountain. The mission of this unpretentious rock has been lost by all of us, so perfectly has it done its job.

This stone is my law. I have placed it to be the base of all my Empire, all of my society. Only should I topple it or place it on a lower tier would it not be so. My children will be programmed by your bonzes to worship my law and enforce the law for all time."

"Ah," the old man closed his eyes and asked, "So you accede the design of your children to me and my order for all time?"

234

"They will always have a choice in their partners," declared Angkor, thinking of Sophia.

"Of course. We shall design the new Khan each generation and decide which of the eight will succeed their predecessor."

"Agreed, Master."

Tok leapt to his feet. "Then may I leave this mat? I should like to feel the grass again."

The antediluvian stones had been placed more than two thousand years before to collect the ribbon of water meandering down the moss-covered hill. It spilled into the rectangular reflecting pond to the sill, then channeled quietly into the Siem Reap.

Afternoon sun filtered through the ageless grove of willows that surrounded the pond. Its light sunlight flickered and danced as the billions of slender leaves twisted in the almost imperceptible breeze. Angkor watched leaves loosen and twist away from their branches. His admiration for the designer of this place increased when he saw none of the leaves touched the surface of the still pond or the patio as they came to rest.

Benches hewn from weathered stone sat at either narrow end of the pond. When seated, you would study the reflection of the person seated across from you. Pitth had spent hours here with his friends when he was a student in this place.

Two figures passed through the curtain of willows on the far side of the pond. Angkor recognized Buru, his seventeen-year-old son. His heart swelled; the last time he had seen his son was five years ago when Sophia insisted on "dropping in" to see the boy while they were returning from Indianola. He had been a gangly boy then, shorter than his mother. Now he was nearly as tall as his father, but slender like his mother. His face was long, narrow like Sophia, his hair wiry black like his father. The boy's stride was confident and fluid as a cat moving through tall grass.

Buru was leading a girl who appeared to be his age. She wasn't pretty, shorter and heavier than Angkor preferred and with milky white skin and rich red hair. They seated themselves on the bench opposite the older man. Angkor narrowed his eyes at the closeness of their bodies. Buru took her other hand in his. The couple shared a quick glance, then he looked to his father's reflection in the pool.

"I greet you, my father."

"I am up here, Buru. Look at me," Angkor instructed.

The boy raised his gaze to meet his father's. "I greet you, Father. Thank you for meeting with me." Buru's voice was polite.

"I greet you, my son," his father replied, evenly. "I am pleased to see you."

"And I you. Mother is well?"

"She is. You could call her on your comm more," Angkor admonished. "She is much happier when she speaks with you."

Buru nodded his head.

"This is my…friend, Annabelle Klerrk, Father."

"I greet you, Emperor Angkor." Her voice was accented, scratchy.

"Annabelle Klerrk," Angkor returned the greeting. " South Africa, yes?"

"My ancestors are *Afrikaner,* yes," she answered. "We emigrated two centuries ago to Luftstra, an independent farm planet." Her green eyes blazed as she uttered the word *independent.*

"I know of your world," Angkor responded. "It lies outside my protection."

The girl bristled.

"Your naming day is in three weeks." Angkor now ignored the girl. "Has your mother or grandmother contacted you about your robe?"

"Grandmother has. She tells me you put it off until the last minute," a small smile formed on the boy's face. "She says you hated the rainbow robe."

"I still do. But it is tradition now, so I have no choice in the matter," his father said ruefully. "I would suggest you meet with her quickly so you have more time to select a, ah, dignified robe."

"Tradition, yes," Buru's gaze returned to the water. "Father, I will not be attending the Naadam festival or the naming ceremony."

"Oh? And where will you be, my son?"

"On Luftstra. With Annabelle. My wife."

"So," Angkor maintained his exterior calm demeanor. Inwardly, he seethed. "When did this marriage occur?"

"We are not married yet, Father," Buru said. "We will move there first, then get married. Annabelle and I have it all worked out."

"And your schooling? There is an accredited university on this Luftstra, I assume?" Angkor was struggling to maintain his control.

"I will not be attending university father," Buru stated. "Annabelle's family owns the largest farm on Luftstra. I will work for them, learning the farm on Luftstra Prime. When I demonstrate the ability to run the farm, Annabelle and I will take over the farm on Luftstra Four."

"And this prepares you for assuming my title one day - how?" Angkor could hardly contain himself.

"He does not want your title!" the girl interrupted.

Buru patted the girl's hand. Returning to Angkor, he said, "I do not wish to be Emperor, father. I have learned much about myself here in temple over the years. You are becoming a legend. I do not wish to be legend, nor do I want to follow a legend. I have found a way to carve out my own life, free of the obligations of your legend. Annabelle and I love each other. We want to make a life together, have children and live out our lives together in peace."

"This is foolishness!" Angkor was beyond control, "You will forget this foolish plan this instant! Buru, you will join me and return to the Keep today. Young lady, I am pleased to meet you. But I will not condone this ridiculous plan. After Buru becomes a man and earns his degree, we can revisit this marriage. But until then, I would suggest you return to your studies here, then go back to your family with my blessing and rethink this plan." He spat out the last words.

238

"Are you demanding as my father?" asked Buru. "Or ordering me as my emperor?"

Angkor's mouth gaped, stunned by his son's insolence. He gathered himself and croaked, "What of your people? What of the Khalkha? All these years, all this study. You have responsibilities, my son. Are you just going to walk away from your duty for this girl?"

"What of my free will?" Buru asked. "You have told me that free will is a fundamental right. Does that extend to everyone save your own son?"

"What of your mother?" Angkor asked, "What are you going to say to her? For that matter, when are you going to tell her?"

Buru hesitated for a minute, then answered, "Mother will understand. She left her parents, after all, when she came of age."

"Her circumstance was different," snapped Angkor. "And she was of age. She was a tea merchant when I met her, not the son of the headman and heir to the Empire."

The wind increased, whistling through the fronds of the willows. The limbs writhed and fluttered in the gust. Thousands of leaves whisked about, circling the patio and pond.

"Be sure of what you are doing, Buru," warned Angkor. "If you do this, if you walk away from your family, your people, there will be no return."

Angkor felt his heart break as Buru wrapped his arm around the girl. "I have made my decision, Father."

A gust of wind struck the line of willows. They bent, groaning from the maelstrom that had struck, stripping millions of leaves from their branches. The magic which kept the leaves from the terrace couldn't hold back the wind; the green cloud of foliage surrounded the couple and Angkor, obscuring them from each other. The wind died, blowing the leaves away, save two. Their stems were joined, gracefully they twisted and danced as they fell, settling on the surface of the reflecting pond.

Angkor stared at the leaves resting on the placid waters. The kami of this place had spoken. So be it. "Then you are dead to us," he told Buru. "Your name will be removed from the lists of the people of the Khalkha. You are banished from our lands. Our ancestors turn their backs on you and your children. Your very name will be a knife in the hearts of your mother and me."

Angkor Khan, Headman of the Khalkha, Emperor of the Terran Empire and father to only one son, turned his back and strode away.

Chapter 24

October 3062

Mars Station

The laboratory door slid open with a hiss and a clatter. Elian reminded herself for the thousandth time to ask maintenance to look at the noisy door.

The thump of the door's opening was accompanied by the scrabbling clatter of pointed feet entering the lab. "Good morning, Doctor Elian Lumburg!" In the eight years they had been working on Mars Station, Elian had been unable to convince Third Scientist Daughter to use her given name.

She readily agreed to allow her Terran peers to refer to her as Three. Her antennae would curl and shake, the Vinithri equivalent of laughter. But she and the rest of the Vinithri simply wouldn't use the Terrans' first names. "Oh, Doctor Elian Lumburg, I could never be so informal," she explained. "It would be so impolite, oh my, yes. As I am part of your nest now, I must maintain the correct level of civility. Even if you monkeys are so, so…" her whole body would shiver and she couldn't speak.

"Good morning, Three. Wonderful to see you," Elian replied. "I trust you slept well?"

"Oh, my, yes, very well, thank you," bubbled the irrepressible Vinithri.

The Vinithri were a constant source of amusement and wonder amongst the Terran researchers. The etymologists had studied hive and nest insects of Terra and her colonies. Those observed were tightly structured and organized and the Vinithri matched insects in these terms. Their portion of the labs were always the neatest and most organized. What was shocking was the amount of laughter and joy exhibited by the Vinithri scientists.

A cluster of Vinithri would spend hours studying their unusual devices, barely speaking, moving in unison on a particular problem or another. Suddenly, one would stop, start gyrating her body and emitting pheromones that the translators would identify as *singing*. The words were incomprehensible to Terran speakers; it sounded like melodious chattering to them. Several Vinithri would rub their vestigial wings and the *scritch-scratch-scratch* added to the alien melody.

Other times, the singing would start, then quickly change to a slow, sad melody. The Vinithri antennae would droop and they would all lower their heads until the nerve ganglion at their necks were exposed.

Elian asked Three about the singing. "Oh, Doctor Elian Lumburg," she tittered, "we live so close all the time. We love being together and the most unimaginable situation for a Vinithri to be in is alone. So, naturally, when we feel a rush of emotion, we start to sing. And when one of my sisters start to sing and dance, I want to sing and dance! And, sometimes, one of us will feel sad. So when she starts to sing about being sad, I want to sing about feeling sad. Don't Terrans do the same thing?"

"We like to celebrate together, yes," Elian said. "But usually when I am sad, I want to be alone."

"That's *terrible*," gasped Three. "When I am sad, I absolutely must be with my sisters. Is it not the same with you and your male, Doctor Rolf Lumburg?" It had been difficult for the Vinithri to comprehend the female Terrans living and working with their males. In Vinithri society, males existed only long enough to mature. After mating with the Queen, they were taken away to die.

Three clattered over to her work station and set to a task immediately. "We had a wonderful treat this morning," she chirped. "Doctor Beau Melesky received what he called a care package from his family in Vermont in Occident. He had something called maple syrup. Oh my, oh my, oh my, Doctor Elian Lumburg, I haven't the words to describe how astounding this Vermont in Occident maple syrup is. When we move into the Keep, will there be this maple syrup?"

Elian smiled at Three's excitement. "Certainly and much more goodness besides. Rolph and I are hoping we will be able to commute from our home in Seattle when we shift our operations there."

Three's antennae drooped slightly. "It will be good to go to Terra, I suppose," she said, "but it will not be our home. Second Scientist Daughter and I have discussed the new Queen's care after she is hatched. I will travel with her to Falleron and help her settle in. Once she is inseminated, I will return to Terra to work on your Emperor's plan for his heirs. I will return to Falleron only should First or Second Scientist Daughter die. Then I would ascend upward one spot and assume the next position."

"Then you would go home to Falleron."

Elian smelt the flat, ozone smell of Three's response. She had lived and worked around the Vinithri scientist to recognize despair.

"No, I would return to Falleron." Three's antennae hung loosely, touching the floor as she bent over in sorrow. "None of us can go home again."

Hours later, the cranky door opened with its screech and bang. Rolph Lumburg entered the lab whistling, carrying an opaque box under his arm. Three's antennae began to quiver. "Hello Three, hello Elian," Rolph sang. He kissed his wife and whistled again at the Vinithri.

Three quivered again. "Oh, Doctor Rolph Lumburg," she quivered. "You sing such naughty things!"

The Lumburg's laughed. "Actually, I came to see you bearing a gift, Three." He set the box on the table and opened a tiny door at the bottom. "You remember our friend *Apis Cerana Royala?*" The two-inch-long, Asian honey bee queen preened on his index finger.

"Of course." Three extended her foreleg; the large bee crawled along the proffered forelock. "Greeting, Majesty." Three's greeting was respectful, as she lay her antennae flat and exposed her neck ganglion.

Rolph opened another door in his gift box. "I'd like to introduce you to another friend, Three," and could not hide the pride in his voice. On his finger was an ant, brown and red, three inches long and fat. "This is *Dinoponera Paraponera Clavat Royala.* She is the largest ant to be found on Terra."

Three extended her other foreleg; the large ant crawled onto Three and waved her antenna. "Greetings, Majesty," the Vinithri scientist repeated. She looked to Rolph. "I assume this represents progress on our mission?"

"Third Scientist Daughter, this represents the solution to our mission!" Rolph could hardly hold back his excitement. "We know the honey bee queen produces a close facsimile of the queen jelly we need to feed your queen pupa. Unfortunately, she produces so little, we would need five hundred thousand queens to produce the jelly over the course of one year. *Dinoponera,* on the other hand, produces copious amounts of the jelly, enough that five hundred queens can produce in a month what five hundred *Apis Cerana* produces in one year. Further, the *Dinoponera* is hardier; we can produce five hundred thousand in less than half the time than the *Apis Cerana.*"

"Wait, wait!" Elian interjected. "Dinoponera don't produce the queen jelly compatible for our needs."

Rolph grabbed his wife and spun her around, "This one does, my love," he said. "She has to be fed *Dinoponera* queen jelly while pupate. But we have spliced the necessary gene sequence into *Dinoponera* so, when fed correctly, will produce the Apis Cerana-Vinithri hybrid jelly we need to produce for the queen pupa!"

The Vinithri scientist's four legs collapsed beneath her. "Is this true?" she gasped. "Have you done this? Are you telling me you have saved my race from extinction?"

Rolph extended his hands and cautiously took the two queens. "Yes, lady, we have found the solution to save your race. Already we have half the Dinoponera queens we need. Within the month, we will have all the queens available to produce the jelly needed to maintain your queen."

Three struggled to her feet. "Then the Vinithri must get busier still," she said. "We need to inseminate the chosen egg now so the pupa can hatch in three months. Then we will be ready to move to the Emperor Angkor's Keep to grow our queen."

A fierce wind whistled and howled around the mountains of Angkor's Keep. It was fitting; Angkor had rarely felt out of control in his life.

Sophia's cries still tore at him. She had fallen to her knees when Angkor told her of the banishment of their son, tearing at her clothes and grabbing Angkor's feet. "No, my husband, no," she wailed. "Not our son! Please tell me you have not done this to our son!"

He had wanted to kick her away while he wanted also to throw himself to the floor as she had done, to wail alongside her.

The anger and frustration had all come to a head and he had no way to release the pain. Instead, he had stalked away, leaving her to her despair.

Now, Angkor sat with his legs dangling over the rail-less balcony of their chambers, overlooking the Gobi. He had wanted none of this. His plans had him and Sophia a hundred million miles away, safe and snug on Ganymede Station. Perhaps Buru would have fulfilled his duty to the tribe and they could have been a family. Suishin's fall had been a mercy for him, never having to be exposed to the hell his life had become. Perhaps he should join his brother in death's sweet embrace.

But he had a mission. Tok and Ng were quite specific. He was to write the law for his Empire. He was to set the Terran Empire on its course for the next ten thousand years. Or some such drivel.

Most of all, he could not do that to Sophia. He had caused her enough pain and misery. For him to kill himself in such a cowardly fashion…No, he would not do that to her.

He heard her delicate footfall approach. The gentle rustle of cloth as she knelt behind him. Her slender fingers began to knead his back and shoulders. "You are so tense, my husband," she spoke in her tender voice. "Here, let me help you." Strong fingers followed the knotted muscles in his shoulders, massaging and pressing the tense ropes down his spine. She always knew just how much pressure to apply, just where she needed to press and rub next.

His tears coursed lined cheeks. Here, in this place with his blessed wife, here he could cry at last. Out of the prying eyes of the public, behind the stone walls shading him from his spying generals. Here, he and Sophia could share their grief.

"He told me you would understand," Angkor said, his voice hoarse. "I pray you do, because what he has done is far beyond my understanding."

She wrapped her arms around his broad shoulders and kissed his neck. "I do understand. As I understand your decision. I don't agree with either of you. But as Buru's mother, I know what it means to follow your heart. And as your wife, I know that you are bound to your honor and the honor of our people.

"There is little I can do for Buru. Now he will have to find his own way, just as I had to when I left Calcutta. It will be difficult for his wife and him. But if they love each other enough, work hard enough and the gods look with favor on them, then we have no need to fear for them.

"I will watch over them, Husband. I am his mother and it is my job to do so."

She gave him a gentle tug; he turned and lay on her lap. Stroking his hair, she said, "You are a great and mighty Emperor. You are the Khan of our people. For them, for all of your Empire, you must be strong and firm. Our people, indeed all of Terra and the Empire must see that you, of all people, honor and follow the law and traditions. For you, my husband, I shall do all the wailing and crying, suffering the indignities life will heap upon you.

"But in here, in our privacy, you can unleash your pain with me."

"What did I ever do to deserve you?" Angkor asked. "I did not plan any of this when I took you away from that vile merchant in Delhi. When I sought your father's blessing, I only thought it would ever be just you and me. I did not want this," he waved his arm around. "I did not want to become Emperor. I did not want to write the law. I still don't want these things. These things that drove our son away. And yet, still, here you sit, holding my aching heart and showering me with love. What did I ever do for all this?"

"You bought tea from a poor tea girl," Sophia brushed an errant hair from his forehead. "And as bad as it was, you drank it, anyway. You treated a poor girl well and won her heart. How could I not do this little thing, after all you have done for me?"

She patted his shoulder. "Now, enough of wallowing in your pity," she ordered. "It is late and I am tired. Come, it is time for bed.

Chapter 25

March 3065 A.D.

"Your majesty, may I present Doctors Elian and Rolph Lumburg, Terran leaders of the Angkor/Vinithri Project?" The Emperor acknowledged the couple's bow and extended his hand.

"I am pleased to meet you both, Doctors." Angkor's voice was firm as his handshake. "And, please, since I am back in a lab today, would you please call me Doctor Angkor? It has been too long since I've heard my preferred professional name."

Elian blushed as Rolph laughed. "Of course, Doctor Angkor," he gushed. "I took the liberty of reviewing many of your papers from your time on Ganymede. Fascinating stuff! Tell me, when you were examining the protein strings of the aminos extracted from Jupiter..." He winced as Elian's sharp elbow jabbed his ribs. "OW! Right, sorry, Doctor Angkor," apologized Rolph. "My wife reminds me we have a tour for you. If you would, Sir?" He extended an arm.

"I should like to introduce our lead Vinithri colleague, Third Scientist Daughter," Elian stated. The Vinithri stood straight on her lower four legs, bowing her head exposing her nerve ganglion.

"Greetings, Majesty," came her delicate pheromones. "I am honored to meet our sponsor, finally."

Angkor bowed as well. "The honor is mine," he replied. "As I am responsible for the near extinction of your people, I am humbled and honored to meet the savior of our new friends, the Vinithri."

Three straightened her neck. "First Daughter said Mother would not approve of grief for her loss, nor would she allow any thoughts of anger or revenge amongst the upper castes. What has happened has happened. We are now friends and allies. So rules the First Daughter, who is the voice of the Mother."

Angkor bowed his head. "The First Daughter is indeed wise. Please, show me this facility. I am eager to see your accomplishments!"

The party meandered through the laboratories beneath the Keep. The Vinithri workers had done their work well. The walls, floors and ceilings were the polished granite stone deep in the roots of the Khangai Mountains. Here and there, veins of minerals from the rich red oxides of iron to the vibrant blue-green of copper.

Channels had been cut in the walls and floor for power, water and any one of a hundred conduits needed to run a facility deep in the mountain. Small labels were affixed with Terran writing and Vinithri scent pads identifying each conduit and pipe. While designed to be a research facility and a school for the eventual heirs of the Empire, it reflected an artistic appearance, beautiful and functional without being austere.

"Be careful about letting my wife down here, Doctors," joked Angkor. "The empress has an aesthetic for decorating. She'll have these lovely walls painted and shrines everywhere if she finds her way down here."

"Here is the nursery, high…Doctor Angkor." Elian opened the chamber door with her passkey. "The cradles will support the Vinithri eggs that will have the heirs' zygotes injected after the design for each is approved."

Twenty-four clear tanks were supported by more of the smooth, granite stone. They were clustered in groups of three around a central column that reached from floor to ceiling. Various tubes ran between the tanks and the column, still others between the tanks in each cluster.

Each cluster demonstrated a cloudy fluid of its own color: red, yellow, blue, orange, green, violet, white and black. "Each cluster represents the file as designed by the committee s assigned to the particular file," explained Three. "The embryonic fluid itself is naturally clear. Sister Doctor Teresa Anne Wallace-Smythe of the Sisters of the Holy Names Order and who runs this part of the facility, added the color to make identification easier and to add to the visual appeal of the project."

"Does she always use a person's full name and title?" whispered Angkor.

Rolph nodded, "Nearly ten years we've been working together. She and the Vinithri all do it. It's a cultural habit."

"As the embryos mature, we will monitor them closely. Any deviations shown in a cluster will be examined and discussed. Corrective measure will be taken. Should an embryo show extensive deviation and does not respond to adjustment, we will of course, discontinue the damaged nucleus," explained Three. "By the time the heirs reach the point of gestation, we shall have eight healthy, superior Terran infants ready to be born, so to speak."

"What will happen should more than one embryo from a cluster mature to the point of being born?" Angkor asked.

"That cannot be allowed to happen, Emperor Doctor Angkor Khan," Three replied. "Only one child from each cluster can be allowed to be born."

"So one child would be killed?" Angkor pressed.

"No," relied Elian. "We have had much discussion on the point, Doctor Angkor. We will be constantly monitoring each heir through the process. With each alteration, each adjustment, we and the individual file director will rate the cluster and decide when it is time for continuation or discontinuation. It sounds harsh and it is. But we cannot take the chance that an inferior leaves this facility."

"So to have eight healthy, perfect children, sixteen will be sacrificed."

"It is the formula we use with our queen," Three explained. "It is why we needed so much queen jelly. When our eight queens hatch, they engage in combat. Any unhatched queen is killed first; the others will destroy each other until only the finest, strongest survive. She will be inseminated and give birth to our next generation."

"It seems cruel, Doctor Angkor," Rolph explained, "but we on the File Board decided the Vinithri model would suit our Empire the best. While our children will not engage in mortal combat as the Vinithri do, the education and physical demands we place on them during their training will ensure they will be the finest specimens available in each generation."

"Are they inseminated yet?" Angkor asked.

Elian shook her head. "No, Doctor. As my husband said, we have studied your *bona fides*. It would be our honor, Sir, if you would review the files the committee has decided on before we proceed."

"Yes, yes, of course!" exclaimed Angkor. "It's been so long since I looked through an electronic sequencer! When can we start?"

"We have one more stop before we go to the sequencing lab," Three said. "The queen should like to meet you before she departs for Falleron."

"You mean queens, don't you," Angkor asked.

"No, Emperor Doctor Angkor Khan," Three bowed, exposing her neck ganglion. "She defeated the last of her rivals last night. The Vinithri have a Queen Mother once again."

The Queen's Chamber was nearly the deepest excavation in the mountain. Like its predecessor on the Vinithri Homeworld, it was wide with a lofted cathedral ceiling nearly to the top of the Keep. When the Queen reached Falleron, she would live out the rest of her days in a place like this, producing the billions of eggs for the next generation of the Vinithri civilization. As such, the chamber in the Keep replicated the low light of the one on Falleron, save the light wasn't quite as dim, allowing Terrans to move about and work in the chamber.

Three and the Lumburg's bowed before they entered the room. Angkor, the Emperor, did not. As a monarch he marched in, head high, staring neither left nor right as he proceeded through the pathway of the Vinithri warriors in the room, exposing their neck ganglion as he passed.

A cluster of royals huddled in the center of the room. One stepped forward and bared her neck. "Emperor Doctor Angkor Khan," and her manner was as if she spoke to a god.

"Second Daughter," answered the Emperor. "I am pleased to see you again."

"Alas, Emperor Doctor Angkor Khan, my elder sister who was First Daughter joyfully died when she heard the new Mother had completed the ritual combat this morning," the Vinithri said. "As such, I am now First Daughter and voice for the new Mother, until her eldest are ready to take over the nest."

"Oh, how sad, First Daughter. Please accept my deepest regrets for the passing of your sister," Angkor stated. "She was an extraordinary being, and I shall miss her."

The new Eldest Daughter startled. "Oh, no, Emperor Doctor Angkor Khan," she insisted, "the passing of my predecessor is not a sorrowful thing. It is a wonderful, joyous thing! Our Mother gave her the task of making our peace with you and ensuring the future of our people. She has succeeded and brilliantly! I was honored when she offered me her neck. It shall be my life's work to continue that which she started. When the time comes for me to offer my neck to the next First Daughter, I hope I meet it with the same dignity and fulfillment as her!

"But to business." She lowered her head again, exposing her neck. "Her Majesty, our new Mother, wishes to meet with you." An opening in the circle of the tall, yellow and green Vinithri appeared.

She was nearly as long as an adult, save her abdomen was a full eighty percent of her body. Her thorax and head were perhaps a three and a half feet long. She was a glittering gold with brilliant emerald green eyes. She didn't bow as her elders had, instead tipping her head to one side as she examined the tall Terran before her.

"You are the Terran Emperor, Angkor Khan, yes?"

He startled slightly. Somehow, he expected her voice to be high pitched, as a child. Rather, it had a timeworn, ancient tone, as though she had seen a dozen centuries and was weary.

"I am," he said. "And how do I address you?"

"I am the Mother," was her tired reply. "Or I will be, soon. My aunts tell me we will depart for Falleron this evening. They wanted to leave sooner, but I insisted on meeting you first. And here you are."

"Yes, Mother," Angkor said. "I am pleased you waited."

"Please come closer," she asked. "My eyes are already adjusting to the light I will have on our new nest. I'm afraid that means I am nearly blind now and will be completely so when I arrive on Falleron. I'd like to examine you closely so I will have a memory of you."

"Of course." Angkor leaned close to the young Queen. Her antennae extended and brushed across his face and head. She emitted a pleasant odor that came out of her translator as cooing.

"I assume you must be very handsome for a monkey," the Queen said with delight. "Although how sad your antennae are so flaccid and limp." She twisted his hair in one of her own flexible antennae.

Angkor laughed. "It is my hair," he explained. "Its only purpose is to keep my ears warm. And I'm sure my wife must find me handsome as you do. She also likes to play with my hair."

The Queen quivered with laughter. "You are a strange people," she said. "I don't understand your having a wife and a husband. But it seems to work for you, so I'll assume it is a good thing." She leaned close to Angkor. "Since we didn't make any drones, I will be inseminated by the seed we have available," she said conspiratorially. "I will be the first in my line not to have to do so. Perhaps the last. But do warn your wife, I find you handsome for a monkey. So if she treats you poorly, I will have my warriors snip her neck and I will claim you for my own!"

The two monarchs shared a chuckle. Then the Mother became serious. "Angkor, my Mother left me a message. She instructed me to do whatever it took to ensure the survival of our species. The First Daughter gave me a message for her predecessor that laid out your agreement between our people. Including the alteration, you made to our DNA ensuring we will remain loyal."

"It was necessary."

"Yes, I am sure. I can see the wisdom in this," the young Queen said, "and it has been done. I could no more raise my hand and strike you than I could fly to Falleron without a ship. What I need to let you know is we, you and I, must carry this secret to our graves. My First Aunt knows nothing of what was on the note, nor shall I ever let her know. I need your pledge that you will keep this secret."

"Of course," Angkor answered. "The agreement was made to ensure the survival of both our species. Now that it is done, I will carry this secret to my grave as you have asked."

The Queen visibly relaxed. "Good," she said. "I swear to you, that I will likewise carry this secret to my end. I have one more request of you, Angkor. It is a small thing. But it I will die happily one day to leave this mark upon your descendants, as an eternal mark of Terra's and the Vinithri bonding." She wiggled her arm to come closer.

Angkor placed his ear next to the translator and heard her whispered request. He smiled as he looked into her jeweled green eyes. "Of course, Queen Mother. I shall see to it personally. Such a wondrous contribution, simple, elegant and a sign for all time of our friendship. Thank you."

"Thank you, Emperor Doctor Angkor Khan," the Queen bared her neck ganglion, "for helping create me and for saving my people. I will go now to Falleron to my duties. I doubt we shall ever see each other again. Fare thee well, my friend Angkor Khan."

Angkor bowed low. "Farewell my friend, Queen-Mother of the Vinithri," he said. "If we don't meet again in this lifetime, perhaps the next."

Chapter 26

January 3066 A.D.

The laboratory beneath the mountain at the Keep was a godsend for the Emperor.

While the machinery of the bureaucracy that ran the Empire was still largely in Zurich, Angkor had found as many ways possible to oversee his Empire from the Keep in the Khangai Mountains.   It was home, familiar territory from his childhood. While he hadn't spent years living in the Keep as did his father and brother, the memories were still amiable.

He and Sophia would break for weekends occasionally to their home in Indianola. It was privacy they made there. The troops who were assigned to his protective detail prided themselves in not being seen by the royal pair. The residents of the small town treated them as Ang and Sophie, just another couple in their small community.

But the laboratory in the Keep was where Angkor spent his every spare moment. He eschewed his own lab or desk for a simple research station amongst the other scientists. His guards were left standing outside the door so *Doctor* Angkor could continue his research.

The only time he exercised any authority was at the request by the Vinithri Queen Mother. It was a small change. Few on the Council opposed it. But those who did were most adamant.

"Eye color is one of the random factors we are counting on," was the argument. "If we start making rules on eye color, like a bunch of proofing nitpickers on Harvest Day, what's next? Are we going to be designing these children to be perfect little robots? There must be some random chance!"

"I gave my word as Emperor," Angkor decreed. "This will be the only visible connection between my heirs and the Vinithri, who made this all possible. It must be so."

The File Committee would listen to the arguments before going to their chamber to reflect and meditate. The decision on the matter of eye color was onerous, so they waited overnight to announce their decision. The Emperor Doctor was correct. As not only Emperor, but the founding father of this line, it was within his right to demand so inconsequential a thing as eye color.

From that day forward until hundreds of thousands of years later when the File Committee was dissolved, the eyes of all the Khan's heirs would be vibrant emerald.

He entered his chambers, exhausted. His morning had involved matters of state, the largely boring minutia that made up the Sovereign's day. Judicial appointments, ministerial reports. A visit from the ambassador of Mer, complaining about the shore leave visit by the Imperial Destroyer *Muay Thai*. The leave had gotten out of

261

hand, dozens of bars damaged, some looting and the virtue of fine Mer maidens impinged. Angkor listened to the report and promised a full investigation. He sent a message to Admiral Schurenburg, asking for the results of the investigation and charges to be filed. Compensation for the physical damage would come from the fleet.

His relief was an entire afternoon at his work station. The sequencing was going well. Geneticists were careful, cautious scientists. Each line of detail would be examined for even the slightest flaw. One strand out of place could render the entire plan imperfect, creating an imperfect heir. The loss of his son Buru, Angkor had decided, was possibly due to an imperfection he had missed.

Their quarters were dark when he finally quit for the evening. Sophia was in Occident, touring schools. Angkor missed her when she wasn't home. Since he had banished Buru, she selected children as her vocation and cause. The newsfeeds showed her nearly every night, touring a school here or an orphanage there.

During his annual tour in the spring, she had convinced him to accompany her to visit the children of his Empire. Angkor joined them in singing songs; he knew a great many tunes from his time in the nomad camps as a child and was delighted when the youngsters taught him their songs.

Planetary officials became concerned. In the past, they could count on Emperor Angkor Khan to examine the economic engines of their worlds and comment gravely on the need for keeping order throughout the Empire. Instead, he and the Empress watched skits, accept flowers and gifts and examined children's schoolwork with the same gravity that the Khan had previously given his Empire.

In dark corners of that Empire, plots began to form.

Angkor took little or no note of the reports of these plotters. His security was assured, he told himself. While there would need to be a reckoning one day with his three oldest friends, in the meantime each was proving to be a strong, loyal member of his Empire.

The lights in his chamber didn't come on when he entered, he noted with some irritation. No matter, the switch was a few feet inside the door. Still, the lights should be on now. He would have a firm meeting with the head of maintenance.

The switch didn't work.

"Please, great Khan, allow me," came a disembodied voice. The lights came up at a low level. There was a hooded figure standing in the opening of his balcony.

"Ryder Finn!" gasped Angkor.

"No," the figure pulled back his cowl. He was Mithranderer, pale blue skin and steel hair. His face was smooth, unlined by the passage of time. His violet eyes, though, spoke of aged wisdom and timeworn concern. "I am Cassius Finn, son of Ryder Finn, servant to Mithranderer. She has sent me here with an urgent question and an imperative mission.

"Mithranderer asks the Terran Emperor Angkor Khan, why have you not written the law?"

"May I?" Angkor indicated the couch. Cassius nodded. "I have been quite busy with an important project," stated the Emperor as he sat heavily on the settee. "One that I need to personally oversee. Mistakes were clearly made with my son. I will not allow it to happen again."

"Mithranderer says, what you need to ensure is the safety of your Empire," Cassius replied. "She says the mistakes you are making now are having a far greater effect on the future of the Empire than a single line of misplaced code."

"I have to be certain!" thundered Angkor. "I cannot, will not allow the imperfection I allowed with Buru!"

Cassius was calm in the face of Angkor's fury. "And in the meantime, the very Empire you seek to have this perfect child rule is staggering and stumbling about. You are building a mansion on a foundation of sand. The builders are shirking their sworn duties, slapping the building up just enough to please their overseer while stealing the finer things for only themselves.

"Mithranderer asks, have you forgotten the murder of your father? Have the perpetrators of this great crime been punished?"

"No," Angkor buried his face in his hands. "No," he repeated, shuddering. "I have failed my father, though I know who the criminals are."

"Why?"

"I need them," Angkor responded. "Xaid is an astute businessman. His investments for my Empire have increased its value immeasurably. Salaam maintains my intelligence mechanism quite efficiently. And Dawlish, my god, Dawlish. What would I do, how would my Empire stand without Dawlish?"

"So your Empire is really a triumvirate, with you as a figurehead?" accused the blue skinned man. "Mithranderer says that was not the agreement, Angkor Khan. Are you the leader of your Empire, or have you acceded your throne to lesser men?"

"It is my Empire," Angkor snapped through gritted teeth. "Does Mithranderer send you to tell me different? Perhaps she has someone else in mind who can do this cursed task? If so, let him stand here, now, and I will gladly turn over this damnable job and retire to Indianola with my wife!"

"No. Mithranderer says you are the one chosen because you are the nexus for this part of time/space. She only desires you to do what is needed to set this Empire for its future," Cassius stated. "Speaking for myself, Lord, I am offering myself and my services to you. My father, Ryder Finn, served your father honorably for many years, He sits now in perpetual communion with Mithranderer in his twilight years. He and I agree that I am the correct deputy for Mithranderer to sit at your right hand to help guide you."

"What of my heirs?"

"The Vinithri you call Three, along with the Doctors Lumburg, has the situation well in hand," Cassius said. "Master Tok has prepared Master Ng well for his role as head of your file committee. You must learn when to delegate important matters to qualified people," his voice went to a whisper, "and when to take matters into your own hands when dealing with your enemies."

"There is always a price to be paid," argued Angkor. "If I agree with your plan, what is the cost to be?"

"The price you pay will be accepting me as your friend," explained Cassius. "I will gladly pay my measure in full to you. The price Mithranderer asks is that you give the whole of your being to your Empire. It is all she asks." He extended his blue hand.

"Ryder Finn was my father's closest ally and friend," Angkor brooded. "And in the end, I suppose, he sacrificed this friendship to ensure the future of my father's dream." He pondered for long minutes.

"It is done," Angkor declared, slapping his knees and standing. "Cassius, I will accept your friendship and advice. Should you do half so well as your father, then it will be an investment cheap at half the price. All I stand to lose is a job I don't want. And my gain is a trusted friend and valuable ally."

The men clasped forearms. "The Buddha said, the value of friendship is greater than its equal measure of gold." Angkor said. "I daresay, I need that friendship today even more than I need the very air I breathe."

"Then, my Lord, shall we get to work?" Cassius produced a stylus and a pad. "We have your laws to write."

Chapter 27

March 3070 A.D.

Spring had come to Cascadia.

There was still a bit of winter's chill outside the cabin at Indianola. The cabin's heater could have easily blocked the chill, but the couple enjoyed the sharp, cool temperatures of the early morning. A window near their bed was a welcome portal to the odor of early spring; moisture hanging heavily on the weighted boughs of the ancient cedar forest, the ferns and Oregon grape awakening from their winter slumber, the piquant of the Puget Sound seasoning the fertile bouquet.

Sophia murmured and rubbed her naked breasts against Angkor's chest. Their lovemaking last night had been epic. *Then again,* "Angkor pondered, *it always is better in this place.* His hand rubbed up and down the warm, soft skin of her back as he glanced about the room. The mirror might take a bit of explaining, the spider web of on its surface. Indeed, he wasn't entirely sure how they had managed that. And she'd be disappointed with the broken kitchen table. They had spent weeks searching for just that table years ago. Repairing it would take some explaining, he was sure. Maybe they should just replace it.

Fewer questions that way.

He kissed the crown of her head. Her flaxen hair, so brilliant and golden in their youth, had begun to dull. She fussed about it as a matter of course, but refused any treatment to restore it to its youthful luster. "I am fifty-seven years old!" she would proudly declare. "I am not ashamed of that; so why should I be ashamed that my hair is no longer that of a silly young girl?"

He sank his nose and inhaled her scent. Jasmine and flowers as he remembered from the first night they had spent together nearly thirty years ago in the tiny room in Calcutta. She wouldn't let him touch her then, that night, as they hadn't married yet. That wouldn't be proper, she had declared, until they were married the next morning.

As soon as the ceremony had been completed, though, she had nearly dragged him back to their room.

Angkor sighed happily. The news reports always depicted the Empress as a soft spoken, demure lady of unfailing manners and politeness. Would they ever believe she was the same woman in the throes of passion? "Mmmm," she moaned. "Good morning, Husband." Her eyes were slits as she awoke and smiled. He leaned down to kiss her.

"GAGH!" she cried, her eyes open wide, turning her head away and gagging. "Angkor, you silly, romantic fool! Your breath smells like a goat and I'm sure mine is twice as bad! Let me brush my teeth first!" Nearly to the bathroom in an instant, she called over her shoulder: "And I have to pee."

He admired her firm, round bum as she disappeared into the white-tiled cubicle. *She certainly has fine hips...* he recalled. He threw the covers aside and followed her to the bathroom. *We haven't showered together in quite some time...*

The airship rose high into the tangerine twilight. Below, the passing daylight slid across the landscape, leaving behind a jewel-encrusted carpet of black. While its engines pressed the ship forward, the terminator line easily outraced the ponderous vessel.

Xaid Singh reclined on a chaise raised from the chambers floor. Its biofeedback sensors formed the cushions to support his form, kneading and vibrating his body. A flute of sparkling was in one heavily ringed hand, while the other tapped away on the keypad issuing from the malleable white ceiling. Lines of data scrolled through the perfumed air.

Commerce continued twenty-four hours a day. Xaid's ship journeyed with a purpose at its altitude while the trigibytes of data were intercepted and analyzed seconds ahead of Xaid's competitors. Seconds were all it took in many deals across the Empire. While intercepting the signals this way was technically illegal, none would complain, fearing their own questionable tactics would be exposed.

"Master?" The voice had shocked many. It was a high, melodious tone, unmistakably that of a young boy. While many had raised an eyebrow, Xaid was too wealthy to concern himself with the opinions of lesser beings. He had a wife, of course, necessary to maintain the correct social standing. She had even dutifully produced him four children he rarely wanted to see. She had her palace in the south of France, the children their tutors and nannies. So long as they caused him no embarrassment and stayed quietly in the background until he needed them, he was content.

"Master?" the voice had called.

"Yes, Joaquim, what is it?" Xaid responded, lost in the flow of the numbers.

"The broadcast you directed me to watch for has started, Master," the ship answered.

"Very well, reduce data to one third, center the broadcast and expand to full size."

The columns of numbers reduced and positioned themselves to Xaid's left. The hologram assembled itself from the ether, forming a handsome couple walking comfortably across the tarmac of Ulaan Baatar, returning from a two-week vacation at their home in Occident, the announcer stated. It was early spring, so he wore a fashionable grey suit and a heavy charcoal overcoat. A traditional Mongol fur cap covered his head.

She was wearing a similar coat and cap. Xaid would have wagered that she wore a sari and blouse. They held gloved hands, smiling and waving brightly at the crowds who had gathered to see the Royal Couple. They smiled and waved until the long black ground car swallowed them up for the thirty-mile voyage to the Keep.

"Volume, up by half," directed Xaid.

"So there goes the Emperor and Empress to meet the heir children on the occasion of their fifth birthday," the announcer's voice couldn't have sounded happier. "The palace has been quite clear; the ceremony is in keeping with the Emperor's Khalkha tribe's tradition. The mother, or in this case, Empress Sophia and the Keep's colony of monks and proctors, have raised the children. The heirs will then enter an intense schedule of education and training as a competition to decide who will succeed the Khan.

These grandchildren of the Emperor Angkor and Empress Sophia…" the voice droned on, though Xaid wasn't listening. A flick of his hand and the holo disappeared, replaced by the columns of numbers. He tried to focus, but the scene he had just witnessed had him seething.

Angkor's destruction of the Shurkorov Corporation had cost Xaid billions. The losses had been recouped over the years, thanks to the production contract Angkor had awarded him. This technology for producing heirs clearly fell into the terms of the contract. All new technology was to be passed into his hands for development for the next five hundred years. Since Dawlish had exposed the Augmenton program on Luna fifteen years ago, Xaid had struggled to regain the upper hand in the competitive and illegal superior human project.

The Augmenton project had moved far out into the rim, far enough away from the Empire to be safe for hundreds of years. There was still the issue with the brains of his investments. The human brain could maintain its sanity for about six months before it began to disintegrate, resulting in the necessity to terminate the expensive test subject. The project, while holding a great deal of promise and profit, was currently costing Xaid hundreds of millions every year.

Xaid was convinced the technology used by his college companion was the solution. If only he could find a steady supply of the Vinithri eggs and DNA sequencing to amend the brains in the subjects, it would result in a success for his investment. Perhaps they could even grow their own subjects.

It would also present Dawlish with the superman army he intended to march across the stars.

Angkor must be made to understand. He had dallied for years now, writing his silly laws that were clearly not meant for Xaid and his contemporaries. He had made an agreement with Xaid and he would fulfill that agreement. Or he would be made to suffer.

"Joaquim!" he commanded, "I wish to speak with General Zoltan, immediately! I do not care what he is doing, tell him I will speak with him."

"Good morning, children!" Ng's voiced reflected the joy he held in his heart for the precious blossoms in his care. That Tok had made him Chief Bonze in this temple was a great honor. That the task of his order was the creation and education of the future Khan for the Empire humbled him.

He could not imagine a greater joy in anyone's life than to live each day with the heirs. They had been "born" self-aware. Within a week, they were vocalizing. Days later, they were speaking in complete sentences. At two months, they were walking, albeit clumsy.

At five, they now had strong, developed personalities. Blue was a natural leader, while Red was a fiery debater. Yellow was introspective and sensitive. Purple was clever, Black quiet and observant. Green was curious while Orange was confident. And White. Dear sweet White, the dreamer. She would spend hours at a window, staring, daydreaming.

They assembled before him, dressed in traditional pants or skirts and jerkins. Their vests matched their names.

Sixteen emerald eyes focused on the proctor as they formed a perfect line. There was no fidgeting as one might expect from five-year old's. They had been created to be superior and superior beings were not nervous. As heirs to the Khan, they would show no fear.

The door opened with no ceremony; the royal couple entered, arm in arm. "Majesty," announced Master Ng, "may I introduce the heirs? Children, these are your grandparents, Angkor and Sophia Khan."

As one, the children kowtowed, their foreheads touching the floor, then rose. As one, they snapped their hands to their hips, their heads tipped imperiously at the couple. "We are honored," they said in a single voice.

Angkor stepped before each child, bent at the waist and studied it meticulously. Four boys, four girls. Each stood precisely three feet high, its hair as black as the void. From there, the file committees demonstrated their mastery of combining Angkor and Sophia's features.

Skin tones ran from cream white to butternut. Their jaws started with one boy echoing his grandfather's square chin to Sophia's refined taper on one granddaughter.

As Angkor bent and studied each child, Sophia knelt and wrapped loving arms, hugging and kissing each youngster. It was better than any test Ng could hope for. The children registered looks of bewilderment, fright, suspicion or happiness. Ng whispered the results into his pad. Later there would be time to analyze the reactions with each child's committee.

Angkor clasped his hands behind his back, as he recalled his father's pose in his mother's yurt so many years ago. "Your grandmother and I are so pleased to meet each of you and congratulate each of you on your fifth birthday. In our tribe, the Khalkha, you are now of the age to start school. However, your proctors tell me that each of you are well ahead of an average child. As a reward, Grandmother and I will dine with you this evening.

Further, in two months is the Naadam festival. On my fifth birthday, my father took me to the festival. To honor my father, each of you will serve as the Khan's honored guest." He bowed to the children.

"They are so darling, don't you think, Husband?" They were cuddled in their bed in the Keep, the evening chill forcing them to burrow deeper under the covers and nestle closer. A gentle spring shower freshened the chilly air outside the screened and barred window.

"Hmmmm," Angkor replied, "they are a fine addition to the tribe. The file committees have done a marvelous job producing candidates for my crown. I wonder which will prove to be superior?"

Sophia elbowed Angkor. "You are a terrible man, Husband," she chided. "We have eight beautiful grandchildren to watch grow up and all you can wonder is who will replace you?"

"It will come to pass, Wife," he told her. "And I, for one, will be glad when the time comes. My father wanted this and died for it. I do not wish to die as Khan. When my successor is ready, I will abdicate and we will retire to Indianola for the best of our years."

"Hmmm, that sounds so wonderful, Angkor," cooed Sophia. "I'm sure the rest of the children will love playing in our woods or exploring the beach."

Angkor startled. "That is not what I…" He felt Sophia quiver and shake, her face burying itself into the grey hair on his chest. "You are a very evil woman!" he declared as Sophia rolled on her back, choking as she laughed.

"As our friends in Indianola would say, Husband," she gasped, "gotcha!"

"No, my dear wife," growled Angkor as he rolled atop her. "I got you."

Chapter 28

April 3070 A.D.

General Dawlish Zoltan picked an imaginary piece of lint from his
impeccable uniform. Decorum demanded a soldier's dress be
perfect when meeting with the Emperor, even when the Emperor
was one of the soldier's oldest companions.

Xaid had been most insistent about this meeting. Dawlish's
lip curled at the thought. *Using him, Marshall of the Imperial Armed
Forces, as a messenger boy!* He had protested that this was a task
far beneath him. However, Xaid had been infuriatingly calm and
insistent. Dawlish would take this meeting to Angkor, he would
present Xaid's demands and be certain the Emperor understood that,
Khan or not, he would be made to comply.

Dawlish resisted the urge to kill Xaid on the spot. Alas, the
crafty Sikh had enough of a dossier on the General to ensure his
cooperation.

The Emperor had assumed the suite of offices his late father
had used. A pair of guards in dress uniforms stiffened when the
general approached, saluting sharply as guardians of the Khan
demanded. The outer office was reminiscent of Angkor's old office;
cream walls over wainscoting. An efficient looking woman stood
from behind an oak desk. "General Dawlish," she lisped, "would
you step right this way? The Emperor is engaged at the moment.
Please, may I take your hat?" She directed him to a small room to

the side, also of cream walls and wainscoting. "I will inform the Emperor that you are waiting for your appointment." She closed the door firmly.

Waiting for my appointment? wondered the General. *What manner of hubris was Angkor pushing now? Enough, save that for later. There are more important matters at hand for now.*

An ancient ancestor clock marked the time with a slow *tick-tick-tick...* Dawlish fumed, the insult from the Emperor plain. He considered an insult of his own, gathering his cap and leaving without a word. But, no. Xaid had been firm. He was to remind Angkor who was in charge.

After nearly an hour, the receptionist appeared before him. "The Khan says he has a few minutes now, General," she announced. "If you would follow me, please?"
He marched through the antechamber, where none of the half dozen secretaries looked up. She opened the double doors to the inner office and announced, "Highness, General Zoltan."

Again, the clear insult. Angkor remained seated behind a large oak desk, scribbling on a pad. At the Khan's side, a blue alien spoke in low, hurried tones, pointing at the pad. The general stood stiffly before the desk as the receptionist closed the door behind him.

Five more minutes passed before the Emperor, not looking up, asked, "Yes, General?"

"I would prefer the conversation were private, Sir," Dawlish requested, attempting to be civil.

"This conversation is private," Angkor stated.

"Not with the alien present, it isn't. Sir." Now Dawlish barely contained his contempt.

Angkor looked up, glaring at the General. "Cassius Finn is my most trusted advisor," he snarled. "Are you implying the trusted advisor of the Khan is untrustworthy?"

"The matters I wish to discuss are between you and me. Not outsiders." Dawlish stated.

"If I say he can be trusted, then you will trust him," Angkor said in a dismissive tone. "If you will not trust him, then you may assume it is of no interest to me."

"Do you forget yourself?" shot back the General.

"Do you forget yourself, General?" Angkor's words were clipped and abrupt.

Cassius straightened. "This may be an opportune time for me to take a break, my Khan," he said, "Fifteen minutes?"

Angkor nodded slightly, never breaking eye contact with Zoltan.   "Well, General?"

Dawlish waited for the door to close. "Our friends would like me to remind you who placed you on your throne," he stated.

"My father set me on this throne," Angkor replied. "You and our…friends, facilitated my ascension, but ultimately it was Tenzing who placed me here."

"So you say," was the cool reply. "But I remind you of a few facts. Suishin and Shurkorov would have killed you had we not intervened."

"So you say," Angkor mocked Dawlish. "I have come to believe that the threat you presented me may not have been as dire as you reported. Indeed, my father had the situation well in hand until you deceived me."

"And yet, there you sit. The recipient of the deeds of men," Dawlish said. "You were a willing participant in the events. You made certain agreements with certain people. Those people want their recompense now."

"Ah, so you are Xaid's lapdog now," Angkor smiled. "From my warlord to his messenger boy. Tell me, messenger boy, what is it your master wants?"

Dawlish's hands slammed down on the ancient desk top. "Do not forget you are speaking to a Turkman!" he roared.

Angkor's slug thrower had appeared in his hand from nowhere, aimed clearly between Dawlish's eyes. "Do not forget you are speaking to your Khan," he hissed.

Dawlish's eyes narrowed. "I will not forget this insult," he snarled. "Xaid reminds you of the contract you agreed to. This technology you have used to create your unholy brats belongs to him for development. You will provide the details and materials to him to develop this science. This will include the eggs supplied by the Vinithri."

Impossible," stated Angkor. "The agreement for the Vinithri eggs is between myself and the Vinithri Queen. And the technology is my own research, not subject to the agreement. You can tell Xaid he will need to find the answer for his Augmentons elsewhere."

"Augmentons are illegal, Emperor."

"You ought to remind your master of that fact, lapdog," snarled Angkor.

Dawlish gathered himself. "You will provide the materials I have asked for," he said. "You will have them ready by the end of the week."

"I will not turn that information over to Xaid," Angkor's reply was set in stone. "The Vinithri will not provide any eggs. Xaid will cease his Augmenton experiments immediately or suffer the consequences.

Dawlish strode to the door. "You will provide the information, Angkor," he ordered, "or it is you who will suffer consequences."

"General?"

"Yes, Emperor?"

"You have not been dismissed."

"May I be dismissed, Emperor?" Dawlish requested, contempt in every syllable.

"My Khan," Angkor corrected.

"May I be dismissed, my Khan?" Dawlish's tone became even more disrespectful.

"Be gone from my sight," the Khan ordered.

"My father spoke to me of this," Cassius said. "Of the terrible sin he and your father made you commit."

"It was necessary," Angkor replied. "Only I didn't know this for some time after the fact. My brother was controlled by the Shurkorovs, with drugs and sex. That I became a servant to Xaid and his cronies was not clear to me until after they murdered my father." He tapped the binder on his desk. "This will go a long way to make my amends for slaughtering Suishin."

"It is finished, then?" the young alien asked.

"Yes," Angkor nodded. "I have forwarded it to my Prime Minister for implementation immediately. Given the nature of General Zoltan's meeting with me, I fear I will need some of its provisions soon."

"Do you fear the Xaid cabal?"

He stared at the three stones closely. He himself had placed them, turning them as he thought he needed. But the water seemingly had a mind of its own. He could see now that Dawlish, for all the power he had given him, was subservient to Xaid. And the third was trickier still. Small, unobtrusive, it seemed to have little influence of its own. But he could clearly see now that his third position gave backbone to the other two. Eliminate that stone and Xaid's position would be clearly weakened.

Dawlish would become inconsequential.

No longer. This," he tapped the binder once again, "is the capstone. With it, the future of the Empire my father and I created is secure. Oh, they will strike at me, most certainly. They may even kill me. But this law will ensure the future of the Empire."

He hefted the book. "Imagine, a law so simple our children will learn it in school. So common sense, our citizens and subjects will revere it. And so solid, any man of power who would stand against it will find themselves confronted by our entire Empire. All the people, Terran or otherwise, living in security, fairness and peace."

"There are those who will fight it."

"And there are many more who will defend it. I am curious to see what will become of our law in a thousand years. Two thousand years. Hell, a million years." Angkor laughed.

"Our law, Khan?" asked Cassius. "You mean your law."

Angkor stared deeply into the eyes of his friend. "Our law," his voice was soft. "Oh, I will get the credit. My name will be praised and remembered. But I will know…Mithranderer will remember your influence, Cassius. The future of our Empire is in no small part due to your influence and guidance. For my people and my descendants, 'thank you' is too small of words."

Cassius gripped his friend's hand. "It is I who am grateful to be allowed to serve. Mithranderer says she will remember and she will remember the Great Khan, Angkor."

"…And here it is, the law for which my father lay the foundation. The law I have spoken to you for forty years. The law for every being in my Empire, from the farmer in his fields where he works to make a life for his family, to the teacher in the school, instructing her students on what it means to be a citizen. The code

that protects the less fortunate, the prisoner, the captive and the subjected people.

The law that binds me and my progeny to it, from how my successors are chosen, to how they shall rule. The law that keeps all our lawmakers in service to the governed.

It is implemented here and now. It exists for everyone this very moment. Your own laws of your worlds are unaffected, save where it conflicts with our law. Copies are being sent to every home, every school, and every library and in every language and medium for display.

To those who would oppose the law, I warn you. This is the law the people want. You violate it or stand against it at your own peril. As some people expressed, the law is severe, but just. Before you say a single word against it, I would suggest you read it and consider whether your opposition is worthy of the ire of the people..."

Emperor Angkor Khan, speech to the people on the implementation of the Law of Angkor Khan, 3070 A.D.

It could not be possible for a more beautiful day, young Cassius decided.

Spring was in full bloom in Zurich. The hills around the city were awash in green as the knolls and peaks shook off their white winter cloaks and exploded into ripening glory. The air, still crisp in the morning and scrubbed clean by the evening showers, tantalized the lungs of those who ventured out.

Even old Zurich shone in the new growth. Flowerboxes everywhere had been planted and the early blossoming flowers were eager to display their finery. The gray and gloom of the winter had been washed off the edifices and they fairly glowed, emoting rebirth for the old town.

Cassius broke fast with the Khan and his lady. Angkor was in fine spirits this morning and why not? His speech had been received well, and the whole of the Empire was singing its praise for the vibrant leader and his new, just law.

He had found them down at the gazebo next to Lake Lucerne, standing knee deep in the water. Angkor's pants were wet. Sophia had pulled her orange sari up out of the water. She took a stone offered by her husband and tossed it in the water, her years-old clumsy attempt to skim the stone.

"No, no, my love," giggled Angkor as he had hundreds of times in the past. "Move your arm flatter and flick your wrist." He demonstrated, bouncing a stone a dozen skips across the still water.

She tried another stone, managing to bounce it three times. She clapped her hands, nearly dropping the hem of her gown in the water, and jumped up and down with excitement. She and Angkor kissed and she demanded another stone.

Cassius cleared his throat. "Good morning my Khan, Lady Sophia."

"Oh, Cassius. Come, Sophia, we're having breakfast with Cassius this morning," They laughed and splashed water at each other as they strode ashore. Liveried servants appeared, drying the couple's feet and helping them don slippers. Others brought tea, coffee and juices, along with cloches of warm food and bowls of fruit.

The young Mithranderer had never seen the royal couple acting so. Both were clearly enjoying themselves, sharing their food and laughing muchly. Cassius wished the Empire could see their Empress this way. Her blue eyes sparkled, she poked and prodded the Khan, tickling him and being tickled in return, far from the staid, demur air she put on for the press.

"You are in fine spirits this morning, my Khan," stated Cassius.

"Indeed!" exclaimed Angkor. "So beautiful a morning in this dreary place. The most desirable woman at my side, the finest friend a man could ask for...Why shouldn't I be happy for a change?"

Sophia had taken a mouthful of tea. Opening her lips, she sprayed a stream from between her teeth onto the face of Angkor and giggled. "Why, you..." he growled, tackling her from her chair with a shriek and a laugh as he nibbled and kissed her face and neck in the sweet grass.

"My Khan, my lady..." stammered Cassius. "As much fun as you are having, we do have a schedule to keep today."

Angkor sighed and sat up. Sophia stuck her tongue out at Cassius and blew a raspberry. "Spoilsport!" she complained. "I have to go change for my trip, husband." She kissed his nose, then bit it and jumped back. Laughing, she gathered the hem of her sari and raced to their residence.

Angkor clapped his friend around the shoulders. "Cassius, my friend," he told the younger man, "We must simply find you a suitable wife. Of course, she won't be Sophia, but you can only hope…"

An hour later, the royal couple stood at the ramp of the near orbit shuttle that would carry her back to Ulaan Baatar to prepare their grandchildren for the Naadam festival. She had changed into a bright yellow sari and was warmly wrapped in Angkor's arms. Around them, the ground crew finished preparing the ship for its flight under the watching eyes of the Khan's bodyguards. They gave the couple a wide, respectful space.

"I know it's only days, my love, "he told her, "but each time we part, my heart longs for you."

"As does mine, Husband." She lay her head on his chest. "Yes, I can hear it. I hear your heart calling to mine."

"I look forward to the day when it is just you and me in our home," he sighed. "Just the two of us in our home by the water. Away from all of this." He kissed the top of her head.

Sophia lifted her mouth to his. When their lips parted, she said, "How lucky this poor tea girl is, to have found her other half in such a fine man."

A shuttle crewman stood nervously beside them. "Sir, Ma'am, it is time to go."

She gave a sad little sigh. "I must go, Husband."

"I will be in Ulaan Baatar next week, my love."

"Your mother and I will have our grandchildren waiting, Husband," she promised him.

He watched her walk up the gangway and enter the ship as she had hundreds of times for the last fifty years. The engines began to hum and vibrate, the air snapping around him.

"Angkor!" he heard her cry.

She was standing in the doorway, her yellow sari pressed against her body by the wind from the engines. She was saying something, but the noise was too great for him to hear. "I love you, Sophia!" he yelled, blowing her a kiss. Her eyes lit up and he saw her lips cry, "I love you, Angkor!" and she returned the kiss just as the door whooshed to a close.

Cassius waited at the side of the gleaming black ground car. Together, they watched the ship lift from the tarmac, turn and soar into the brilliant blue sky.

"Ah, Cassius, my young friend," Angkor slapped the Mithranderer's back jovially. "It is much too fine a day to race back to the office and go to work. What say we ditch the office and grab a powerboat. I have just received a case of fine Mongolian butter beer begging to be…" His face glowed from a distant flash. Angkor's face went slack, his eyes wide.

"Sophia…NO!"

The expanding dirty grey- black cloud was tinged with the red and orange of the expanding fireball. Debris of the ship spun and tumbled away from the cloud, each trailing smoke as it sought its way back to earth.

287

The low rumble of the shuttle's explosion hit them seconds later.

Chapter 29

June 3070 A.D.

The journey of the Ganga starts in the Himalayas to the north. The winter snows on Sagarmatha and her sisters form glaciers which melt slowly through the summer months. Each trickle meanders it ways downhill, merging with other droplets to form a tiny rivulet. The rivulets gather together as a creek. The creeks become streams. The streams form ever-growing rivers.

And the rivers gather to form the sacred Ganga. It cuts through the heart of the ancient civilization and returns to the sea.

To the Hindi, it is the pathway to *Moksha,* the liberation from the cycle of life and death. For more than five millennia, the people of the River Goddess have bathed in her cleansing waters. In death, their ashes join with the cycle of the Goddess, to the sea, high in the clouds and gently back to Sagarmatha and her heavenly sisters.

A month after the explosion, they found Sophia's remains. The wreckage of the shuttle had been strewn throughout the rugged Alps in a wide arc. They told Angkor she was found along a glacial stream in a small glade of edelweiss.

They reverently gathered what remained of the Empress, placing her in a simple casket and transporting her to Delhi at the Khan's request. She was placed in stasis, for it would take time to gather her family.

Angkor dispatched a rail fold ship for Luftstra to gather Buru. The wall between them was as solid as granite, but the

Brahmana had been quite specific. In life, Sophia had been a devoted daughter of the *Bhadrakali,* third of the Hindi gods. In death, her *Shraaddha* ceremony, returning her to the tender mercies of the *Ganga,* must be performed with equal devotion for her journey through the afterlife. Buru had a sacred duty to perform on the banks of the river - the *Antyeshi,* the ritual cremation.

Cleansed and swaddled in the red cotton shroud, Terra's empress was borne on the shoulders of cousins and carried to the ceremonial crematorium yards from the river. Marigolds were placed around her and she noiselessly slid into the chamber. The thousands gathered prayed in silence as Buru stepped forward as tradition demanded. He had promised himself he would be stoic, not embarrass himself by falling to pieces at this moment. He wiped his face with a yellow silk kerchief, hoping no one could see how close he was to tears. The attendant opened the panel, revealing the red button.

Buru gathered himself and with a shaking hand, pressed it.

In ancient times, the cremation would go on for hours as the fires did their work to free the soul from its body. This machine worked swiftly and silently. Minutes after Buru pressed the button, the attendant entered the room holding an urn decorated with yellow flowers. Buru startled visibly as the urn, still warm, was pressed into his hands. He was swift in presenting his mother's ashes to Angkor.

At the river's edge waited the Brahmana, holding a small silver spoon. Angkor opened the top of the urn so the holy man could scoop a portion of the warm ash. He held it over the water and prayed, "Lady Ganga, we give to you now Sophia, daughter of Ham and Aie. Dutiful wife of Angkor. Mother of Buru. Grandmother and friend. She has been a pious daughter of your Lord Bhadrakali. We ask you take her in, cleanse her of all her sins and give her residence in your palace beyond." He upended the spoon just as a gust of wind came up. Sophia's ashes cascaded from the spoon, were caught upon the light breeze and scattered. As she settled near the water, the lightest of her remains swirled and danced above the surface of the Holy *Ganga* before gently settling on the surface and beginning her journey downstream to the sea.

The Brahmana spread his arms. His voice was clear and loud, joined by the thousands around him in the singing of the *Bhajans,* the song of the thousand names of Vishnu.

The servant held a silver tray bearing the note. *"Son, I should like to meet with you before you depart. Father."*

Buru was tempted to crumple the note and throw it to the floor. On most any other day, he might very well have done just such a thing. But they had gathered to honor Mother. As angry as he was with his father, he could not act dishonorably on this day.

The room was a small study near his father's office. Books lined the walls, a pair of creased leather chairs lounged on either side of a polished wooden table. On a delicate lace cloth sat Sophia's urn with a framed image of her next to it. Father, wearing a fine blue suit, stood staring out the lone window in the room.

"Ah, Buru, good," his father motioned. "Sit, please, my son. Tea?"

Buru nodded his assent. Angkor poured three cups, placing sugar and milk in one and setting it before Mother's urn. *Just as she liked it,* recalled Buru. Angkor set the sugar and milk next to Buru and placed a pat of yak butter in his own cup. Buru made a face.

"I know, your mother would chide me for drinking my tea Mongolian fashion," said Angkor. "I take it you never developed the taste, either."

"Milk is fine, Father," answered his son. They sat for long, silent minutes. Angkor sipped his tea and said, "You were right. That night, your mother told me she understood why you did what you did. It has taken me many years to understand. Your mother's death brought it finally into full focus for me. You would have hated this job worse than I hate it and in turn, would have hated me. I could not live with myself if I knew you hated me.

"But she understood what I did, as well. She also told me she disagreed with both of us." He flashed a small smile. "Leave it to your mother to see three sides to our dispute." Buru snorted.

"I have been watching you, Buru, "Angkor continued. "I know you are a landowner now and a member of your local government. I understand you are considering a run for your world's Council?"

"Mother told you this."

"Yes and many other things. I knew she wrote you and slipped away from time to time, on the excuse of going to Indianola,

292

to see you. She always came home happier after seeing you. I am sure she would not want us to continue this dispute."

"There is no dispute, Father," said Buru. "I have made my decision and I stand by it."

"Yes," his father said, his voice full of regret, "and I am very, very proud of you." His eyes welled with tears. "I only wish your mother would have heard me tell you that."

"I think she knew," Buru said, his eyes also wet. He pulled a portable holo from his pocket. "You have three grandchildren, Father. Jaakob, Andruu and Pia." An image of the children rose from the table. "My wife and I have another on the way."

"Oh my," gasped Angkor. "Your daughter has her mother's eyes."

"And her attitude as well." For the next hour, Buru slowly showed his father images of his family. Angkor laughed, cooed and expressed surprise at the antics of his son's children. When the images finished, he blew out a happy sigh. "A fortunate man, you are, Son. Yes, a most fortunate man."

"I don't recall this image of Mother." Buru picked up the framed image.

"That's funny," Angkor said. "I took that the morning you were born. Your mother hated it; she was so tired, being up all night with our surrogate. But she refused to leave her side, wanting to see you enter the universe. Of all the images I have of your mother, it is my favorite."

Buru set the image back next to the urn. "No, son, I want you to have it," Angkor said. "I have thousands of images of her, and I have her here in my heart." He tapped his chest. "But this one, given the circumstance, this one I want you to have."

"Thank you, Father," said Buru. He replaced his holo-emitter in his jacket and stood. Fumbling with his mother's image, he faced his father. "I need to go. My shuttle is waiting. There is one more thing I want you to know. On Luftstra, we have read your law carefully. We are having much debate about it. In my own home, my wife and I argue about it constantly. But she approves of much of your law. I would not be surprised if Luftstra applies for membership within the next ten years."

Angkor stood and opened his arms. Buru shook his head. "No, Father," he said. "We had a good conversation today. But I am not ready to forgive you completely. Yet. Please, let us give it some time."

Angkor lowered his arms. "You will call me?" he asked. "From time to time? And perhaps send me more images of your family?"

"From time to time, Father." He gripped the doorknob, then faced Angkor once more.

His father was holding Sophia's urn to his chest and was weeping. Buru now realized how aged his father had become. His rich, black hair was streaked with grey, his face lined with deep furrows. Father's hands, always so strong, were shaking slightly and had a dusting of spots across them.

Buru inhaled deeply through his nose. "Mother was murdered, Father."

"Yes."

"I want revenge."

"Not so much as I, my son."

"Do you know who did this?" Buru asked.

"Yes."

"I want to know who is responsible!"

"Go home, Buru," Angkor ordered. "I need to do this carefully, quietly. Be assured, Son, your mother's murderers will be punished for their misdeeds to our family.

And I will be certain they suffer."

Chapter 30

June 3070-July 3071 A.D.

Upon returning to the Keep, Angkor disappeared into a laboratory he commandeered for himself. He emerged after a week, haggard and demanding gastroenterologists and endocrinologists. The first who attended him he deemed unsatisfactory. Calls went out to the great research universities of the Empire and the finest in both disciplines were assembled for the Khan.

He selected a dozen of each at random and they disappeared behind the doors of his laboratory again. Four weeks later they emerged, the doctors returning to their studies, the Khan to his stable. He stopped only long enough to change into traditional travelling clothes, breeches, boots, jerkin and cap. Angkor selected a roan pony and departed deep into the desert, demanding no guards or attendants. Ever-cautious security officers orbited the lone horseman at an altitude that their Khan couldn't detect. Cognizant of the fact that Angkor wanted time to clear his head in the emptiness of the desert, they allowed him an empty desert. But only empty enough.

His travels took him deep into the Gobi. Ten days he rode, stopping only to tend to his pony and refill his water bag. Rations needed only a bit of water and heat from his portable power supply. He had long ago learned to sleep and eat from the saddle.

On the tenth day, surrounded by only scrub and rocks, he climbed off his horse and sat. The pony wandered about, nibbling at the thorny, dry plants struggling to survive in the harsh world. Angkor sat, elbow to knee, holding his chin. The computations and patterns flowed through his thoughts; he turned them and they rolled through again. After five days, he decided there was an error. He whistled to the pony and rode back to the Keep.

Once again, the call went out for the scientists. Angkor selected a different group and sequestered them in his lab again. After a month, the scientists left. Angkor again rode a pony out of the Keep, this time heading north into the mountains. Again, his reflections revealed an error.

Again and again, four more times, scientists were summoned, worked with the Khan in his laboratory, only to be turned out so the Khan could go into seclusion to review the progress. His sojourns into the desert and the mountains grew longer. His weight loss became obvious; aides tried to fuss over him when he returned. The Kurultai members met with the bonzes in the Keep who were raising the heirs, seeking which was the readiest, should the Khan break down completely, necessitating his replacement. Ng, the chief bonze would only smile and say, "We are on schedule. When the time comes, the new Khan will be ready."

It was after the turn of the year. The scientists who came to serve the Khan departed as their predecessors had, five times before. The Khan had dressed in his warmest traveling clothes and departed across the frozen desert. He was grateful to find his aides had correctly guessed his destination, erecting a well-stocked yurt for him and his pony.

For ten days, the winter winds howled and tore at his shelter. He heard it not. The temperatures plummeted, but he paid it no mind. The formulas ran through his head over and over. He checked each line, each character, then checked each again. He could find no error.

With a final nod, he saddled his horse.

He studied the image closely. The arch of her eyebrows, the left a tiny bit lower on one end than the right. The long slope of her nose. The tiny curl of her soft lips. The tip of her chin. He missed her, every inch of her. He had wondered if the pain of her passing would ever fade; it was as real today as it had been at the moment he watched her die.

He kissed her image. "Tonight, my love," he told her. "Tonight I strike down your murderers. I know you would not want me to do this for you. But I am a Khalkha warrior and they have touched my woman."

The room was perfect. Angkor had selected the dining room with a magnificent vista of the mountains. The setting sun washed the room in golden light, a sign, he was certain, that she approved.

It was the finest table ever set in the Empire. The linens were premium ivory, the silver gleamed from hand polishing. Five settings of gilded china and lead cut glass. Angkor put Sophia's image next to his setting where he could look to her. A discrete knock, then a servant opened the door and announced, "Sire, your guests are here."

"Show them in," ordered Angkor. "Notify my *major domo.* Exactly in the order in my instructions, particularly the cocktails."

Xaid swept into the room, followed by Dawlish and Salaam. "Angkor, my dear friend," Xaid's fawn skin-covered hands reach out to Angkor. He dressed impeccably, of course, in a white silk suit, his turban stiff around his head. A gleaming opal in silver peaked his dress. "Thank you for inviting us to share this meal with you." Salaam also extended his hand and greeted his old friend.

Dawlish, in his General's uniform, saluted his Khan, albeit with a suspicious eye.

"My friends, sit, please," Angkor beckoned to the setting. Once all were settled, the wine steward filled their glasses with a rubicund wine. "One year ago today, my precious wife crossed over to the next world," Angkor said. "Tonight, on the first anniversary of her death, we honor her and her traditions by holding *Shraddha,* the ritual meal for the dead. Gentlemen, Sophia." They raised their glasses and returned the salutation.

"I have many surprises for you this evening, my friends." promised the Khan. "First, my dear, if you please?"

An apparition appeared in the corner. The column of light extended into three dimensions, then slowly arranged itself. Sophia, in her younger days from the market, wearing a familiar sea green sari. She glided to the table, taking her place next to Angkor. The men gaped at her soft, curled hair wafted in an unseen breeze, her opal eyes sparkling from an inner light. She demurely smiled and said, "Good evening, friends of my husband."

299

"Angkor, what manner of madness is this?" demanded Salaam. "My friend, this is not Sophia. This is unnatural, obscene. Where did you come by this…thing?"

"Be calm, my friends," soothed Angkor. "This was a gift from an engineering student from Iowa University in Occident. I believe he meant it as a memorandum for me. Don't worry, I know it is not my Sophia. It was a kind gesture. Observe.

My dear?"

The holo-Sophia turned to Angkor, "Yes, my husband?" it asked.

"Don't you have something for me to show our guests?"

I do!" she glided over to a tabernacle mounted to the wall. She unlocked the chest and carried the urn within to the table, placing it at the setting next to Angkor. "Thank you, my dear," he said. "You may shut down now." The holo-Sophia nodded and deresolved into an eight-inch disk hovering where her waist had been.

Angkor plucked the disk from the air, walked to the balcony and flung it into the night. "I will not need this after tonight," he told them. "Tonight, I complete the ritual mourning and may continue with my life."

A second glass of wine was poured. "My friends, I give you the honored guest of our celebration tonight, my wife Sophia." The men stood and raised their glasses to the urn and drank.

They dined mostly in silence. Salaam and Xaid tried to speak with Angkor, but his responses were single words or grunts.

300

Dawlish eyed his Khan, casting furtive glances at his friends. His inner voice screamed of danger. He had no overt reason to be cautious. Nevertheless, he maintained his guard.

The supper finished, a cheese plate was laid out. They were served a flute containing a milky yellow drink. "My friends, this is a special preparation I created for just this evening," Angkor said. "I started work on it years ago and tonight it is perfect. I can think of no one I would rather share it with than you, my old friends.

"Each morning I wake up with the light and promise of the new day before the weight of my life comes down on me and I remember that Sophia is gone. I turn to her as I did for more than thirty years to kiss her just one more time and she isn't there.

"I remember something she read me once. 'Let us be grateful to the people who make us happy; they are the gardeners who make our souls blossom.' Today marks one year since my soul and my wife died." He raised the glass and drank.

Angkor watched as his friends drained the beverage. Xaid had an unpleasant look on his face. No matter, Angkor hadn't cared what the potion would taste like. Only that it worked.

The servants removed the glasses and placed a tiny glass before each man. In each glass was an amber syrup. Angkor picked his up and stared into the glass.

"To me, the most tragic fact of my wife's death is she was murdered. Murdered by you, her friends."

"What madness is this!" demanded Xaid. "You call us here to honor our friend! Your wife! And now you accuse us of her murder! Have you gone completely mad?"

"Yes, Angkor, how could you possibly say such a thing?" said Salaam. "Were she alive today and here right now, surely she would admonish you for such foolishness!"

Dawlish picked up the small glass. Turned it in his fingers, stared at it. "Poison," he said finally.

"Yes," said Angkor. "And if I were you, I'd drink that quickly. Two of you are receiving the antidote. The third? Well, I may or may not have their antidote in my hands."

"Give that to me this instant!" Xaid tried to leap across the table. Alas, too many years of soft living and opulent meals had expanded his waistline. He flopped on the table, then slid off, overturning the perfect setting. He clawed at the tablecloth whining and blubbering.

"I warn you, Xaid, you do not wish to spill your cup. It may have your antidote. It may not. As for my trophy." He tipped his head back and poured the fluid into his mouth.

Dawlish eyed the Khan, then swallowed the contents of his glass. "You said you've been working on this for years?" he asked.

"Yes," Angkor nodded, "since the day you murdered my father. Ryder Finn supplied me with the original autopsy. The weapon was a military grade sniper rail weapon. The same weapon used to assassinate Ameranda Whitehorse. But it was not one of your soldiers who murdered my father. There is a single entity in the

Empire who could accomplish both the Whitehorse killing and my father's murder."

Salaam placed his fist over his mouth and coughed.

"I would drink your antidote, gentleman," Angkor said. "The poison I devised is quite exquisite and fast acting."

Xaid glared at the emperor, then drank the liquid swiftly. Salaam held the glass up questioningly. "You'll never know for sure if you don't drink." Angkor's voice was not unkind.

Salaam drank. And immediately coughed it up, spraying the fluid and half his dinner on the table.

"When I realized that you murdered Tenzing to put me on the throne, I became cautious. My laboratory was built to create the Vinithri queen and my heirs. But it also served for me to examine each of your DNA. As time went on, I shelved the project, thinking you were loyal subjects to my rule. But Dawlish convinced me otherwise. You are a fine officer, old friend. When you confronted me in my office, demanding I treat you as the Chief of Staff years ago, I could see our decision to promote you was the correct one.

"But when you came to me at Xaid's bequest, an errand boy, to try and collect the Vinithri eggs and our method of designing my heirs, I realized that you no longer served me or my Empire. I should have had you killed then and there. I should have done more to protect my Sophia."

Salaam started coughing again, wrapping his arms around his stomach and groaning.

"Cassius and I raced to finish my law. That would protect us, I was certain. Surely, with the punishments I had written in, I felt perhaps it would deter Xaid's ambition," Angkor looked down. "I was wrong."

"I expected you would come after me. Sophia was our friend, a friend to all of you. Surely, I would never have expected you to send your lapdog, Salaam, after my wife."

Blood began to ooze from the corners of Salaam's mouth, eyes and ears.

"Let me explain what is happening to you, you *hashashin* dog," snarled Angkor. "The compound I gave you was formulated off three sets of DNA. You three. I could drink a gallon of the chemical and never get anything more than a mild stomach ache from the volume of fluid.

"For you three, it attacks you two ways. First, stomach acid is very similar to hydrochloric acid. I accelerated your endocrine glands to continually produce this acid. Phase two breaks down the lining of your stomach and thereby the sphincter valve between your stomach and small intestine. Your small intestine draws liquids and nutrients into itself, dispersing the acid throughout your circulatory system."

Salaam had fallen to the floor, crying and groaning. He worked his jaw, trying to speak through a mouth already clogged with blood. Angkor leaned over the dying assassin. "Does it hurt?" he gloated. "Are your guts on fire? Are your veins ablaze from the acid boiling in your very blood?

"They wouldn't let me see my wife after they recovered her. They told me she was found in a glade of edelweiss. I was able to get my hands on her autopsy report. The explosion seared her lungs, but not fatally. She had third and fourth degree burns over one hundred percent of her body. Her body, deaccelerating from flight speed to terminal velocity ripped her clothing from her body. At some point, she lost an arm and both her legs because of the speed.

"Can you even *conceive,* you dog, how badly I want you to hurt right now? If I could, I would make you feel this agony for months and years. I suspect you'll be dead in a few minutes. Far, far quicker than the fifteen minutes it took my wife to fall to earth."

Salaam gasped and grunted, his body writhing under Angkor's watchful gaze. He gave a sudden jerk and squeak, then he was gone.

Angkor settled back in his chair, looking relieved and pleased. "Now for you two," he said.

"Your antidote will keep you from death for one week. You will report to me to receive your dosage and a further week of life. Serve me well and live. Disobey me or bore me and you will die like this dog. Do not attempt to save any the antidote to manufacture yourself. You are only receiving enough for a single week of life. Further, this is a genetic weapon. I know all of the geneticists who could replicate my formula. The antidote has my mark on it; they will know it if they see it. And they will let me know.

"General, you are to prepare my fleet and build it to defend my Empire. You will work with Admiral Schurenburg and prepare

305

him to replace you within five years. Succeed and I will give you a comfortable retirement. Fail me and die.

"Xaid. You bastard. It's been you behind all this all along. You, your money, your lust for power. Your well-heeled friends operating above the law. No more.

"I had to finish my law. Thanks the gods above I did before you could act. The law is in place, it is inviolate. It brings the lowest man to the level of the high and mighty. Hear now the decision of the Khan.

"I take away your name. All your properties and possessions are mine. Your family belongs to me. You are no longer a person; you are a thing. Property to be owned. You are worthless. You will be sent to my gardens to toil until the day I tire of you and dispatch you to my composting factory. Guards!"

Two burly soldiers entered the room. The Khan pointed at the thing which had been Xaid and directed, "Take it to its cell. Tell the head gardener he has a new slave." The guards grabbed the protesting slave, knocking its turban from its head. Long black hair fell. "Wait," called the Emperor. He picked up a knife and sawed the Singh's hair and threw it on the floor. The Khan beckoned; the guards pulled the weeping slave from the room.

Dawlish stood and gave the Khan a respectful bow. "You are dismissed," ordered Angkor. Servants arrived with a gurney. "Take that to my laboratory," ordered the Khan pointing at Salaam. "They will know what to do."

Angkor gathered up Sophia's urn. Clutching her to his chest, the Khan went woodenly down the hall to his chambers. He kicked off his shoes and curled up on his single bed, wrapped a tired body around Sophia and cried himself to sleep.

Chapter 31

August 3073

The Intelligence colonel stood ramrod straight before the Khan. He fixed his eyes to a spot just beyond the Khan's head. One did not look the Khan in the eye, lest the stare be misconstrued as defiance. His black uniform was impeccable, of course, its grey piping accenting the somber livery. It served its purpose. Often enough the very sight of an Intelligence officer in uniform was enough to cause even innocent suspects to quiver and soil themselves. Of course, if they were being interviewed by Imperial Intelligence, there was likely a good cause for the fecal accident.

"Sir, this is the data stick we found in the recorder on his desk," he said matter-of- factly. "The message addresses you directly. It is the opinion of Intelligence that you should view the file."

Angkor rolled the data stick between his fingers before placing it in the port on his desk. The holo image of Dawlish seated behind his own desk appeared.

"My Khan," the holo stated, *"I have faithfully served this uniform, first with distinction in the Turkman Army in my youth. When your father called, I proudly served as Chief of Staff of the Terran Union Army. You asked me to rebuild your Army and your Fleet when you became Emperor. I have done so with humility and gratitude with the faith you have shown me.*

I have betrayed your faith. Worse still, I took advantage of our friendship, manipulating you to Xaid's desires and to my own.

In the end, my worst disloyalty to you was to facilitate the murder of the Empress. I justified my decision by convincing myself that if we demonstrated our power, you would acquiesce to our demands.

I misjudged you. The starry-eyed medical student I knew back in Delhi would not have been capable of such savagery and revenge. I should have known, having been a firsthand witness to what you did to the old tea-seller.

My Khan, you charged me with creating an Army and Fleet to defend your Empire. I have done so. You have charged me to make Admiral Schurenburg ready to assume my job within five years. He is now ready. Therefore, my duty to you is at an end.

Angkor, I wish I could call you friend again. But I relinquished that right the moment Sophia's shuttle exploded. Your punishment was of the utmost cruelty and still, befitting. I have appeared before you every week and begged for my life. Each time I drank your elixir, I died on the inside. Each week facing you, guilty of murdering my friend, Sophia, and being disloyal to my oaths to you.

It has become too great a burden for me to bear. I cannot live another day with my shame."

He placed a slug thrower against his left temple.

"Long live the Terran Empire! Long live the Emperor, Angkor Khan! May you rule for a thousand years!"

309

The report of the weapon was loud, sharp. The pressure wave from the low velocity round compressed his brain until the right side of his skull warped and fractured, sending bone, flesh and hair across the room. A scarlet fan of blood and tissue followed.

Dawlish collapsed facedown onto his desk, his heart fibrillating spastically as the signals from his brain ceased. Blood poured from the wound until his heart, too uncoordinated to pump any longer, stopped.

Angkor noticed a split second before the holo faded that someone had started to pick up the recorder. He removed the data stick, twisting it in his fingers again, then handed it to the Colonel.

"The body was dismembered per protocol," the colonel reported. "The remnants scattered into various compost factories around Terra. There will be an announcement of his death, of course. His family has been encouraged not to have any services. There is still the issue with the slave."

"Send it to Luna Station," instructed Angkor. "Exo-bio research. I expect it to be disposed of within a month."

The colonel nodded. "It shall be done, my Khan," he replied. "I shall place the order immediately. The data stick will be sealed in the General's file."

"His case is closed, then."

"No, my Khan," the colonel answered. "There are still interesting…anomalies in his file. We will be investigating those anomalies until the Director is satisfied there is no more information to be extracted."

"What happens with the file at that point?"

"A closed file goes into long term storage," said the Colonel. "The Director feels information, no matter how obscure, is power."

"Thank you, Colonel," the Khan said. "You are dismissed."

The Colonel clicked his heels in the manner of an ancient Prussian officer, turned sharply and marched to the door.

"One more question," called the Emperor, rather delighting in the Colonel's abrupt cessation of movement. "Who does Intelligence maintain records on?"

"Intelligence maintains records on all who serve the Empire," said the Colonel, "and anyone who gains our attention."

"Does Intelligence maintain a file on me?" Angkor asked.

The Colonel stiffened.

"Imperial Intelligence maintains files on everyone who serves the Empire," he said.

Angkor had secured a laboratory of his own following Sophia's murder. Within a year, he had developed the poison he used to exact his revenge on the perpetrators of that crime. Now, two years later, the lab had become his refuge.

He maintained a small staff for any number of projects that attracted his attention. The actual time he was able to spend in his retreat was limited; he still had his duties in Ulaan Baatar and Zurich. He was also expected to routinely tour the fifteen colonies that made up his Empire.

But, when the opportunity presented itself, it would not be uncommon for him to be found amongst the scanners and tools of his chosen profession. His staff would boast of his stamina, staring into an electron microscope at the inner workings of mitochondrial DNA from a sample for days straight, reporting the chemical markers he found and relaying the sequence. His attention to detail was a marvel, his curiosity boundless. His staff redoubled their efforts when Doctor Angkor was in the office, not wanting to fail their mentor in any fashion.

His legendary focus was on a protein sample obtained on an asteroid in the Mer system. The sample itself was barely a dozen of cells in any one direction. Angkor had seen the preliminary scans and taken an interest. He signed on to studying the sample closer and was deeply engaged when the visitor chime sounded. It was not time for lunch and his schedule for the day was clear; he had verified that this morning with his secretary. Ergo, unless the Galactic Council was invading (and that was quite unlikely, for if they had, security wouldn't be politely signaling him, they would have already smashed open his door and dragged him to safety,) then it was a distraction he could ignore.

The chime interfered again. So, while it was below the level of invasion, the caller clearly thought their need was greater than Angkor's peace and quiet. *It certainly better be!* as Angkor pressed the button for his comm.

Doctor Elian Lumburg appeared before him via the holo. "Ellie!" exclaimed the Khan. "Wonderful to see you! To what do I owe this pleasure and disturbance?"

"Doctor Angkor, it's good to see you," she said. "Listen, if you're not too busy, one of my teams has made a discovery I think you'd be interested in? It involves your heirs project. I've sent a pipper. It should be at your lab presently."

The door chimed. "It's here now, Elian," Angkor said.

"Excellent. We'll see you shortly, Doctor."

The pipper was the invention from the engineering student in Occident, the device that had brought Sophia's holo to the unholy triad's dinner party. A metallic disk about eight inches in diameter, it held a miniature lift plate and a holo emitter. Programed with an image of the owner, it acted as an escort or messenger, albeit with a limited vocabulary and intelligence.

Angkor hated the device.

A holo of Elian greeted him at the door. "Good afternoon, Doctor. If you would come with me?" They proceeded through the sprawling complex beneath the Keep in the Khangai Mountains. Angkor thought highly of Doctor Elian Lumburg from their time on the Vinithri queen project. Hence, he had named her as director of this complex, working closely hand in hand with the Heir File Committee and Master Ng.

He observed the progress of the children. They were nearly teens now, and a lively bunch. The intelligence progress was astounding; already two held doctorates, four others were nearly writing their theses. The children's physical prowess was never in doubt. Were he to allow them to compete, he very much doubted there was any life form at this level of physical age who could match them. Indeed, they could most likely outperform most adults.

Master Ng expressed concern at the children's emotional development. While they got along well with each other and their proctors, they appeared oddly undisciplined at times. It was probably due to their lack of interaction with parents, and was a recent development of the last seven year years.

Since their Grandmother Sophia had died.

She had been a constant in the children's lives. She never missed visiting with them daily while she was at the Keep and rarely went more than a month without seeing them. "The children are reacting to the loss of Grandmother in this way," said Ng. "They have plenty of adults around them. But no adult family member. It leaves them hurt, feeling alone in the universe."

Angkor tried. His own father, Tenzing, was rarely available when Angkor was the age of these heirs, and when he was available he was stiff, formal. Only after Suishin's death had the two been able to communicate. Although Angkor could certainly understand his father's word over his brother's grave; *I'm glad it is you who are here with me today, Angkor. This is how the plan said it would be, although today I would give anything for it not to be so.*

The Khan prayed, even as the virtual holo continued, that he would never have to stand over the grave of Buru or any of his grandchildren.

"We are here, Sir." The holo had stopped at a nondescript door marked "Forensics Lab 2 Doctor Theodore Gebow". The holo pressed the door chime and deresolved when the door opened, leaving the messenger disk hovering waist high. Angkor resisted the urge to kick at it; he really hated the damned things.

"Doctor Angkor, welcome!" Elian called. "Please, I'd like you to meet Doctor Gebow."

Theodore Gebow was a short, heavy Terran, with unruly curly white hair and thick black framed glasses sitting on a pimply nose. He had a white goatee and dressed oddly, surgical pants and a rumbled plaid shirt that was crookedly buttoned. The pocket held a collection of implements Angkor didn't want to consider.

"Oh, my," Doctor Gebow's eyes bugged beneath his thick glasses. *Glasses?* wondered Angkor, *In this day and age? I have heard there were those on who corrective gene therapy didn't work. But they were generally left blind.*

"Doctor Gebow, I am Doctor Angkor. I am pleased to meet you," Angkor said. "Elian said you have a discovery I would be interested in?"

Doctor Gebow's awe of the Emperor was obvious as he stared for several moments, his jaw slack and his eyes wide. Elian gave him a nudge. "Oh, right, the S subject," He hurried to his desk station. "I have been assigned to examining subject S since his being brought here two years ago. The cause of death was extraordinary! He was...dissolved from his own gastric juices."

315

The stasis chamber in the center of the lab went from opaque to clear. Angkor felt a surge of pleasure. The stasis had been applied to Salaam close enough to his death that the anguish on his face was clear, frozen in time. The blood had stopped flowing from the body, but it still glistened, appeared fresh. Angkor only wished he could have slowed down the melting process. It would have been more gratifying had Salaam been forced to suffer longer.

"I was examining his neural processes, first in the affected area, then those radiating outwards towards the brain." Doctor Gebow sounded like a professor in Angkor's college days. "When I got to a relatively clear section of nerves, I found an anomaly." An arm with a cylinder attached to the end lowered itself from the ceiling and hovered over the body's chest. "As you can see, Doctors, the nerve cluster here appears normal. But when I looked closer at the nerve endings," The image on the screen zoomed in, exposing the end of the nerve cells. "You can just make it out...here."

Angkor examined the image more closely. What appeared was a normal looking nerve endings, except..." Doctor Gebow, would you transfer this image to the hologram imager?" Angkor heard the clatter of a keyboard, the image transferred to the projector in the middle of the lab. There it was, amongst the cilia of the nerve endings. A thin silver thread. "That can only be a micron thick!" exclaimed Angkor, "What is it?"

"Point seven five microns actually, Doctor Angkor," said Theodore. "And my analysis identifies it as Thembrodium, a rare

316

element found on worlds that have or have had salty oceans at one time. It develops from nerve cluster decomposition, crystalizing into a very tiny element. It is extraordinarily dense and conductive, perhaps as much as ten times the speed of human nerves. The element is so rare; an ounce is valued on today's market at one million credits for a single troy ounce."

"Why would Salaam be carrying several millions of this…Thembrodium in his body?" Angkor asked.

"As much as one third an ounce, sir. A fortune, yes," Gebow smiled, "But that is not the big surprise. Watch."

The arm moved above the cadaver's open mouth and peered inside. The holo reformatted, focusing on the soft palate. The image focused inward into the tissue, revealing an odd cube, its corners rounded off. Several of the grey strands connected to the box. "Here's the big surprise, Doctor," said Theodore with pride. "The ganglion cluster. It is connected to Thembrodium strands into his cerebral cortex and throughout his nervous system."

"To what ends, Doctor?" asked Angkor. "What does this achieve?"

"If I want to send a low watt signal," Doctor Gebow explained, "I need a big antenna. With antennae, bigger is always better; the bigger it is, the more sensitive. Conversely, if I want to receive a low watt signal, the same principle applies. A low watt signal needs a large antenna to be received. What has happened here to subject S is: he has a transmitter that uses his body as an antenna. He broadcasted and received using this micro transmitter."

"I presented this information to our geneticists with the chemical composition," Elian said. "During feeding both in vitro and early childhood, we can replicate this process in the heirs. Resulting in..."

"Telepathy," answered Angkor.

"Exactly," Elian said, "The first generation will be extremely primitive, perhaps reading emotions or tactile sensations. But we believe that within five generations, they will be able to communicate with each other with a simple thought. Perhaps two or three generations beyond that, read other beings' minds, perhaps even controlling other bodies. A few generations later, telekinetics."

"The superior being," whispered Angkor. "*Homo Sapiens'* replacement, *Homo Superior.*"

"Exactly, my Khan," said Elian. "And the sequence will find its way into the population slowly, from the less superior heirs. Eventually, perhaps as few as six or seven thousand years, the whole of our species will have this talent.

"This is the gateway to your Empire's rule of a hundred thousand years."

Chapter 32

May 3083 A.D.

The Kurultai Council was in an uproar!

The gathering in the great hall of Ulaan Baatar had been guardian of the Mongol Empire for three millennia. In ancient times, the Council would meet around a great fire on the steppe, no one sitting higher than any other, not even the Khan. Eventually, halls of various types were built, each with the basic layout, no one leader seated above another. In 2883 A.D. Soushui Khan from the Oirats had constructed this hall. She had read the stories of the Council meeting on the open steppe and was determined to return to that part of the ancient ways.

The building was erected on the outskirts of the city. The low walls barely concealed the steppe beyond. The sweeping roof was retractable, so the Council could meet under open skies as their ancestors had. It was closed only on the coldest of nights.

A great fire pit centered the meeting place. Circling around the pit were simple wooden chairs for the chieftains of the various tribes of Mongolia. As in ancient times, Soushui Khan had decreed, none shall ever be seated above another.

This night, one hundred chieftains from the greater and lesser tribes, gathered around the fire. Angkor Khan, Headman of the Khalkha and Leader of them all, had come to them with a request.

Over those centuries, there had been much asked of them, all for the greater good of Mongolia. For the last half century, Tenzing and his son Angkor had asked even more of the Council, always for the greater good of the people of Mongolia and the Terran Empire.

But this, this struck at the heart of Mongolian traditions, whether those of the Khalkha, Buryat, Oirats or any one of the dozen smaller tribes represented by the Council.

Tradition demanded at the age of eighteen, the new warriors of the tribe appear before their Council and declare themselves adults and warriors. It would also be the time the Khan would anoint his successor, either Crown Prince or Princess.

Historically, the Khan presented a single child. On a dozen occasions, twins were presented. In an extraordinary event in the twenty fifth century, a set of triplets became adults on the same day. That Angkor Khan had eight grandchildren claiming their rightful place amongst the warriors of the Empire was unheard of. The Council struggled with the sheer number, but conceded the Khan would be allowed to accept all the heirs as adults in the same ceremony. What they argued was Angkor's decision to allow the head of the monastery at the Keep to announce the future Khan.

Seraht, Headsman of the Oirat, was the most vocal. "For three thousand years, the first amongst us has stood before the Council and received our approval before we announced the divinity of the Crown Heir," he argued. "Even your father presented you to us for approval before he told the world. Now you would have us break this tradition?"

"My predecessor, the Great Genghis Khan, crowned his son before he presented him to this Council," responded Angkor. "In times past, it has been clear to all the world who the heir would be before coming to this august body. Always we have placed our faith in the *Khutu Khtu*, the embodiment of the living Buddha, to guide us. Indeed, my grandchildren have lived their entire lives under the tutelage of Master Nom Ng, Master Bonze of the Keep, recently of the Temple of Angkor wat.

"Each of these children were designed and created by the very virtues and requirements you, the Kurultai Council, demanded of the new Khan. Each has been forged, by education, meditation and actions in preparation for becoming new leader of this great Empire. We have, all of us, worked so hard and sacrificed so much, to achieve this Empire. Do we decide that our decision twenty years ago is no longer valid? Are we to question the wisdom of the servants we entrusted with this holy task? Do we now render the sacrifice…the very lives sacrificed, for this cause? To throw their lives away for nothing, because we fear to change that which is traditional for that which is best?"

"My Khan," stammered Seraht, "our concerns are not about fear…"

"It is all based on your fear!" thundered Angkor. "You are terrified of losing your place, your position amongst our people. What would they say if they could see you now, the sniveling cowards too frightened of the pathway to the future? Pah! I am through with you. I have come here to announce the decision will be made at the naming ceremony next month. Vote how you will. But if I must, I will pave the road of our Empire's future with the bones of cowards."

June 3083 A.D.

She and her mate lived here on a tall stone pillar. Most of the year, the hunting was sufficient. But at the start of the hot season, the others would come. They would gather, create a great commotion for many sunrises. Then, they would leave.

While they were there, the food would come out in abundance. Great piles of garbage would be created; the rodents she, her mate and their young feasted upon would gather and grow fat. They mated and created the hundreds she and her family would need to survive another year.

The sun had risen. The thermals she would ride began to form. The food would soon be scurrying from their dens to gather trash to feed their young.

She spread her grey wings and soared into the morning light.

Angkor wriggled his rump in his saddle.

"A problem, my Khan?" asked the stable boy.

"No," said the Khan, "just getting comfortable."

"Of course, my Khan."

Angkor gave the stable boy a disapproving glare. His condescending tone annoyed the Khan. True, he didn't ride near as much as he should. But running an Empire left little time for dalliances such as riding. Still, he had been riding for over seventy

322

years. His bottom hadn't ever been this uncomfortable. Perhaps he needed a new saddle.

The other leaders of the tribes, the Oirat, the Buryat and the rest formed with him in the van of the horde. In ancient times, there would be tens of thousands of warriors following them. But today was a parade, a show for the attendees of the Naadam festival, so there were only a thousand Mongols in this horde.

Normally, the Khan left this show to the Council to lead. They rotated amongst the headmen for the position of honor. However, the ceremony today would be celebrating the Naming Ceremony of the Khan's heirs. It would be the first such ceremony in over fifty years, since the current Khan had become a man.

"My Khan, look." Seraht, headman of the Oirat pointed. The grey and white *Shikra* climbed from her home in the stone pylon and winged her way on the hunt. "A good sign." The other leaders nodded their assent and clapped Angkor on the back, congratulating him for such a potent sign.

The Khan pulled his sword from his scabbard and raised it high. "Hooo-OOOO!" the horde cried, "Hoooo-OOOO! Hoooo-HOOOO!" On the third cry, Angkor whipped his horse about and galloped through the yurt village surrounding the festival grounds. He led them unerringly through the streets to the pavilion at the center of the temporary city.

The cries of "Hoooo-HOOOO! Hoooo-HOOOO! Hoooo-HOOOO!" surrounded the horde as they tore through the city as in ancient times. It was a glorious start to the day, horses thundering across the steppe, through the streets, the Khan leading them.

They gathered on the stage to the cheering crowds, their horses taken away by servants. Angkor swaggered to the edge of the platform, fist on his hips. "I am the Emperor Angkor Khan, son of Tenzing Khan, leader of the Mongol people!" he cried. "Are there any who care to defy me?" His golden robe shone in the sun, the simple crown Sophia had designed still sat proudly on his brow. The crowd answered his challenge with the "Hoooo-HOOOO!" of the Mongol people. Angkor stomped majestically to his simple throne. A mighty clash from a brass gonged silenced the crowd.

A young Mongol girl, perhaps as old as seven, walked down the aisle formed by the crowd. Her tiny form crossed the vast plaza before the dais wearing the simple clothing of a nomad. She carried a yellow silk pillow with great care. The multitude was silent as she passed, all falling to a knee.

She positioned herself before the Emperor. "Majesty," her bird like voice carried across the arena, carried by a concealed microphone, "May I present the Empress, Sophia Marshall?" Angkor removed the silk cloth from the gleaming diadem sitting on the golden pillow. He indicated the throne next to his own. "My Lady," he said.

The girl set the pillow on the throne, turning it so the graceful point faced the crowd. She kowtowed to the diadem. In turn, Angkor kowtowed to the small girl. "Thank you, Child," he whispered to her.

The spectacle began. Mongols, horsemen of the steppes for centuries, rode in complex patterns on the parade ground before the leaders of Terra. Musicians banged drums, clanged cymbals, blew horns, strummed, stroked and plucked at a variety of stringed instruments.

A bright spectrum of color splayed across the arena as dancers from around the Empire sang and pranced. The Khan knew many songs and laughed and clapped his hands in time, adding his lusty baritone when a familiar song was sung.

The ceremony came to a pause. Angkor sprang to his feet and declared, "My friends! Fellow Terrans! Honored members of the Kurultai! Guests and friends from off world! Welcome to our festival. I now declare the Naadam to…"

"HOLD!"

The voice was firm, resolved. Angkor smiled proudly. The combined voice of the eight hushed the whole of the assembly as he had hoped.

The crowd and performers parted as the eight rode down the main venue side by side. Each heir was dressed in a robe similar to Angkor's, save the colors matched their individual file. Eight powerful chargers carried them, shield in their right hands, a short bow in their left.

They formed a line at the base of the dais. The boy dressed in black announced, "We are here before our Grandfather and our Grandmother and the whole of the people to claim our position as men and women of the Khalkha tribe and to demand our seats at the warrior's table!"

"Men?" roared Angkor. "Women? I see no men or women here! I see children, dressed in adult's clothes, riding adult's horses! Begone, go back to your mother and bother us no more." He girded himself.

It was a single *THUMP!* Angkor was not sure where his grandchildren would aim. He had shot between his father's legs. His grandchildren had outperformed him; a neat circle of arrows had buried themselves in the planks around him.

Sixteen emerald eyes bored into his. Eight steel barbed war points, aimed at his heart. Each bow arm was straight, unshaking, the bowstrings taught, pulled to the eight cheeks.

"Who are you?" he demanded. "Who are these men and women demanding my attention?"

One by one, they lowered their bows and stood high in their stirrups declaring,

"I am your grandson, Janus Arcadia."

"I am your grandson, Keerma Lui."

"I am your grandson, Rahnie Lau."

"I am your grandson, Pintare Gyn." "

I am your granddaughter, Pershma Soi."

"I am your granddaughter Gui Ou."

"I am your granddaughter, Mea Gehn."

"I am your granddaughter, Lily Marshall."

"Lily Marshall?" wondered Angkor. No matter, it was her decision. His arms opened. "Welcome grandchildren, though children no more. You are invited to join the warriors at the warrior's table!

"But before we breakfast, we have to attend to one more duty."

The newly declared men and women mounted the stage and formed a line facing the crowd, arms crossed and chins high.

"Since ancient times, when the heir achieved his place at the warrior's table, the Khan would present him to the Kurultai Council for their approval of the new Crown Prince or Princess. Today, we honor the tradition of our ancestors by naming my heir before you, our people and the Kurultai Council for approval. These eight before you were designed and bred to this role even prior to their birth. Each is physically superior, each is astounding in knowledge and morality.

"Twenty years ago, the Kurultai Council charged the bonzes from the Khmer temple at Angkor wat to create a curriculum to raise my grandchildren to be superior. And, today, these are the finest human beings in existence. It is only right the finest of these eight be named my successor. I call upon the Master bonze of my Keep, Nom Ng, to reveal my successor."

The elderly bonze bowed before his old friend and student. For the occasion, he was wearing brilliant marigold robes, with a scarlet sash and a wide brimmed hat matching his red sash. He accepted the sword Angkor proffered. The whole host of priests in

327

the assembly chanted as Ng marched slowly around the eight heirs. The chanting stopped when his raised his hand.

"My brothers and sisters were charged with making each one of you the Khan. We shouldered this task gratefully, for the order of the Buddha was to achieve enlightenment through perfection. In this, we have succeeded brilliantly! Each of you can become our next great leader. But there is one who stands above, albeit by the slimmest of margins.

"We have known each of you before you were born. From the time your zygote divided for the first time to this moment, the destiny of the Khan has been set in the stars. We have consulted the Gods and demons, the Erinyes and the Xinhua. We met this morning and arrived at our final decision."

He stepped forward and knelt at the feet of the young man wearing blue. He raised the sword and said, "My Khan."

His brothers and sisters bowed. The leaders of Terra and the whole of the assembly knelt before the new Crown Prince.

Janus Arcadia Khan accepted his father's sword from the bonze, raised it high above his head and uttered his first command. "Rise," he said.

Chapter 33

May 3129

Dusty roads and fields had existed as early as the seventeenth
century A.D. in this part of Occident, further back than when the
land was part of the old United States. The country was named for
the timeless river, Mississippi, and on Sunday the locals still got up
early and dressed in their finest before going to church.

Old Creech arose even earlier. As caretaker of the Duck
Crossing Baptist Church, it was up to him to drive the old bus
around the parish and pick up the children for Sunday school.
Missus Jackson, the Reverend Jackson's wife, would be waiting for
them by eight and would raise holy hell if he didn't have all the
children there on time.

The bus was a hundred years old if it was a day. Its
hydrogen engine rattled and belched, shaking the whole bus.
Ancient panels, loosened by a thousand Sunday trips, torn and faded
seats repaired hundreds of times by strips of tape and the persistent
tap-tap-tap coming from behind the computer module gave the bus
character, at least according to the Reverend Jackson.

Still, every Sunday, Creech climbed into the driver's seat and
enter the start sequence. The bus shuddered and wheezed while the
engine turned over. With a loud bang, a blue flame would shoot out
of the exhaust pipe. The engine ran unevenly for a few minutes
before settling into the uneven purr of an alley cat trying to decide

between the moldy cheese and rotted fish carcass it found in the trash bin.

Creech pushed the gearbox lever, wincing as he did every Sunday when trying to find to forward gear. It clunked into place and he eased onto the dusty road on his rounds.

His first stop was Wendy Welch, age fourteen. She was a thin girl who sang like a nightingale in the choir. She would lead the other children in hymns as Creech drove about picking them all up.

"Good morning, Miss Wendy," he drawled at the pretty girl as she climbed on the bus to take a seat primly in the first seat on the right.

"Good morning, Mister Creech," would come her soft reply. "Lovely day." It could be pouring down rain and the girl would always say it was a lovely day. She would start humming as he drove to the next stop. As the children boarded, she would greet them by name. The bus would pull away and she would start to sing, the children joining in. "The Old Rugged Cross" would be followed by "Jesus Loves the Little Children."

The last pickup was Polly Preston, age six. Her golden hair would be arranged in ringlets and she wore a blue dress. "Good morning, Miss Polly," Creech told her.

"Good morning, Mister Creech," she replied. She held up the tiny bundle. "Mama says she hopes you enjoy the egg/ bacon biscuit this morning."

"Thank your momma for me, Miss Polly," he told her. It was the same every Sunday. Missus Preston made a fine egg/bacon biscuit and gave it to Polly for the bus driver who took her to Sunday school.

He started for the church as the children began his favorite song. *"Shall we gather at the river? The beautiful, beautiful river..."* when the black ship roared low over the bus, the shock wave shaking them like a rabbit in a hound dog's mouth. He slammed the brakes until the bus stopped shaking. Screams and crying filled the bus interior, non-stop from the terrified children. Wendy stood and raised her hands. "Listen everyone, listen!" she called. "We're fine! Jesus is watching over us. Come on now, join with me." She began to sing in her pure, sweet voice, *"Jesus loves the little children..."*

There was still sniffing and a few still crying, but tiny voices joined Wendy in singing the comforting tune. Little Polly, afraid of nearly nothing, had wandered to the back of the bus and stared out the back window. "Mister Creech?" her voice warbled, "it's coming back."

The Bougartd raider leveled, its guns sighted on the bus. Creech had thrown the bus back in gear and dirt sprayed from the tires and he desperately sawed the wheel back and forth, praying he would make the bus a difficult target.

The first half dozen rounds exploded behind the doomed bus. The seventh round immolated little Polly Preston, the next round entered the hydrogen fuel cell of the bus, igniting the volatile gas. The bus erupted in blue fire, scattering the its debris and its occupants in a quarter mile circle in the fields.

The raider circled once more, then went hunting for more targets.

"Grandfather! Grandfather, wake up!" Janus' voice was as irritating as it was frantic.

Angkor opened an eye. "Go away," he hissed. "I am sleeping."

"Grandfather! Wake up!"

Janus had raised his voice to the Khan. It must be important.

Angkor opened both eyes and struggled to sit up. "All right, all right," he grumbled. "What is so important you have to wake an old man who is just trying to sleep?"

"Grandfather, you are needed in Command," Janus lowered his voice to a respectable tone. "We are under attack."

The old Khan's eyes snapped open. "Help me," he commanded. A pair of servants appeared and dressed the ancient and fretting monarch. A soldier stood at attention behind Angkor's hover chair. While it was two hundred yards to the Command Center, at one hundred and twenty years old, Angkor was unable to walk the distance. "Hurry! Hurry!" urged Angkor, pounding a bony fist on the arm of his chair.

"ATTENTION!" came the cry as he entered the palace's headquarters for planetary defense. It was not a large room. The real command center was thousands of miles away, buried deep beneath a mountain in the Alps. But from here, the Khan was given real time updates and could direct the defense of Terra.

The holograph table dominated the center of the room; it had Terra displayed, hundreds of red arrows darted and danced across its face. "My Khan," reported General Gebyu, "we are tracking three hundred of their ships across the globe at this moment. They are lightly armed, mostly chemical explosives and pulse energy weapons. Their attacks are random, hitting mostly civilian targets. As you see, we have launched fighters and are engaging them."

"Who are they?" demanded the Khan. "How did they manage to enter the atmosphere without our planetary defenses stopping them? Where is my fleet? I do still have a fleet, don't I?"

"They came out of other space between Luna and Terra," the General said. "Marvelous bit of navigation. It gave us only moments to react. I have recalled the fleet; the lead elements will be here within the hour. Our planetary based fighters are doing quite well. The raiders are larger ships and don't maneuver as well as ours. Really, my Khan, I believe the threat is negligible."

"Tell that to my dead subjects," grumbled the old man.

"Highness, there is an incoming message," a fresh-faced officer called from an alcove. "She insists on speaking with you."

"Main holo," directed General Gebyu.

The image of Terra wavered to be replaced with a ten-foot-high image of a Hecht. Her head turned to and fro, then settled on the Emperor.

Angkor's eyes narrowed. "Grrrscnk," he hissed.

"You honor me, monkey," the Hecht said. "Grrrscnk was my mother. I am Grrrscnt, Premier of the Hecht Homogeny. Are you the monkey she called Angkor Khan, Leader of the monkeys of Terra?"

"I am Emperor Angkor Khan of the Terran Empire," he announced, stiffening his body to attention as he faced the creature. "What is the meaning of all this?"

"Mother warned me of your arrogance," Grrrscnt said. "She said it was her own fault for spending all those years on Terra playing with her food. No matter, monkey. The meaning of all this should be quite plain. The Galactic Council is still quite put out by your little Empire. You have managed to beat the Solarians and the Vinithri. So, now it falls to the Hecht to put you in your place.

"The ships attacking you are the Bougartd. Nasty creatures; don't taste good at all. But they are quite compliant and do the job they are contracted to do. And, to your dismay I am sure, they are loyal members of the Council. So, I have hired them to destroy your defenses so the Hecht can take possession of a new feed herd."

She leaned closer to the image. "I am sorry to see you have grown so old, monkey Angkor Khan," she ridiculed. "Mother often spoke of eating you. I was going to make you part of my victory celebration, but it seems you have grown old and gamey. No matter, I hear there are plenty of suckling Terrans for me.

"Now, we are going to start the next phase of the invasion. I will give you this one chance to surrender. What say you, monkey?"

The Khan struggled to his feet. "Never," he croaked. "You may bomb us to dust, but we will never surrender to the likes of you."

"No, not to dust," responded the Hecht. "Your cities, yes. But my plan will leave plenty of you to feed our new colony. Goodbye, monkey." The holo dissipated abruptly.

"Proximity alarm!" a cry came from the back of the room. "Two, no three large ships emerging near Mars." Then, after a long pause: "Dear gods, Hecht dreadnaughts."

"Launch everything!" the Khan ordered. "Alert the weapons platforms. Call the fleet, tell them to hurry!"

Satellite data appeared on the holo. The Hecht dreadnaughts were uneven lumps with random appendages intended for terrible usage. Terra's defensive satellites launched hundreds of missiles. Hecht counter fire destroyed most of them, but the remaining dozens hit the dreadnaughts repeatedly. Scattered fires erupted on all three of the Hecht ships, but the massive war machines maintained their single-minded course straight at the heart of the Terran Empire. They split up when they reached Terra, each entering a looping orbit. Terran fighters and cutters raked fire down the sides of the odious vessels.

"Launch alert!" cried a voice.

A canister released from the ship over Pan Asia. It entered the atmosphere nearly vertical. "Tracking sir. Tracking," They all waited until the voice called, "Target is Zurich. The device is…antimatter, sir."

"More launches." They stared at the screen as the dreadnaughts released more canisters across the globe. Seconds later, the list began: "Denver, Moscow, Johannesburg, San Paulo, Seattle…"

Angkor clutched right arm with his left and let out a gasp of pain.

"Orders!" came a cry. "We need orders!"

"Grandfather?" Janus dropped to a knee beside Angkor, "Grandfather, what are your orders?"

"Proximity alarm! Luna orbit!" A terrified officer shouted. "It's the fleet!"

The holo image changed. The unnerving look of space unfolding revealed five mighty Space Fold sleds. Each carried four destroyers, which peeled away as they entered real space and flung themselves at the Hecht dreadnaughts. Missiles launched by the destroyers struck the ponderous vessels, followed closely by twenty smaller, more agile warships. The dreadnaughts returned fire, destroying *Punch* and *Bullyboy,* but it was clear they were being overwhelmed.

"Proximity alarm! LaGrange Point!" The holo shifted again. A pair of spindly Vinithri cruisers appeared.

"Grandfather, it's the fleet. What are your orders?" Janus shook the Emperor, then gasped.

The left side of Angkor's sagged, his jaw fell open and a stream of drool fell messily onto his uniform. The Khan couldn't hold his head up. A dark red drop trickled from his ear. He moved his mouth, but unintelligible noises were all he could form. Angkor groaned in pain and frustration.

"I need a med team to Command, immediately!" Janus snapped. "General, contact the Vinithri, now! All fighters are to switch vectors to the anti-matter bombs. Tell the destroyers to press their attacks. We have to drive off those dreadnaughts before they drop any more weapons."

"Sir, I have the Vinithri," a call came.

The image of the dreadnaughts shifted to an imposing Vinithri. "I am Third daughter of the Vinithri, ally of the Terran Empire. Whom am I addressing?"

"I am Crown Prince Janus Khan of the Terran Empire," answered Janus. "I greet my ally, Third Daughter, and welcome your fleet. There are anti-matter weapons that have been released by the enemy that are threatening our cities. Can you intercept them?"

The Vinithri spoke with her crew. "Not all," she reported, "but enough, I should hope. We honor our agreement with the Terran Khan." She exposed the black neural ganglion between her head and thorax.

The holo shifted back to the Hecht dreadnaughts. All of them were burning now, as the slender Terran destroyers, less than a tenth the size of the Hecht ships, danced and darted, firing their weapons from close range and zipping away to prepare for another run.

A brace of Hecht fire caught the destroyer *Grappler* and it exploded. A second destroyer, the *Ju-Jitsu,* had its starboard engine nacelle shot away. It spun in a nauseating gyration before exploding. The *Muay Thai* staggered from a glancing blow. It arced away from the battle, burning, then turned back toward the enemy, wavering not once as it rammed the lead dreadnaught.

The massive ship shuddered, fire erupting through the grey hull. It pulled out of orbit, shuddering once more before bursting into a ginger and hoary blossom of fire. The remaining dreadnaughts began a ponderous climb out of orbit. The *Samurai* exploded, its fragments shredding the second dreadnaught. Its sub-light engines faded and it glided past Luna. As the Terran ships tore at the crippled enemy, escape pods began to pop from the dying ship.

"I want prisoners," Janus ordered.

There was a flash, high above the northern pole. "The Vinithri have intercepted one of the bombs, my Lord," came the report. "They locked an energy grapple to it and sent it over the pole where it exploded. They are engaging the remaining weapons." Two more flashes bounced on the holo before a Major stood and announced, "Sire, the weapon targeting Zurich is about to strike."

"Visual," ordered General Gebyu.

It was late in Zurich; street lights outlined the condemned city. The ageless capital of the Empire was awash with light, the spires of the cathedral highlighting the old city. Around the lake, the orderly streets and building of modern Zurich gleamed in the dark. Small vessels crisscrossed the placid surface of the unseen lake. The satellite shifted, showing a glowing object falling toward the city. At ten thousand feet above the city, the object opened. A dark spot

338

appeared that began to swell, turning grey, then silver and becoming brilliant chrome sphere five thousand feet in diameter, where the perfect ratio of one to one annihilation was achieved. The atmospheric gasses that had been consumed by the antimatter created a vacuum, growing only until the last of the matter/antimatter annihilation was complete. The atmosphere and energy released was drawn back into the vacuum and compressed. When it reached critical mass, it exploded.

The shock wave struck the city as a hammer to a fragile Christmas ball. At the center, the buildings were compressed, the earth compacted a hundred feet deep. The crater was three miles in diameter, the shock wave roaring away from the crater, uprooting the countryside for fifty miles.

The only sounds from the dead city were the hot, swirling winds that carried away the silent screams of thirty million lost souls.

The command center at the Keep was equally silent, watching the city die. An alarm sounded. "Moscow," came a muted call.

They watched as the ancient city on the Volga died.

The alarm sounded the third time. "Silence that damned thing!" snarled Crown Prince Janus. "What is the status of the battle?"

Seconds later the Hecht dreadnaught reappeared. It was past Mars, accelerating away as Terran destroyers continued their attack.

There were only four destroyers visible; the rest had been crippled or destroyed.

Space in front of the Hecht ship began to distort. "They are trying to enter otherspace," General Gebyu announced. "I want them stopped!"

The destroyers pressed their attack. The *Fisticuffs* raced in front of the dreadnaught and contacted the edge of the face fold. The great destroyer distorted, was dragged into otherspace and exploded. But the fold collapsed, preventing the Hecht escape. The three remaining ships' attack became more frantic.

The Hecht ship slowed. Escape pods began erupting. Before command could say anything, the destroyers began firing.

No prisoners would be taken from the third Hecht ship.

There was no cheering. The bomb fell over Cairo. The Vinithri ships grabbed wildly at the remaining weapons while the Terran fighters fired at the falling pods. A cutter rammed one, trying to alter its course. Instead, the bomb opened, consuming that ship and another dozen more.

Delhi and Seattle died under the chromium spheres...

Medics had arrived, manipulating the Khan's hover chair into a gurney. Strange noises came from the Khan as they frantically cut away his uniform, shoving needles into his arms and a breather over his face.

Angkor grabbed at Janus. The Crown Prince took his grandfather's hand and held it tightly. The Khan had aged in the hours of the attack, his skin ashen and grey. Only the hand clutching

Janus' showed any life, shaking slightly. The rest of Grandfather was flaccid, limp.

But his eyes glared at Janus. He moved his jaw, "H-h-h-h?"

"How many Grandfather?" Angkor nodded. "We destroyed one dreadnaught," he answered. "The other two are ours."

"Nnnnnn…" the old man shook his head, "S-s-s-s-t-t-t."

"Cities, Grandfather?"

Angkor nodded.

"Five, Grandfather," Janus said. "Zurich, Moscow, Cairo, Seattle…and Delhi."

"D-d-d-deaaaah," gasped the old man. His eyes clouded with tears.

"Crown Prince, we need to move him to the clinic." The medical was gentle, but firm.

"Of course." The Emperor had released Janus' hand. The medics moved the gurney swiftly out of the room. Janus gripped the doctor and demanded, "What happened to my Grandfather?"

"Simplest terms?" the doctor asked. "The Emperor had a stroke. A severe hemorrhagic if early indications are correct. Not surprising, given his age and the stress of his job." He pried the Crown Prince's hand from his arm. "Now, please excuse me. I have to go tend to my patient."

Chapter 34

The Emperor was dying.

They moved him back to his suite and placed him in his bed. Servants bathed him and dressed him in his favorite nightclothes. He indicated he wanted his wife and now cradled Sophia's urn in his arms.

The doctors placed him on a ventilator immediately. The stroke had damaged his ability to speak, so he was fitted with a voder. After three days, the feeding tube was inserted. Only his grandchildren and the very highest officials were allowed to visit, but for only a short time. The Khan, it was explained, needed his rest.

Janus visited twice a day. Grandfather was fading in and out; he would hold his grandfather's hand so Angkor would know he was there. He told Grandfather stories of growing up in the Keep and of his time in the Temple. The Khan would smile, listening to his grandson's recollection of so many adventures he himself had experienced. When the Khan was lucid, Janus discussed affairs of state.

The dead were estimated conservatively at one billion. The majority came from the cities and the surrounding areas.

Seattle, built on the Puget Sound, had become a five mile, circular bay. The tsunami resulting from the compression had scoured region from the Willamette Valley to Kimat in the far north. All the governments of Occident were pledging and racing support to the devastated community. Likewise, Persia and Europa raced battalions and brigades to Cairo and Zurich to salvage the ruined cities.

The Volga River had looped through Moscow on its way to the sea. Even in the modern era of mag-lev trains and heavy lift dirigibles, the Volga had historically transported goods through much of the Russian interior, much like the Mississippi River in Occident. With Moscow now a vast crater, the Volga began to create a lake, while downstream of Moscow the river bed was fast becoming a winding dry chasm. This would not do for the hearty citizens of the Russian Federation. They had already seen too much death and calamitous devastation of their cities throughout their history.

The Russian premier stood on the lip of the slowly filling hole. He shook his fist (with a convenient holo cam there to capture it, of course) and vowed with an iron voice that Moscow would be rebuilt, better than before. Even if it took a thousand years. Already, heavy construction equipment was building a dike to restore the flow of the Volga.

Around Delhi, a crowd gathered at the rim of the crater. It bisected both the Yamuna and sacred Ganges rivers. Both rivers were now filling the crater, forming a lake where there was once a bustling city.

Twenty-four hours after Delhi died, a *Brahmana* poised himself at the lip of the crater, his arms raised. He began to sing the *Bhajans*, the ritual of naming the thousand names of *Vishnu.* There were few bodies to cremate and even less fuel to support the cremations. Those gathered around the now sacred lake clapped hands and sang the ritual for the victims of the city.

Sixty of the Bougartd raiders crashed onto the surface of Terra. One hundred thirty-five Bougartd crew members found themselves stranded there. To their misfortune, seventy-eight were captured by angry Terrans before troops could arrive to take custody of prisoners. Their deaths were neither quick nor painless, since Terrans had perfected the art of torturing their enemies to death for many millenniums.

Twenty Hecht escape pods containing two hundred ninety-six Hecht were secured near Luna. None of the crew from the third Hecht dreadnaught survived.

The Captain of the Hecht ship captured near Luna was invited to dine with the Crown Prince. Her hind leg had been injured during the fight and after she was captured a Terran surgeon had amputated it. A few days later, she was escorted under heavy guard to supper with Janus in the Keep. The table was set for monkeys, she noted. But there was an elevated table facing the main dining table, clearly meant for her. The guards secured her neck chain to a staple affixed at the table. She could just stand, but would have to bow to do so.

Janus sat at the center of the table, generals and other officials to his left and right. He stood and addressed the Hecht officer. "I greet you, Grrrscdd, former Captain of my prize now in orbit around Luna. These officers are my War Council. I am Janus Arcadia Khan, Crown Prince of the Terran Empire."

Grrrscdd stood as far as the chain of her neck would allow. "That means nothing to me, little monkey," she snarled. "I demand you take me to my crew so I can verify you are treating them according to the Conventions of War by the Galactic Council. I further demand you notify my government of our capture so negotiations for our release can be arranged."

"Captain, Captain, I assure you your crew is being taken care of," Janus replied. "Please, let us be civilized beings, yes? Sit, my chefs have prepared a special dinner for us that I am sure you will find memorable."

She tugged at the chain, hissed, then sat. Her guards pointed their weapons at her as a waiter appeared with a platter bearing a large slab of meat. Grrrscdd picked it up and sniffed. It was a haunch of Hecht, spiced and burned, as Terrans were known to do. Obviously, the Terrans expected her to be offended by serving her a piece of one of her crew. Clearly, they didn't understand the Hecht. She ripped a piece off with her teeth, chewed and swallowed.

"How is your leg, Captain?" Janus asked.

"I appreciate the skill of your physician, monkey," answered Grrrscdd. "I am sure she would find a job with your people as a butcher, as adroit as she was in removing my leg."

"You misunderstand me, Captain," Janus said. "I can see how well my physician removed your leg. My question is how well did my chef prepare it for your supper?"

345

Strange creatures, these monkeys. Though Grrrscdd appreciated the insult. She tore off another piece and ate it. "A pity your chef ruined by burning it as she did. Of course, I understand monkeys burn all their food. Disgusting." Grrrscdd believed she was as skilled at insults as well as this monkey. "I can assume you are feeding my crew as well?"

"Whether your crew is fed or not is no longer your concern." Janus ate a morsel. "Mmmmmmm, delicious. My compliments, Captain."

"Now, as for your crew. It is unfortunate for all of you that Terra didn't sign your conventions. Nor will you have any protection under our laws. As such, I have given consideration as to what to do with your crew and your allies, the Bougartd. There will be no negotiation for your release. You are all now my property. You will be kept at our facility on Europa. I would advise against escape; we will simply open the building to the atmosphere. You will be put to work, of course. And since we have little knowledge of your physiology, you can expect half to two thirds of your crew to volunteer for examination and investigation."

"You mean experimentation!" shot back the Hecht.

"You bombed our cities," exploded Janus. "You murdered at least a billion of my people. You have no moral defense, no reason, and no excuse that should be given even the slightest consideration for any form of mercy."

"You're a barbarian!"

"Yes, we are," smiled Janus. He selected another morsel of her leg. "Mmmmmmm, delicious."

Angkor drifted in and out of lucidity. When he was aware, he accepted the warmth and love from his visitors. Janus kept him aware of what was happening within the Empire. He smiled at the joke Janus played on the Hecht captain and sucked on the sliver of the leg he was brought. Grrrscnk had always teased about eating him.

His dreams were nightmares. Suishin visited him often, mocking his failures. Sophia would join him, wailing that Angkor had promised to care for her…and had failed miserably. Tenzing stood over his bed, disapproving.

Salaam, Xaid and Dawlish came to him. "Had you only listened to me," Dawlish scolded, "none of this would have happened. All these deaths…" the apparition shook its head.

He could hear the wails of the billion. Faceless specters milled through his room, drifted over his bed. "I'm sorry, so sorry…" he told them, over and over. But still the phantoms came, driving him deeper into his despair.

A long lost, but familiar figure in saffron, appeared at his side. "My friend, you came to see me," the Khan said joyfully. "Where have you been all these years?"

"My friend Pitth," his spiritual center answered, "as I told you, I have been with you always. I am here because today you need me the most."

"Today?" Angkor became angry. "Today? What about when the aliens attacked? Where were you then? When my friends deceived me and I murdered my own brother? When my wife..." he broke down and began to cry.

His center stroked his steel colored hair. "Pitth, my student, my friend," he said, soothing. "All these things and more were written in the pages of time long ago. You placed your stones masterfully and today you should revel in what you have created, not mourn what you have lost."

"What I have created!" Angkor grew furious. "What I have created was death, loss, devastation. All I have done was kill, destroy and to what end?" He sobbed, "Look at the five cities. That is what I have wrought."

"Indeed?" replied his center, "Would you like to see what you have truly wrought?" He beckoned.

A mist formed. Angkor startled as Janus entered, looking older and wearing the hideous golden robe and fur cap his mother had purchased for his own naming day. He kowtowed, then stepped away, followed by another young man dresses identically, who repeated the gesture. Then another and another.

One entered, his clothing monochromic, bound in a heavy chain. He kowtowed and turned to join the others. "Wait," called Angkor, "who are you?"

"I am, I will be known as...Eight," the trussed man responded.

"Eight," Angkor considered. "Such an odd name. Why are you bound and your clothing so dark?"

"I am, I will be a perversion of your line," was the morose response. "I sought to destroy all you created. I will die at the hands of my dearest friend. My daughter has, will remove my name for all time. I am bound in penance for my misdeeds."

He turned and joined the others in the mist. Angkor watched as men and women, all dressed in the golden robes, passed.

The line continued. A slight woman with hair as golden as the sun was bowing to him. "Wait," he called to her.

"Yes Grandfather?" Her hair was long, past her waist and flowed as blown by an unfelt breeze. Her eyes blazed a familiar emerald green.

"What is your name, child?" he asked.

She stood straight, hands on her hips, looking down her tiny nose. "I am; I will be Queen Annika Khan. I will enlarge our Empire more than a thousand-fold."

Angkor sighed. "Daughter, you have your grandmother's beautiful hair."

The small woman kowtowed. "You honor me, Grandfather."

She turned and the line continued.

A massive being appeared wearing scarred battle armor. The panoply was dull gold with a rainbow of stripes on the upper legs. "Who are you, Grandson?" the Emperor asked.

"I am, I will be General Svere Khan," he answered, saluting. "I am; I will be the only Khan not your reincarnation. Extremists

349

tried to usurp the Empire. I served as Emperor until the heir was ready to assume the throne."

"What of the extremists, General?" Angkor demanded.

"It took me ten years and nearly a quarter of the Empire's lives to stamp the heretics out," the General reported, his green eyes blazing. "For that, I will be remembered as Svere the Slaughterer." He saluted and once again the line continued.

Men, women, tall and short. Hair of every color, bodies heavyset and slender. All had one physical trait in common.

Asian eyes, emerald green.

Hundreds, then thousands passed by, each bowing deep to their founder. With some, Angkor held short conversations, as he had with Eight, Queen Annika and the General. He didn't know how long they were there, watching the endless line of future Khans passing by.

A tall being, neither male nor female, stood before him in the familiar golden robe and fur hat. Emerald eyes looked kindly on Angkor. It was disconcerting seeing this Khan as it was wavering, turning translucent then solidifying, as though it were here but not here. *"Was it a ghost?"* wondered Angkor. "What is your name, Grandson?" he asked.

Its smile was beatific as it kowtowed. "I am, I will be," it paused, "The Last."

"The Last," repeated Angkor. "Then my Empire will die one day."

Its laughter was like a dozen tiny bells. "Oh Grandfather!" it answered. "In my time, we are beyond anything as mundane and prosaic as death. Sol has long gone cold and our Temple lays safe beneath a layer of ice miles deep. Each of my predecessors was designed to be an improvement of the previous. I am the result. We, Terrans, have evolved. To the younger species, we are as Gods. As such, I have no reason to meddle in their affairs, save to ensure they follow your law.

"Today, we walk amongst the stars. Not just in our own galaxy, but in as many as we can see beyond. We are ancients now and I spend my time speaking of great things with the other ancients of the universe. This is your legacy, Emperor Angkor Khan, first of the Terran Khans."

The whole of the assembly kowtowed once again and faded as the mist thickened. "Come young Pitth," his center sounded sad. "It is time for you to say good bye."

Angkor pulled the mask aside and croaked, "Janus. I want Janus right now."

He was hurried to his grandfather's side. It was time. Angkor pulled at the mask, so Janus helped him remove it. The Khan beckoned him closer.

He placed his hand on Janus's head. "You are Emperor now," he said. "You are the sword and shield. You are defender of my Law. Keep our Empire forever strong and free." He kissed Janus on the forehead and said, "It is done."

His eyes closed. A smile formed on his face as Emperor Angkor Khan, First of the Terran Emperors, died.

The Emperor Janus Arcadia Khan personally announced his grandfather's death. *"He sacrificed himself to build the Empire and died protecting us all. I swear to you all, this day, that I shall give of myself as my grandfather did, to protect and to serve our Empire."*

As his ancestors had, Angkor was dressed in his finest robe and sat in state on his throne in Ulaan Baatar for three days. Mourners from across the Empire knelt before the Khan and swore their fealty in this world and the next. In a break with tradition, the new Khan allowed his seven brothers and sisters to stand at his side as they observed who properly paid Grandfather their respects. And who did not. In the coming months, Imperial Intelligence would be kept busy with the knowledge.

From there, soldiers bore their leader to the Keep, now known as *The Temple of Angkor Khan,* as declared by grandson and heir, Janus Khan. Angkor himself had sealed the old tomb of the previous Headmen of the Khalkha. "It is appropriate," he had told Janus. "The chamber containing my Father and our ancestors is the place of the old order, the Headmen of the Khalkha. I am the Founder of this new line. You are the first of a new breed, the first of the superior Terran Khans." The new tomb was built beneath the arched cathedral that had once housed the Vinithri Queen.

Corbodium is the hardest crystal in the known sciences. To cut one, the crystal is phased partially into the fifth dimension where it becomes malleable.   A sarcophagus was created by the scientists of Angkor's Temple. The bonzes placed him within it, along with the urn containing the ashes of his wife, Sophia. A stasis generator would prevent deterioration of the Great Khan for all time. The corbodium casket was closed and returned to the third dimension. Sealed within the crystal, the Great Khan and his lady were protected for all time.

The tomb had been designed and built by both Terran and Vinithri scientists. The first of the three chambers was reserved for preparing any who entered. The second was the ossuary for all the Khans who would follow. Janus was assured it would always be exactly as large as it needed to be.

The third was a gold lined chamber for Grandfather and Grandmother. Janus had personally inspected the tomb years before. Written on the gilded walls was his Grandfather greatest achievement.

The Laws of Angkor Khan.

Chapter 35

Year 10,136 of the Galactic Union (August 3129 A.D.)
Hrrrhncht, First Premier of the Hecht Homogeny, stood regally in
the accused box as it was driven before the dais in the Galactic
Union's Grand Hall. As Premier, she was expected to be here to
witness the decision of the High Court of the Council, a duty and
burden she gladly accepted.

Hoots and hisses, growls and cries greeted her as the carriage
was paraded before the nine hundred species who were members of
the Council. A handful of feces landed at her feet, just one of the
dozens of missiles being flung. Her predecessor, Grrrscnt, daughter
of the thrice-cursed Grrrscnk, had placed the Hecht in this situation.

With Grrrscnt dying in her dreadnaught over Terra, and none
of her daughters old enough to battle her, Hrrrhncht had seized
control of the Homogony. Now, as Premier, her first duty was to
stand before an angry Galactic Union and answer for the Hecht's
failure.

Arrived at the foot of the dais, the crowd was allowed to
express its fury for exactly five minutes before the gong announced
the start of the proceedings. The chamber was immediately silent,
though the threat of riot lay just below a veneer of civility.

"Our box is empty," noted Hrrrhncht. *"This does not portend
well for us."* As one of the fifty founding members of the Council,
their place of honor had always been on the central aisle, the second
from the left away from the front. Normally, the Ambassador and

her staff would be seated there in their finery. The empty seats could only mean the Supreme Court's decision would go badly.

Heavy curtains at the rear of the dais opened to darkness. Lights came up slowly, from red to the brightness of the room, revealing the three robed figures of the Supreme Court of the Galactic Union.

Tradition spoke to justice being blind. As such, in the ten-thousand-year history of the Union, the identity of the three justices on the Supreme Court had never been revealed. They would only appear together in their robes, seated (it was assumed) behind their bench. Each would speak into a microphone inside their robes, broadcast by a voder which translated their native tongue and voice.

"Hear now the judgement of the Supreme Court in the matter of the Galactic Council versus the Hecht Homogeny." The voice was of a young man, albeit scratchy and hoarse. "The Founders of our great society, of which the Hecht are a part, wrote:

"In the matters of our success, we shall always remember that success is a process of careful consideration, discussion and debate. As such, though ponderous, we shall never forget that our real strength will always come from meticulous planning and flawless execution. There shall never be any action unless it has been thoroughly examined and approved by the Council.

"Conversely, failure must always be recognized swiftly, less it becomes a poison to the Assembly. Once failure is discovered, it must be dealt with swiftly, finality and without mercy.

355

"Premier Hrrrhncht, the Hecht have been found guilty on two counts of failure. The first was on the failure to secure Terra with the aid of the Vinithri. The second was the unapproved and disastrous failure of securing Terra a second time with the aid of the Bougartd.

"Previously, the failure of the Solarians and the Vinithri were grounds to expel them from our Union. We are aware of the historical significance the Hecht have had on this Union since its very beginning. As such, we are loath to expel you. Rather, we reduce your status to that of observer, removing you from every office and committee of this Council. Your seat is moved to the row in the furthest reach of this hall. You are declined an invitation to rejoin this Council for a period of time not less than five hundred standard years. You are denied any tribute from this Union, nor may you exercise any trade agreement with any Council member world unless that treaty becomes approved through this Council. Do you accept these terms?"

Hrrrhncht gripped the rail of the accused box. Her crest rose a brilliant red. Nevertheless, she bowed and said, "The Hecht accepts the ruling of the Supreme Court."

"Then, be gone from our sight." The justice's bench slid back and the curtains closed.

The craft containing Hrrrhncht trolleyed back up the center aisle way toward the atrium. The Council, its anger satisfied, ignored the former leader from their midst.

Not bad, mused the First Premier. *This banishment to the back rows I can work with.* She began to formulate her plans.

May 3139 A.D.

Aboard the *Siene,* the Emperor Janus Arcadia Khan sipped a cup of tea from a priceless porcelain cup and set it carefully on its saucer. The purser had explained the setting had been personally selected by the late Empress Sophia during the late Emperor Angkor Khan's journey to the outer worlds of the Empire immediately before the Khan's father, Tenzing, died. From what he remembered of Grandmother Sophia, Janus rather doubted she had selected the fine china.

Janus had opted to have afternoon tea with his closest advisors in his private forward lounge. Mars grew ruddy and fat in the bay window that dominated the room. The Khan had ordered the approach vector screening of the Mars Shipyard and graving docks. His advisors were aware, of course, that the ship was near completion. Only he and Cassius knew just how close.

"Majesty, we are in the orbit you requested. We are standing by for your orders to approach your shipyard." The voice was in his head, a benefit taken from the body of the *hashashin* assassin. It had been unnerving at first, receiving communication directly into his brain without a standard com. He adapted quickly, though, and thoroughly enjoyed having conversations with people weren't in the room while he was attending some boring function or odious meeting.

"Very well. Begin the approach as we discussed. *"*
"Ladies, gentlemen." Janus said. "For years, we have been discussing my Grandfather's plans for protecting and expanding our Empire. After the Battle of the Five Cities and Grandfather's untimely death, we were handed a bountiful gift from our enemies.

"The hulks and wrecks left behind by our enemies provided us with the secrets of powering our fold vessels more efficiently. Imagine nearly unlimited power, using hydrogen fuel and the secrets of the universe hidden from us by the Galactic Council. Now that we have taken these secrets from those who would oppress and destroy us, we are on an equal footing with them."

"I take it they didn't give up those secrets easily." Lazarus Stein, his Financial Minister sipped at tea, spilling a trickle in his full grey beard.

"Easily enough," drawled Jeffery Andersen, his Intelligence Minister. He wore a crushed, wide brimmed hat and was a mountain in black, save for a large silver buckle. "Y'all would be amazed what a critter will tell you with the proper persuasion."

The whole room chuckled.

"Gentlemen," Janus said. "Behold, after ten years, the result of our labors."

It was difficult to make out at first, a spider web of silver reflection against the curtain of blackened space behind it. As *Siene* drew closer, the framework of the space dock became apparent. A tapered cylinder extended a quarter mile past one opening of the dock and, as two smaller docks were being pulled away, revealed six barrels affixed to the stern of the cylinder. Small worker pods and drones swarmed the vessel.

"Half a mile long. A quarter of a mile in diameter. Two launch bays capable of operating seventy-five of our most modern *Brigand* fighters. Four single barrel meson rifles, mounted in turrets for combat and planetary assault," quoted Janus. "Fifty missile batteries, two hundred close-in lasers for fleet action and defense."

Janus spread his arms. "I give you Terra's Dreadnaught Mark 1!"

The *Siene* orbited around the space dock, eager eyes examining the slumbering beast. From the belly of the ship, they could see three of the meson turrets, arranged around the fattest points of the ship. Sweeping close to the belly weapon, they could see inside the mirrored barrel, the orange glow of the meson generator reflected deep inside the ship. Smaller turrets tracked the shuttle as it passed the black and grey flanks of the warship.

The yacht circled the dreadnaught three times, then parked off the port bow of the deadly vessel. "Glorious, my Khan!" breathed the Prime Minister. "Truly glorious! When will he be ready to deploy?"

Janus spoke into his comm. "Execute!"

The work pods and drones arced away from the dreadnaught. Clamps and arms on the dock released and raised away from its mighty hull, while position and navigation lights burst into glory along the black and grey hull. The six engines glowed vivid blue/white as the ship departed the dock and entered orbit independently for the first time.

"The Imperial Navy Dreadnaught 01, the *Revenge.* His brothers, I.N.D 02, the *Requite,* and I.N.D 03, the *Reprisal,* are being launched from their graving docks at my shipyards at Uranus and Jupiter Stations   Each vessel has docking racks for two *Fisticuffs* class destroyers. Together, they form our first Task Force and will patrol our colonies. Within five years, five more dreadnaughts will be delivered from these three shipyards, along with a new class of destroyer.

"In addition, I am expanding these three shipyards and building two more, at Tantalus and Vega. Within ten years, we will have ten dreadnaughts of this class and two dozen destroyers.

"By that time, I expect the next generation of dreadnaughts to be ready to build, along with new destroyers. My shipwrights assure me we will be ready to build out first attack carrier within fifteen years.

"The Galactic Council generously supplied us with the tools we need to protect ourselves. What they did not take into consideration is the extent we are willing to go for our revenge.

I only wish I could live long enough to witness my descendants carrying out my plan…"

It was cold. Gods, it was cold. The power in his suit was gone, so he would soon be dead. Hypothermia? Hypoxia? It didn't matter at this point. The alien was gone from Doctor Boradt's mind. He was grateful for that mercy.

"Well, small thing, what are you doing here?" Doctor Boradt opened his eyes. A biped stood beside him, dressed in the golden robe and hat that the Guardian wore. "You must be the plaything my Guardian spoke of. Tell me, small thing, was thy Legend what you expected?"

Boradt waved his cilia weakly, unable to speak." Ah, you are dying," the being said. It kicked him lightly. His suit came to life, warm fresh air reviving the dying Voudoo.

"Thank you, Lord." Gasped Doctor Boradt. "No, he was not what I expected. He was a murderer. He killed his own brother. A despot, a dictator. I was wrong; his legacy was one of blood."

"His legacy," mused the being. "I am part of his legacy. You may call me the Last, the ultimate of the Terran Emperors. My Grandfather created the line which led to me. I walk the Universe with the other Gods and hold this place safe and holy, for it is the birthplace of Gods.

Would you care to see the true legacy of my founder?"

"I would be honored, Lord."

Doctor Boradt startled. The room was dark, black as the void.

Illumination rose slowly, revealing brilliant gold walls covered with glyphs and illuminations. Doctor Boradt's breath caught as he recognized the Law, written in the nearly forgotten original Terran standard. "Behold, the Founder and what he left for us," said the Last. "The Law of Angkor Khan. The very foundation of society throughout this galaxy. The other Gods have examined it and found it good. It is spreading throughout the whole of the Universe."

Doctor Boradt raised his antigrav so he could see into the casket.

The Emperor Angkor Khan looked as if he had just fallen asleep. He was wearing the original Rainbow Robe and the black furred hat of the ancient Mongol Khans. In his wrinkled and spotted hands, he held an urn painted with delicate yellow flowers. His grey hair was neatly brushed, as if the hairdresser had just left. Doctor Boradt imagined the hair beneath Angkor's nose vibrated as he slept.

They were back in the high ceiling chamber once again. The Last was seated on a magnificent throne. "Do you recall the conversation Angkor had with Tenzing months after his son Buru was born? Angkor's proposal of using rail ships to scatter Terran DNA across the galaxy, seeding it with Terrans to expand the Empire?

"Four hundred million years ago, one of those ships visited your world. The scientists found your world suitable for

362

colonization. It took many years to create a lifeform that would survive on Vaudoo. From the day that we planted your ancestors to this day, you have been following the programing we designed within you. You are a descendent of the Terran Empire, the one thousand eighty second seeking to find Terra."

He steepled his fingers. "I will not kill you, nor will I cause your death. I will instead banish you, safely, to live out your days as you see fit, save you will not do so here. Farewell, little thing. Perhaps one day we shall meet your people walking with us amongst the stars."

Doctor Boradt found himself floating in those stars. He activated the suit's thrusters and rotated slowly, gasped as the whole of the Temple Galaxy came into view.

He studied the Temple for an hour, finally determining where Vaudoo was. His home system was an invisible smear of light in the long trailing arm. In the opposite arm, he fancied he could see the dying ember that was the home of the great Empire.

He noted his power and atmosphere indicators were not dropping. He was not an old man, not by any means. Even having an average Vaudoo lifespan, he could expect to live for as many as seventy to eighty years.

There was no question he would not live long enough to return home. He tapped his thrusters until he was looking outward to the trillion sparks of light across the void. Each was a new galaxy. If the Last was to be believed, even now he was walking amongst those galaxies with the rest of the Terran race as Gods.

His cilia twisted excitedly as he pushed the thrusters forward, aiming at a spark he could barely distinguish. Perhaps he might find these Gods…

"Like" us of Facebook: "Tales of the Spinward March" for news, notes and artwork

Coming in Fall 2017:

Tales of the Spinward March, Book 2:

"The Red Queen"

Made in the USA
Lexington, KY
17 September 2017